Pamela Fudge works as a part-time administrator at Bournemouth University and has written poetry since she was a child. She started writing fiction in 1983 and has had short stories published in most of the national women's magazines in the country. She tutored courses for Poole Adult Education Service for eleven years and for the Writers' News Home Study courses for two years.

SECOND BEST

Stacey Trent has almost given up on love when a whirlwind romance with Nick Cable persuades her otherwise. Believing they are to be married she turns her back on home, career and friends to be with him — only to discover that the promise of a future together is just a tissue of lies. Stacey is left to the mercy of his older brother, Lex, but he's had enough of clearing up Nick's trail of 'weeping females'. However, circumstances force them together, and an attraction grows between them. But will Stacey convince Lex he is more than second best?

PAMELA FUDGE

SECOND BEST

Complete and Unabridged

ULVERSCROFT
Leicester

First published in Great Britain in 2009 by
Robert Hale Limited
London

First Large Print Edition
published 2010
by arrangement with
Robert Hale Limited
London

British Library CIP Data

Fudge, Pamela, *1946* –
Second best.
1. Brothers- -Fiction. 2. Love stories.
3. Large type books.
I. Title
823.9'14–dc22

ISBN 978-1-44480-367-9

Published by
F. A. Thorpe (Publishing)
Anstey, Leicestershire
Set by Words & Graphics Ltd.
Anstey, Leicestershire
Printed and bound in Great Britain by
T. J. International Ltd., Padstow, Cornwall

This book is printed on acid-free paper

This book is dedicated to my sisters,
Barb and Pat. They have shared my life,
shared my dreams, and encouraged me
to believe in them.

Acknowledgements

For this book I'll write a poem
That comes right from the heart
To all those who supported me
When my life was torn apart
Twice they picked me up
And set me on my feet
A greater group of people
You could never hope to meet
Friends of mine for many years
And others who were new
All gave me the strength to live again
Which was what I had to do
But most of all my family
Who never let me down
They fill my life with laughter
And that's my favourite sound
To all of you this comes with love
And a grateful thank you, too
Because everything I achieve
Is all because of you.

Pam Fudge
www.pamfudge.co.uk

1

Screwing the last nut firmly into place, and heaving a huge sigh of relief, I threw the wheel brace into the boot of my precious Mini Cooper — a convertible, no less — with a distinct lack of care and even a good deal of unnecessary force. The jack followed soon after, landing with a pleasing clash of metal against metal, which gave me a brief moment of satisfaction, as did kicking the newly replaced wheel peevishly in passing.

It was childish behaviour for a woman in her mid-thirties and I was well aware of it. I *loved* the car, really I did — but not today — *definitely* not today. Of all the times and places to get a flat tyre, this had to have taken the bloody biscuit. The only good thing — and as far as I could see there *was* only one — was at least I did know how to change a wheel. It was probably the only useful thing my dad had ever taught me, when I'd got my first car — and my first puncture — while I was still in my teens. Luckily some skills are never forgotten, which was just as well as far as I was concerned, since I hadn't seen even one car since I'd turned on to this particular road.

All done, I climbed back into the little car to continue a journey that, with hindsight, seemed to have been fated from the moment I set out. Fighting the urge to check my watch, I glared at the surprising amount of grime that had managed to spread itself on to my hands and underneath my prettily painted nails — mostly chipped and spoiled now, I noticed. I'd thought modern cars were supposed to be cleaner, but I supposed that didn't include the wheels.

A strong desire to know the time wasn't going to stay suppressed for long and, giving in, I gingerly lifted the ribbed cuff of my cream sweater with the tip of one finger, and felt my heart sink into my muddy boots when I saw how late it was.

Nick would be worried sick, and there was no chance of even texting him with the battery of my mobile phone every bit as flat as the tyre on the wheel I'd just removed. He'd probably already left a dozen 'where are you?' messages. Charging the damn thing had been just another job I'd meant to do before leaving home, but with so much else to see to it had ended up being one more thing I hadn't got around to. I tried not to think what the others might be.

Reaching for a scrap of tissue that I suddenly spotted peeping out of my bag, I rubbed hopelessly at the stains on my hands and suddenly realized he might even think that I'd had a change of heart and wasn't coming, or just get tired of waiting altogether and leave. That possibility had me turning the ignition key hastily, and then slapping the steering wheel in frustration when the car refused to start first time.

'Come on, come *on*,' I pleaded. 'Do it for Stacey. Don't let me down now.'

The engine merely whined a protest at the second attempt. I bit back a scream of sheer frustration and swore savagely instead. Holding my breath, I willed it to behave, and on the third try it fired cheerfully into life and I breathed again.

'I should think so, too,' I told the car grimly. 'I shall imagine you stacked up in a scrapyard more often now I know you're telepathic.' Pulling away hastily and a trifle jerkily from the grass verge, I added, 'But I do promise not to put your service off ever again if you just get me to where I want to go this one time.'

Driving along the rapidly darkening country roads I could only hope fervently that I wasn't lost, on top of everything else, because adding that to the equation would just be too much. I'd never seen the point of satnavs — until now, that is — they're not the sort of thing someone like me would have much use for when most of my time was spent just pootling around my home town.

It was easy to see, with the benefit of hindsight, that I should have set off a great deal earlier than I had, but how was I to know there would be such unexpectedly heavy traffic at midday on a Friday, slowing my progress to a snail's pace practically from the minute I'd left home when I didn't normally start my weekends this early?

Everything seemed to be stacked against my making the journey on time and in one piece, I thought with a superstitious shiver and then dismissed the idea as fanciful.

What on earth had made Nick suggest that we meet right out here in the back of beyond anyway? The question presented itself for the umpteenth time, and I had to ask myself, too, why he hadn't at least suggested that we should drive out together? It would surely have been the sensible thing to do.

I suddenly found myself laughing softly at the thought, happier now that the car was behaving, and reminding myself, unnecessarily, that Nick never did the sensible thing. It was his unpredictable and charming ways — not to mention his dark good looks — that had made me fall in love with him in the first place, and with a speed that still made me dizzy whenever I thought about it. He made me feel sixteen again and it had just seemed so right when — ridiculously soon after we met — I had been swept, eager and laughing, into his arms, into his life, and almost, but not quite, into his bed.

'You're such a little prude,' he'd teased, seeming only amused by my prim reluctance to embark on an affair almost immediately after the meeting that had changed my previously well-ordered and rather solitary life so spectacularly, 'almost a virgin, in fact,' he went on, 'especially in this day and age when no one thinks twice about embarking on meaningless affairs. A complete contradiction — look at you, blonde, beautiful, as sexy as hell and yet pure as the driven snow. It's a combination I'm finding extremely hard to resist.'

I was thrilled by his comments and touched by an understanding I hadn't been expecting. I'd been so sure he would roar with laughter when he discovered I'd had less than a handful of lovers at my age, but he'd appeared to find it endearing. Of course, I didn't tell him it was actually more accident than design on my part. I'd seen so many relationships and marriages fail over the years, including my parents', and though I was desperate for the stability of a family on the one hand, I couldn't help but realize that the fear of failure had made me cautious to the point of paranoia on the other.

Meeting several Mr Wrongs in a row in my twenties definitely hadn't helped. Indeed, it meant that in latter years I'd rarely been tempted from the comfort zone that included a well-paid job, a nice flat in a good area and a reasonable social life to bother with the highs and lows that were such a huge part of the dating game. I think I'd told myself there was a lot to be said for the quiet life so many times over the years that eventually I'd started to believe it.

Then, just when I'd about given up on all those faraway dreams of love, marriage and a family of my own, Nick Cable had erupted into my life and changed everything, including my own warped view of life in general and men in particular. I hadn't imagined that someone like Nick existed in this day and age and the fact that — despite being in his late thirties — he was free, too, and yet wanted all the same things as me, I still found hard to believe.

'Not quite as squeaky clean as you, I'm afraid,' he'd admitted ruefully, when I said as much, continuing, 'I've come to the age when

I realize I've had too many pointless flings and even a few near misses where marriage is concerned, but something has always made me reluctant to make that final commitment. I have a feeling that may be about to change.'

I had shivered deliciously, sincerely hoping that meeting me might have something to do with his change of heart. I was sure he understood, without me explaining, that I had not consciously been holding out for the promise of a wedding ring, but we had only known each other a relatively short time. I have to say he did appear to accept without question my belief that a physical relationship should not be entered into lightly. All I wanted was to be completely sure of both his love for me, and mine for him, before taking such a big step.

The relationships in my past were mostly long term — I certainly didn't go in for one-night stands. I fully accepted that few people were likely to reach their thirties unscathed, but every affair that ended badly for me had left a nasty taste in my mouth and a horrible feeling of having been used. Eventually I'd pretty much come to the conclusion that enough was enough and I was better off alone. And then, after all this time, along came Nick who had the same ideals, including the belief, which few men seemed to have, that fidelity in a relationship was everything.

However, we weren't children and I didn't think it fair to keep Nick at arm's length until he went down on to one knee. The days of no sex before marriage were long gone, and anyway I wanted him as much as he wanted me. The thought of being in his arms made me weak with longing. Heat raced through my body at the thought of the pleasures that lay in store for both of us. It had been a long time for me but I finally knew the wait had been worth it.

Nick really was everything I wanted in a man and it soon became apparent that I was everything he wanted in a woman, too, because even as I was busily planning an evening of seduction for the next time we met he'd phoned me out of the blue.

'Nick,' I couldn't believe it — he rarely rang unless he said he was going to and not always then if I was honest, 'what a lovely surprise. I wasn't expecting to hear from you until the weekend.' I had a sudden thought, 'Oh, please don't say you can't make it . . . '

'We have to talk,' he began, 'this has gone on for long enough.'

My heart almost stopped beating at his words and the serious tone he was using. 'Nick?' Even I could hear the desperate note in my voice. 'Nick?' I said again.

Then he'd seemed to change and laughed suddenly. 'Marry me,' he'd said without preamble, surprisingly and very suddenly making the commitment that I really hadn't expected of him, and certainly not so soon. 'Throw a few things into a case after work on Friday,' he'd gone on to urge persuasively. 'We can spend some time together at my place in the New Forest, arrange a special licence and plan our future together.'

'Marry you?' I'd squealed, thrilled, but hardly daring to believe he meant it.

'Of course, it's what you want, isn't it?' He'd sounded almost brusque, though I couldn't believe he would imagine I'd turn him down.

'If it's what you want.'

'I want *you*,' he'd said deeply, and my toes had curled inside my shoes at the clear meaning in the husky tone.

He'd made no secret of his desire for me from the very start, and it had frightened and excited me all at once. I couldn't be any other than I was, but I had still been terrified that he would eventually get fed up with the strait-laced ways that he'd seemed to find so quaint at first or, even worse, coax me into a hasty affair that would end like all the others.

'But why the rush?' I'd felt obliged to ask,

knowing that tomorrow wouldn't be soon enough if Nick really did want to marry me.

'Can you think of a good reason to wait?' He had laughed again, and then telling me he had to go, he'd issued hasty instructions as to where and when we should meet; then he was gone with a seemingly casual, 'I'll see you there,' that was so filled with promise it brought a flush to my face that lasted long after I'd put the phone down.

My friends were aghast when I shared my amazing news, especially those I worked with, 'Charming though he undoubtedly is, you hardly know him or the first thing about him,' was Valerie's opinion and, being a colleague and older by several years and, therefore — in her eyes at least — wiser, she obviously thought she was perfectly entitled to give it. 'How do you know he can be trusted? He could be stringing you a line.'

I put that down to sour grapes from someone who'd never wed, had evidently given up on the idea entirely for herself and thought I should do the same, but then I discovered it was a sentiment echoed by Samantha, who shared my office, was more my age and happily married to boot.

I was incensed, accused them both roundly of being judgemental and grudging me my new-found happiness. Then, determined to show them how wrong they were, I proceeded to burn my bridges in grand style and with a speed that made my head spin if I was being honest. My request to take annual leave with immediate effect being rejected out of hand by my normally placid boss was the final push I needed.

'You, of all people, know this is our busiest time, Stacey,' Simon pointed out in what he clearly thought was a reasonable tone, 'with people clamouring for financial advice after expensive summer holidays and the festive season just around the corner. It was *your* idea to make our services readily available and comprehensible to Jo Public rather than just the business sector and those with money to invest, and it's worked beyond our wildest dreams. With the credit crunch biting we have more business coming our way than we can handle and, until we can take on more staff it's all hands to the pumps, I'm afraid, and so the answer has to be no. What can possibly be so important that it can't wait until a more reasonable time, anyway?'

'You're right, of course, I just wasn't thinking.' I smiled sweetly, but inside I was absolutely furious and even more determined to get my own way.

I liked Simon Manning, I really did, and he was normally one of the nicest, most reasonable people I knew. We had worked side by side for years, building up what had started as Manning's Financial Management, a very small firm of independent financial advisers, consisting at the beginning of just the two of us. I was secretary, personal assistant and general dogsbody, but he had listened to my ideas and put them to good use — along with his own — until we had become a real local success story, for which he gave me my share of the credit. But, I reminded myself furiously, that didn't mean I had to explain my every action to him. If it was too much trouble to allow me two paltry weeks' annual leave — to which I was perfectly entitled — then he could stick his bloody job permanently.

2

It took me only days to pack up my flat, put most of the contents into storage, and leave it in the hands of a letting agency. I left handing my notice in at work until the last day. Without allowing time for second thoughts I chose a time when Simon was out visiting a client, left an abrupt letter of resignation in his in-tray and, using my holiday entitlement to ensure I could leave immediately, I turned my back on the past to make way for my future with Nick.

Samantha and Valerie had done everything to try and stop me but, surprisingly, it was Valerie Winstanley who came hurrying after me and, in a complete about face told me with sweet sincerity, 'It's very wrong of us to be so disapproving and distrustful of a man we actually barely know. Some things are meant to be and clearly you and Nick love each other very much. If you don't follow your heart you may live to deeply regret it.'

There was a lot more and she was clearly putting aside her own very real concerns to wish me all the very best and I was grateful for it. She even hugged me, which I found touching since she really wasn't a touchy-feely kind of person. Having no family to speak of I had always been grateful for my friends, and at that moment and in my eyes Valerie had turned out to be a friend indeed.

It was only now, following winding roads in the unfamiliar depths of the forest, and peering out into the gathering gloom, that doubts began to creep in.

I was vaguely aware that Nick did have a family — albeit a small one — and at last I took the time to wonder why he had never introduced them to me and whether he intended to invite any relatives at all to the forthcoming ceremony.

The frown that wrinkled my brow cleared when I acknowledged that conventionality probably wasn't for Nick. No doubt it would just be the two of us and witnesses on the day, for it would only be for my sake he was bothering to get married at all. It just proved how much he must love me, and the thought made goose bumps roughen my skin. For the first time someone was actually putting my wishes first.

Taking a deep calming breath I began to look for the turning that Nick had described. Curious, in spite of myself, I also began to wonder about the family he'd barely mentioned in the admittedly short time we had been together.

I remembered him mentioning once — briefly, and almost in passing — that his father and mother had died in a road accident when he was quite young. He seemed very fond of the grandparents who had taken on his upbringing, though, so it did seem strange that he hadn't at least wanted them to meet me.

Since he hadn't referred to any siblings I presumed he was an only child like me, and my heart went out to him. I'd lost my own parents when, in my teens, they'd divorced and moved to live as far away from each other — and me — as was possible, so we had a lot in common. I was surprised there was no mention of aunts, uncles or cousins and neither had Nick really introduced me to many of his friends, either. Both of my parents being only children, too, meant I had no other family to speak of, but Nick had been introduced to my friends — which probably hadn't been such a great idea in hindsight, given the judgemental attitude they'd shown to our relationship, so perhaps his was the better way. A relationship, after all, was really only about the two people involved.

Happier with that thought, I gave myself up to focusing all my powers of concentration on finding the elusive turning that every gap in the tall trees seemed to promise. Easier said than done, I found, as one particular conversation with a colleague of Nick's suddenly came rushing back to haunt me, making me feel uncomfortable all over again.

'Ah, you must be the Annie who keeps enticing Nick away from his business and family commitments.' The sarcastic tone wasn't flattering at all, and as my hand tightened round Nick's mobile, I had to bite back the smart retort that might just have put the obnoxious man in his place. Who was he, and how dare he speak to me like that?

'I'm Nick's friend, yes,' I replied carefully. I would much have preferred it if this person — who seemed determined to be unpleasant, if his tone was anything to go by — didn't make use of any form of my name, let alone that particular abbreviation of Anastasia that only Nick ever used, but I held my tongue, reminding myself he might be someone important to Nick's business, or something. Instead, I'd offered helpfully, 'Nick's taking a shower. Can I give him a message?'

'Yes,' he ground out hatefully. 'You can tell him from me that I expect him to leave the undoubted delights you have to offer and get

16

his backside back here sooner rather than later. You might try reminding him that he does have responsibilities.'

I'd felt myself blushing hotly from the top of my blonde head to the tips of my lightly tanned toes, but the furious denial of the affair he was hinting at never got a chance to leave my tongue, as he had gone on forcefully, 'Just make sure you give him that message, word for word. I suppose you are capable of that?'

'I . . . You . . . ' The phone went dead before I'd recovered my powers of speech and my temper sufficiently to string a sentence together coherently, let alone deliver the stinging set-down he so richly deserved. I stared at Nick's expensive mobile, momentarily speechless, before throwing it thoughtlessly and with all my might across the room. I wasn't sure if I was pleased or sorry when it bounced harmlessly among the cushions on the couch.

'Insufferable, ignorant, obnoxious . . . ' I'd still been fuming when Nick came into the room, and for once I was too angry to be embarrassed at the casual way he strolled about my flat with only a carelessly tied towel preserving his modesty.

'That's what you get for answering other people's mobiles,' Nick said shortly, a slight smile taking the sting out of his words. 'You should have let it ring. Must have been my charming partner on the phone, I deduce. He does seem to have that effect on people. What did he say?'

I remembered that he had looked extremely annoyed at the high-handed message, though I had failed to pass on all of the disgusting little details his partner had taken such pleasure in adding, but, annoyed or not, Nick obviously intended to obey what was almost an order, and that had surprised me.

When I'd questioned him about that, Nick told me, 'Lex has a good business head on his shoulders, but he does depend on me more than he should. He's been with the firm for years. My father had left a will, you see, leaving my grandfather in charge until I could take over. I was just a boy at the time and Lex had the experience. He has ideas above his station, I'm afraid. I'll have to go. I won't be gone more than a couple of days.'

He was as good as his word and I hadn't given it another thought until now, when I found myself hoping the rest of Nick's friends and colleagues would be more amenable when I did eventually get to meet them.

'Oh, bugger.' I was dragged back to the present as I realized I'd just sailed past the turning I had been looking for. Slamming on the brakes I skidded to a halt, and swore roundly before reversing back to an entrance that was almost concealed by overhanging bushes and trees. There was the wooden sign Nick had mentioned but it was too dark to read what was on it.

The road I found myself following was little more than a lane, and it led so far back from the road that I'd almost decided that I'd gone wrong after all, when I passed between a huge pair of stone pillars, and on to a wide sweep of gravelled drive. In the headlights of the car the house looked large and imposing but — I noticed with a sinking heart — it was without so much as a glimmer of light from any of the windows to welcome me.

'He'll be round the back,' I laughed at my own doubts. Nick would be there. Of course he would, he wouldn't let me down. I wished I could believe that, but the blank appearance of the house and a silence that was broken only by the sound of the car engine quite definitely told me otherwise and the first feelings of doubt assailed me.

At the rear of the building I had to force myself to switch off the engine and get out of the car. It was very apparent that the house was completely deserted, and without even the benefit of the Mini's headlights the forest crouched, dark, and somehow menacing, all around me.

I just hoped Nick wasn't playing one of his stupid games because a sudden 'Boo!' or tap on the shoulder was going to be the death of me for sure.

Peering nervously about I forced one foot in front of the other and rapped, hopefully, first at the back door and then, even harder, on the front. The sound echoed eerily through the house. Both doors were, of course, firmly locked.

Standing there in the black darkness and surrounded by tall trees that were probably beautiful by day, but now made my surroundings seem isolated and terrifying, I felt very close to tears. Everything that could go wrong with my journey, had, and now I was finally here at last, tired and filthy, it was to find that Nick either hadn't waited, or had never arrived.

Well, there was nothing else for it, I would just have to try and find my way back the way I had come. The thought was not a pleasant one, especially now the light had gone, and the knowledge that most of the roads lacked streetlamps was daunting to say the least.

I dithered for a moment, but then reminded myself that I couldn't simply sit and wait all night in the vain hope that Nick would eventually arrive. Anyway, if I left, there was always the chance I might meet him on the way. It was my only hope. I might well have managed to recall a home number if he'd given me one, then I could at least have rung him at the first phone box I came to. As it was, the chances of my remembering the line of digits for his mobile were next to none, though I supposed I could drive until I came to a pub, order a meal, and ask if there was any chance they might recharge my phone while I ate.

I tried not to wonder, now it was a little late, why he had been so definite that he always rang me, and why I hadn't questioned it before. The explanation that he was often in business meetings and that some went on late into the night had seemed plausible enough at the time, I supposed.

I also tried not to wonder why Nick would choose to sleep on a couch in my poky flat each time he came down to Dorset, when he had a house like this a few miles away in the forest. I simply told myself firmly that he must have had his reasons and trying to ignore the fact it almost seemed as if he'd been trying to keep me hidden away.

Dismissing, with a huge effort, the doubts that were beginning to pile up, I climbed resolutely into the car, and reached for the ignition key. The engine didn't even whine this time. There was just an ominous click when I turned it, and I knew very well I'd be going nowhere for the time being.

Frustrated tears burned my eyes, and I had to squeeze them tightly shut and nip my lip quite sharply to stop myself from giving in to the strong desire to just bawl because everything had gone so wrong. I gave myself a mental shake and decided there were just two choices, to sleep in the car or find a way to get inside the house.

Thank goodness I was wearing trousers, but getting into the house still wasn't easy. I'd never liked heights, and climbing on to porches in the pitch dark was definitely not my idea of fun, but when the moon at last made a brief appearance I could see that the small window above had been left enticingly open just a fraction. It could hardly be classed as breaking and entering because I was, after all, there by invitation.

A handy wheelie-bin was brought into use and the undignified scramble that ensued eventually saw me fall in a heap onto the landing floor, a bit bruised and scratched, probably covered in green moss, but still in one piece and at least I was inside.

I wasn't really surprised, when I managed to find a light switch, to discover that the electric wasn't working and the keys to the doors — both front and back — could not be found, which was hardly surprising since I couldn't see a bloody thing and had to feel my way around. It just all seemed par for the course of the kind of day I'd had.

There was no way in the world I was going to attempt a return journey down over the porch to retrieve my case and I wasn't of a mind to explore further. I was too tired, too dispirited, and it was too dark anyway. It was too difficult to look for a bright side, but somehow I managed to convince myself that a reasonable explanation would arrive with Nick in the morning.

I made my way back upstairs and felt my way into the first bedroom I came to at the top of the sweeping staircase. I stripped to my underwear and climbed wearily beneath a plump duvet.

There was no warning, none at all. One minute the room and, as far as I was aware the house also, was dark and completely silent, the next the door flew open. A broad beam of light spilled across the bed where I had been — until that very minute — drifting off to sleep.

'What the . . . ?' a deep voice exploded.

I knew immediately the voice didn't belong to Nick and shot up in the wide bed, heart hammering and adrenalin coursing through my veins. Belatedly grabbing at the duvet and clasping it tightly to my breast, I found myself staring at the terrifying reality of all my worst fears rolled into one. There was a man — a stranger — right in the room with me.

3

From the light coming in from the landing it was clear the man was tall and strongly built. Any hope that I might manage to fight him off when he made his move faded to nothing. As dark as I imagined Satan to be, he took a step forward and his shadow loomed over me. Time seemed to stand still as our gazes clashed and held, and then I did the only thing I could think of and opened my mouth to scream, long and loud.

Had I closed my eyes? Surely not — but I didn't even realize he'd moved until a bruising hand cut off the sound almost before it was uttered, and most of my breath at the same time.

I was being attacked and instinctively fought back like a wild animal caught in a trap. I didn't need to remind myself that I was probably fighting for my life, and there was little time for conscious thought anyway, before I was tearing at the cruel fingers with nails that gouged deeply into tough, sinewy flesh.

There was an oath, a muttered, 'Christ, you little bitch,' and then my flailing hands were seized in the punishing grip of the intruder's spare hand and I was pushed hard back against the pillows.

I stared up at the figure leaning over me. His face was in deep shadow. I was petrified, quite sure that at any moment those strong fingers would be closing around my throat and squeezing the life out of me. The same life began to flash before my terrified gaze — including the wedding day I would now never see — when he spoke again.

'I'll let you go,' he hissed in a savage undertone, glaring at me menacingly, before adding, 'but only if I have your promise that you will not only remain silent, but also keep those vicious claws to yourself. Now, do I have your word?'

I tried to nod, knowing I had no choice. Futile to scream anyway; I had already realized that much belatedly, since I knew, as well as he must, that the house was miles from anywhere and there would be no one to hear me.

The minute he released me I was off the bed and running for the open door, but I was not quite fast enough. He moved with a speed that took my breath away and was there well before me, slamming it shut, cutting off my only way of escape, and throwing the room into black darkness.

I was already backing away on silent feet, when the room was suddenly flooded with the brilliance of the overhead light, and I stood, blinking like a startled rabbit in the unexpected glare, with no choice left but to face my attacker.

He lounged with deceptive ease to one side of the closed door, as if daring me to try and get past him, allowing his insolent gaze to travel, almost lazily over my scantily clad body, from the top of my tousled blonde head to the pink varnished nails of my bare feet.

My toes curled deeply into the blue pile of the carpet, as I became all too aware of just how little I was wearing. A silk cami, the white lace practically transparent, offered no protection at all from his all too interested gaze. With my heart thumping, I felt for the duvet on the bed behind me, snatched it up and, with trembling fingers, swathed it around myself, shielding my body from that lascivious regard.

'Almost a pity to cover such perfection,' he drawled hatefully, and my flesh crawled as I realized all over again just how vulnerable I was, alone in this huge house with this — this . . . ?

'Who are you anyway?' I lifted my chin and looked right at him, doing my best to indicate a confidence I was far from feeling, but aware that I had failed miserably when my voice quavered in the most pathetic way. I tried again — harder. 'I *demand* to know who you are.'

He didn't reply immediately, and the time he took gave me a chance to study him. If nothing else, I told myself, I'd be able to give the police an accurate description when this was over. I refused to consider any other scenario than the one of me managing to make my escape.

He didn't look much like a burglar, if I was being honest, and I was trying to be, despite my very real fear. But then again, total honesty would force me to admit I hadn't had enough to do with the criminal element of society to be able to pass judgement on the way law-breakers might or might not look. The pictures I had seen of such people in the newspapers were always notoriously poor reproductions anyway.

His immediate advantage over me was that he was fully clothed, and wearing a suit, of all things. Hardly dressed for housebreaking, I had to admit, but then I acknowledged that neither had I been.

The silence between us lengthened, and the more I studied the man, the less I felt seriously threatened by him. If he was going to murder me, or — or anything else — he

28

would surely have done something about it by now.

He seemed to be waiting for me to speak again, and sheer nervousness almost prompted me to do so. I had to remind myself that he was the interloper here, and therefore the one to be offering explanations. I went back to my perusal of him.

He was tall and he wasn't a youngster — not a teenager by any stretch of the imagination, somewhere in his early forties at a guess. I let my gaze run almost idly from his dark head down to what looked like pretty expensive leather shoes, and back again to his face. Too swarthy to be called handsome, I thought disparagingly. A beard that was little more than stubble gave him a disreputable appearance and his thick, black hair stood on end, probably as a result of our recent struggle. I almost recoiled when I saw the blood oozing from a deep scratch that ran from nose to chin and wondered when that had happened. I would never have considered it was in me to be so vicious, but then I *had* been acting instinctively and in self-defence.

His eyes — darkest blue or maybe grey — met my much lighter gaze steadily, and the black brows dived into a deep frown above the arrogant jut of his nose. He took one step towards me, but stopped immediately as I took one back and uttered a little shriek.

'All *right*, all *right*,' he muttered hastily, holding up his hands in a placating gesture, palms towards me. 'I won't come any closer, but perhaps you wouldn't mind telling me just what the *hell* you are doing here?'

'What the . . . ?' I was almost speechless — almost, but not quite. 'Well, that's rich coming from you,' I fumed furiously, forgetting to be afraid, or even cautious. 'You come barging into my bedroom in the middle of the night, and then you have the infernal cheek to question me? How *dare* you?'

The dark eyes surveyed me steadily, narrowing just slightly. They were definitely blue, almost navy. I could see that now, quite clearly. The man seemed momentarily at a loss, I was pleased to notice, and I wondered again what exactly he was doing there.

I jumped nervously as he moved one arm, but he only jerked his jacket sleeve back a little to expose an expensive gold watch. 'Ten past eleven,' he stated, adding sarcastically, 'hardly the middle of the night, is it?'

Was that all? I was more than a little surprised. It felt as if I'd been asleep for hours. I almost said so, and then reminded myself that the time had nothing to do with anything, and he'd still made no attempt to explain his presence.

30

'Don't change the subject.' I was pleased with my firm tone. Best to make it quite clear I would stand no more nonsense and that I wasn't some young girl he could terrorize, 'Now, you've quite obviously come to the wrong house, and I would suggest — no, demand — that you leave immediately.'

The man smiled then, and though there was no real humour in his expression, I couldn't help but notice that he appeared a lot less threatening now that he looked a little less grim.

'You demand that I leave immediately, do you?' His tone was deceptively silky, and I forced myself to nod emphatically. 'Now, why on earth would I want to do that when I've only just arrived?'

This was too much, and I could feel my temper rising so fast that I found the remnants of my previous and very real fear had completely disappeared. I drew myself up so that every inch of my five-and-a-half-foot frame counted, and thrust my chin forward and up a little so that I met his gaze squarely.

'Because you are an intruder and quite obviously have no business here. You've taken a wrong turn or something. Surely you realize that, and that you shouldn't be terrorizing a defenceless woman in this way?'

This time he laughed. He threw back his

head and he actually laughed. I found myself watching him, quite mesmerized, until I forced my attention back to the matter in hand. Stamping a bare foot ineffectually into the deep pile of the carpet, I hissed, 'I don't see *anything* to laugh at.'

'You don't?' he demanded, thrusting a pair of torn and lacerated hands forward for my inspection, and muttering, 'Defenceless? Huh! Says who?'

I forced myself not to flinch this time, telling him, quite forcefully, 'It was no more than you deserved, the way you burst in to my bedroom and manhandled me.'

The man took a deep breath. Almost, I couldn't help thinking, as if he were trying to keep his patience, and only managing with great difficulty.

'Right,' he said, as if he had reached a decision, 'this has gone on for long enough.'

'Yes, it has,' I replied smartly, glad that he was beginning to see sense at last and had now realized that I wasn't some chit of a girl he could intimidate. 'If you leave now, without any fuss, I won't even bother to phone the police,'

'How very kind of you.' The sarcasm in his tone was biting. The mention of the constabulary appeared not to faze him one little bit, I couldn't help noticing. I felt a hint of nerves fluttering again in my stomach, but chose to ignore it.

More than a little tired of his confident and high-handed manner, I suddenly lost all patience. The return of anger drove away again any hint of fear. It had been a dreadful day from start to finish, and being threatened by an intruder who seemed disinclined to leave was the last straw.

'Oh, get out,' I spat furiously. 'Go on — get out of this house — this minute.'

The laughter had died from his face long since, but I was quite unprepared for the sudden fury that darkened his eyes to jet, thinning his lips and carving grim lines on his face.

With a sense of deep foreboding, I realized that I should have kept calm, and tried to coax him from the house. A little belatedly I acknowledged that I'd been wrong to give him the benefit of the doubt. He was probably a dangerous criminal, for all his reasonably normal appearance, and now that I had provoked him, Lord knew what he might do. I remembered the strength in those punishing fingers and, shivering violently, pulled the duvet tighter around my body, knowing, as I did so that it would offer scant protection if he decided to attack me.

Gathering the shreds of my nerves carefully

together, I tried using another approach and a more reasonable tone.

'Look, I'm expecting my fiancé at any time,' I explained. 'This is his house and — '

'I don't think so,' he cut across my words so determinedly and with such emphasis that I fell silent immediately. 'This,' he insisted with spectacular simplicity, 'is *my* house, and you can hardly be my fiancée since I've never set eyes on you in my life before.'

He was lying about owning the house, was my first thought. That Nick had been lying about owning it was the second and though I tried to dismiss the very idea as impossible, it suddenly wasn't very easy to do.

'You're lying,' I accused, going for that option and trying not to allow any hint of uncertainty to creep into my tone. 'This is Nick Cable's house, and I am here by his invitation.'

'Ah.' The one short word was uttered almost under his breath, and his expression cleared a little, though the grim lines remained.

'What's that supposed to mean? Do you know Nick? Is that why you're here?'

'Oh, yes.' His voice was deceptively soft. 'I do know Nick. I know him very well indeed.'

I was stunned momentarily into silence as the penny finally dropped with a deafening clang. Whatever I had been expecting, it certainly hadn't been this. I stared into those dark eyes in complete consternation, wondering, belatedly, why I hadn't recognized that deep, sarcastic, and now all too familiar tone before. This, then, was the famous Lex.

'You're his business partner, aren't you? But this *can't* be your house. Nick said . . . '

I fell silent as, for the first time, I really began to doubt the truth of what Nick had said. I felt sick as it quickly became obvious to me that only someone who knew the house well would have known where to turn the electricity on. Why Nick should bother to lie about owning it was beyond me, but the untruth had made me look absolutely ridiculous, I realized crossly.

The next minute, in spite of myself, I felt my lips twitch into a tiny smile, possibly prompted by the sheer relief of realizing I was at least safe. How ludicrous it all was, humorous even, the more I thought about it. I tittered a little hysterically, and couldn't seem to stop — until I caught sight of his face.

He was looking — if possible — more furious than he had before, not less, and was glaring at me with very evident dislike, the well-shaped mouth curved into an ugly sneer.

'Nick asked you to meet him here, I take

it?' he queried, but as if he already knew the answer.

I nodded, wishing with all my heart that Nick had kept our rendezvous, as planned. This was not how it was supposed to have been at all, and I was still quite certain that Nick *had* said it was his house. Why on earth would he bother to lie about such a thing?

'We — we're to be married,' I offered. 'He — he didn't tell you?'

The full lips were pursed, the dark head shaken emphatically, before he demanded, 'Oh, that's what he told you, did he? Or is it just what you assumed?' Without waiting for my reply, he went on, 'He doesn't usually go that far.'

I thought he looked suddenly weary and again the whisper of doubt insinuated itself into my mind. Try as I might it refused to be dismissed, Nick should have been here. He had promised that he would be. He had let me down, and it wasn't even the first time, now that I thought about it, though he'd never let me down as spectacularly as this.

'I don't know what you're talking about.' I didn't quite feel able to give up yet. Perhaps Nick would still come. There would be some simple explanation, there usually was. 'He'll be here, he's probably just been held up.'

'God!' He slapped one scratched hand to

his forehead, and I jumped, staring at him when he ground out angrily, 'How can you be so bloody gullible? You ... What's your name, anyway?'

I should have told him to mind his own damn business, but the question, barked at me like that, elicited a response before I had even thought about it.

'Anastasia Trent.' Even as I replied, I couldn't think why I was using the full name I'd always detested — the name Nick had thought so sweet and romantic, but still hadn't hesitated to abbreviate to Annie instead of the Stacey I much preferred. I waited for the smirk and the smart remark that usually accompanied the revelation of my name, but this time it wasn't forthcoming.

'Never heard of you,' he said abruptly. Then, with calculated cruelty, 'Just another in a long line of Nick's little 'interests'.'

'What on earth do you mean?' It was beginning to feel as if the ground was shifting uncomfortably beneath my feet, and I was becoming ever more chilled, despite the thickness of the duvet. I asked the question almost automatically, but had an awful feeling that I already knew the answer.

'He said that you were the best thing that had ever happened to him? He said that he had never been in love like this before? This time he even offered you marriage — if you're to be believed.' His voice went on relentlessly, ruthlessly smashing all of my fragile and so recently built dreams into millions of tiny pieces with every word that he uttered. 'When what he really wanted was to get your delectable body into his bed — with no strings attached.'

'No. It wasn't like that.' It was too horrible. It made all that had been so wonderful seem nothing but a sordid sham. It also made me the biggest fool of all time, and I couldn't bear it.

'It was like that,' he insisted, his face set in hard lines. 'It was *just* like that, and the sooner you admit it, and go back to where you came from, the better for all of us.'

'You act as if you hate me,' I said it wonderingly, still reeling from the shock of his blunt attack, 'but you don't even know me. I certainly don't know you. You could be lying through those nice white teeth for all I know. In fact, I'm quite sure that you are.'

I forced myself to be angry, as angry as he was, because he must be wrong, he had to be. The alternative didn't even bear contemplating.

Ignoring all the other things I had said, he repeated, 'Hate you?' He laughed. It wasn't a pleasant sound. 'I hate what you are — and all of your kind. Holding out for a wedding ring, were you, and a share in the Cable money? Some of them have tried that before, too. Not very original, is it? Or even very modern these days, but then you are a little older and therefore possibly wiser than the women he usually goes for.'

'Oh, you — you're hateful. It wasn't like that. I love Nick, and he loves me — '

He had moved before I had time to take evasive action, and I found myself grasped by the shoulders and shaken hard, before he thrust his face close to mine to ask me abruptly, 'Oh, yes. And if he loves you so bloody much, perhaps you can tell me why he's marrying another woman *tomorrow?*'

He thrust me from him in patent disgust, and I fell on to the bed, still swaddled up like a mummy in the thick folds of the duvet. I didn't move. I knew that I couldn't have even if I'd wanted to, and stared up at him, believing him at last, though I couldn't for the life of me have said why.

'Oh, don't look at me with those great blue eyes.' He sounded outraged. 'You must have known what Nick was after and, I can assure you, he *always*,' he emphasized the word, 'loses interest once he gets it. Hard luck.' He shrugged. 'Why not put it down to experience? You can always try again. Sooner or later some other man of means is bound to fall for those sullied charms and offer you a wedding ring.'

'You bastard.'

'Don't attach that label to me,' he retorted grimly, yanking me to my feet. 'I'm just the poor devil who gets to clear up the mess of weeping females Nick always leaves behind, and with such monotonous regularity that I'm getting just a little tired of it, if you must know. I had hoped his impending marriage was going to change things.'

He looked impatiently round the room until his dark gaze settled on the clothes I had neatly folded over a chair. Seizing the garments, he flung them on to the bed.

'Now, I'm telling you to go, so I suggest you get out of *this.*' The duvet was wrenched from my nerveless fingers, swept from my body and tossed savagely across the room, 'And into something more suitable for your departure — and the sooner the better.' On that decisive note he walked to the door, threw it open, and walked back towards me to insist with great emphasis, 'In actual fact, *immediately* wouldn't be too soon for me.'

'Oh, Alexander, dear, I . . . '

The two of us stood practically chin to chin, both furiously angry and breathing heavily, and into the room had wandered a little old lady dressed neatly in twin set and pearls, who stopped short and stared at me in patent surprise, with not a little curiosity brightening her faded blue eyes.

'I wondered why you were taking so long.' Her words tinkled into the stunned silence that followed her appearance, and the lined faced looked curiously from one to the other of us. 'Who is this, Lex?'

The whole thing had been unreal from start to finish, so I shouldn't really even have felt surprised by his words when he eventually spoke, but I was actually staggered by the speed and the ease of an introduction that left me completely stunned and totally speechless.

'Grandmother.' He drew the elderly lady forward with great panache, as if he introduced scantily clad ladies to her every day of the week, and I could not help but be impressed, until he spoke again. Then his words drove every sensible thought out of my head.

'Let me acquaint you with my fiancée, Anastasia Trent,' he said.

4

I was so shocked, I felt as if I'd been struck dumb. My mouth formed hot words of denial, but no sound was produced despite my best efforts. I just could not believe it. This was the second time in less than a week that I had suddenly found myself engaged — but this time it was very definitely to the wrong man.

The elderly lady looked as stunned as I felt, and I watched her jaw drop in a comical replica of the way my own mouth was obviously hanging open. Despite the very evident surprise the announcement gave her she seemed to recover her wits and her good manners remarkably quickly. I could only be impressed by the speed of it, and then at the warmth of the welcome I was offered.

'How wonderful,' she enthused, coming to stand in front of me and looking into my eyes with a gaze that was uncomfortably perceptive, despite her obviously advanced years. 'She's lovely, Alexander dear,' she went on, after an unhurried scrutiny, 'so, why have you kept her such a secret?'

Ha! I almost laughed out loud and the look

I directed 'Alexander dear's' way clearly told him to now get out of that one.

'I couldn't steal Nick's thunder, now, could I? One wedding in the family at a time is quite enough to deal with, don't you think?'

Again, the ease and speed with which he produced such a reasonable response astonished me, keeping me silent for just as long as it took for him to shepherd his grandmother from the room, with the promise that we would be down in a moment speeding her on her way.

The door had barely closed behind her back before I was demanding furiously, 'What the bloody *hell* do you think you're playing at?'

'Keep your voice down, will you?' His angry tone more than matched my own. 'Give me time to think for a moment.'

'Give you time to think?' I fumed. 'It's a little bit late for that, isn't it?'

'I didn't notice you coming up with an acceptable explanation for your presence in my bedroom, clad only in the flimsiest of underwear,' he retorted hardily, flicking a dark and extremely disapproving gaze in my direction, 'and one that wouldn't shock an innocent old lady to the core.'

Dark colour flushed my face to an

unbecoming scarlet. '*Your* bedroom . . . But I thought . . . '

'Oh, come off it, my dear woman. You clearly didn't think at all before you rushed to throw yourself eagerly into my, admittedly charming, younger brother's arms. I doubt it mattered much at all to you whose bed you were in.'

He made it all sound so sordid, and even I had to admit that, to him, it probably looked that way. My cheeks burned uncomfortably, and I was about to rush to my own defence when I suddenly realized exactly what he'd just said and what it meant.

'Your *brother* — Nick's your *brother?*'

'Yes,' he said sarcastically, mimicking my shocked tone as he added, 'Nick's my brother, and that can't have come as a total surprise to you — unless you embarked on your affair without knowing the first thing about each other. He must have spoken of me — about his family.'

'Of course he did.' I thought I managed to sound emphatic, while at the same time gathering my scrambled wits together and trying desperately to recall whether Nick *had* ever referred to this Lex person as anything other than a business partner. To my own dismay, I really didn't think that he had, and yet another damning lie was added to all the others he'd apparently told me.

I struggled on because I felt I had to defend myself, and my actions, 'It really wasn't the way you make it sound. I've told you how it was and I can't help it if you choose not to believe me. Nick asked me to meet him here. We were to make plans for the future. He said we would be married as soon as it could be arranged . . . '

I stopped then, knowing it was useless to continue, when his grim expression told me quite clearly that if I'd actually believed such flimsy promises, then I was an even bigger fool than he already took me for.

'You should have told your grandmother the truth,' I said eventually. 'You really didn't have to protect my reputation like that.'

'Don't flatter yourself,' he ground out, moving away from me as if just being near disgusted him. 'Protecting you, or that playboy brother of mine, was the last thing on my mind.'

'Then, why . . . ?' I was mystified. The man was a mass of contradictions, but I could have sworn, seeing him with the old lady, that his heart was almost in the right place, at least where some people were concerned.

'To protect *them*.' He jerked a thumb towards the door in an impatient gesture that spoke volumes. 'My grandparents don't deserve to be hurt or offended, as they surely will be if they ever discover just what an unsavoury reputation Nick has managed to acquire in the years since he reached puberty, because you can't really believe that you're the first to fall for his particular line in bullshit. Having been his guardians since he was a young child, they'd be sure to assume his behaviour was somehow due to his upbringing, and try to take the blame.'

This was all becoming stranger by the minute, and I shook my head slightly as if to clear it.

'Oh, don't look at me so innocently with those big eyes of yours.' He sounded thoroughly exasperated. 'How would your family feel if they could see you like this?'

The question was unexpected, and I flushed beetroot-red once again as it hit home. It wasn't my parents I was worried about, since they were safely overseas and couldn't have been less interested, but my friends were a different matter and I recalled with a sinking heart just how desperately they had tried to urge caution.

Not only had I failed to heed their warnings that I barely knew Nick but I had thrown their concern back into their worried faces, even going so far as to accuse them of grudging me my new-found happiness.

However, despite all of that, it wasn't too difficult to imagine their shock and dismay if they ever learned of the position I now found myself in.

I suddenly felt thoroughly ashamed. It didn't even help to tell myself I'd been duped, and by an expert, if this man was to be believed. I really was old enough to have known better. In spite of past experiences that normally made me over-cautious to say the least, I'd still allowed myself to be carried away by a fairy-tale scenario that had seemed too good to be true right from the start. What on earth I'd been thinking of, I really had no idea.

'I'm so sorry. I seem to have caused you a whole lot of bother, but if you would let me go down and explain . . . ' I felt it was the very least I could do in the circumstances. 'After all, it's obvious none of this is any of your fault.'

'Well,' he folded his long length into the small leather armchair that had until recently held my clothes, and drawled smoothly, 'I'm glad you finally appreciate that fact at last.'

'You still didn't have to tell your grand-mother that we were engaged to be married,' I pointed out hastily, unwilling to take *all* of the blame.

'Perhaps not,' he allowed, relaxing back

into the chair as if he were quite prepared to discuss the matter at length, his dark blue eyes were studying me with a disconcerting amount of interest.

I was immediately reminded of my state of undress and was horrified to think I had been preparing to stand and discuss the situation with this arrogant stranger still only dressed in the flimsiest of underwear. Burning with sudden embarrassment, it was all I could do to prevent myself crossing my arms across my body in a tardy attempt at maidenly modesty.

The duvet he had thrown was still on the floor, and I stared at it longingly. But to get to it I would have to pass close by the chair where he still lounged with apparent ease. The thought of going anywhere near him made me decidedly nervous, despite the fact that I had long since convinced myself that he had no design on my person. I reluctantly decided against that method of covering myself.

I could always hold a pillow in front of me, and I only had to stretch out a hand for one of those. The thought was tempting, and my hand itched to comply, but I felt quite sure that such a belated and obvious attempt at modesty would make those well-shaped lips curl in the disconcerting way that was already becoming familiar, and consequently I would end up feeling more foolish than I already did.

'So, you admit that was a mistake on your part?' I picked up the conversation along with the first item my hand felt when I reached, almost casually, towards the clothes that he had flung so furiously on to the bed earlier,

'It was the best I could come up with at a second's notice.' He watched me pull on the cream sweater, his eyes dark and unfathomable, before adding, 'I didn't hear you come up with anything better. Would you really have preferred me to tell my grandmother that you were waiting in my bed for my about-to-be-married brother?'

I flushed a deep and fiery red yet again, realizing I seemed to have done nothing but blush since I had met the damned man, and objected, 'That's not fair. I wasn't . . . Well, I was, but not in the way you're implying and I thought it was me he was marrying.'

He leaned forward and tossed me the pair of trousers that were lying across the end of the bed, telling me in a hard tone, 'Oh, come on. It's nothing but the truth. How cosy you would have been if only *he'd* turned up, and *I* hadn't.'

'We weren't going to stay here.' It wasn't entirely the truth, but I was struggling to defend myself, wondering all the time why I was bothering and why I didn't just tell him straight out that it was none of his bloody business? I answered my own question. Because it was his business, of course, I had to admit fairly. It had become his business the minute I had climbed into his house and into his bed — except, in my own defence, I hadn't actually known that either was his.

Damn Nick, damn him and his lies and deceit, I fumed, temper preventing the tears that I couldn't possibly cry, not after his brother's sarcastic comments about weeping females. Damn him for putting me in such a position. I still couldn't believe he'd done such a thing, after all his promises and the avowals of love that I had been stupid enough to believe.

'Oh, sure.' He clearly didn't believe a word, and I gave up. Ignoring him, I reached for my black boots. The watching gaze became sharp as he told me, 'You won't want those on indoors.'

I thrust my foot firmly into the first one, before demanding of him, 'You surely can't really be expecting me to stay here?'

I reached for the other boot, but he was on his feet in an instant, snatching it away and holding it out of my reach. 'I can, and I do,' he said emphatically.

'Oh, for heaven's sake.' I lost all patience

with him, and made a grab for my footwear, which was immediately thrust behind his suited back. I refused to get involved in a childish tussle for ownership, and settled for suggesting, in the most exasperated tone, 'Just tell your grandparents the truth, for God's sake. Your brother is not a child now, to be shielded from disapproval, and their opinion of me can't matter as they don't even *know* me.'

'You just don't listen, do you?' He thrust a grimly set face into mine. He was so close I could see the dark stubble on his tanned flesh in minute detail, and even smell a hint of cologne.

I noticed almost against my will the silver flecks in the deep blue of his eyes, or maybe they were sparks from the anger I, and my situation, provoked in him. I shivered. The sooner I was out of here the better, I reminded myself, and turned my attention resolutely back to the matter in hand.

'That's all I have been doing since you barged through that door.' I let my fury match his, meeting those dark and angry eyes without flinching. 'Listening to you insult me, and then to your clever introduction that's only made matters far worse for both of us. Now you can just let me have my say.'

I heard him take a deep, and savage breath,

before he muttered, 'Go on then, see what you can come up with, but it had better be good, and nowhere near the unsavoury truth, I warn you.'

'Telling lies runs in your family then, does it?' I spoke thoughtlessly, more from my deep annoyance than anything else. I was quite unprepared when he seized me by both arms and almost hauled me off my feet. I bit back a terrified scream and struggled wildly. 'Put me down, damn you.'

'You're classing me with my brother,' he ground out furiously, the sparks in his eyes pretty awe-inspiring now, 'and I won't *have* it, do you hear me?' He shook me until I was sure I heard my teeth rattle.

Shocked into silence, I could only stare up at him.

'Oh, you . . . ' he began, and then suddenly stopped speaking, a watchful expression replacing his former anger, before, quite gently, and to my utmost amazement, he drew me into his arms.

Even before he had lowered his head, I was shockingly aware that he was going to kiss me and I froze. The minute his lips touched my own, though, the hands that I had placed against his chest flattened on his shirtfront and I resisted him with all of my puny strength. At the same time I tried desperately but ineffectually to twist my head away. He held me fast, my efforts making little or no impression at all.

Eventually, he lifted his dark head and smiled into my eyes. Stunned into a shocked silence I simply stared back. Then he turned, still holding me, to say over his shoulder, 'We're just coming.'

Only then did I realize that his grandmother was standing in the doorway and that he must have heard her coming. I really didn't know which of us I was more furious with at that moment, him, me, or the old lady the whole false display must have been for.

I just could not believe that I had allowed him to kiss me in that way. What on earth was the matter with me? I seemed to have become another person, from the moment this bloody man had walked through the door, scattering my fragile dreams with a few carelessly spoken words, and pitching me into a situation that was becoming more unreal with every passing minute.

My fingers spread against his chest once more, and I shoved with all of my strength, I might have been pushing against solid granite for all the impression I made. The blue eyes darkened warningly, and the hold on me tightened inexorably.

'You'll have to forgive us,' he told the

older woman lightly. 'We're just getting reacquainted.'

There was the softest chuckle, before the door closed very quietly, and I made another, greater effort to thrust him away, hissing at the same time, 'How dare you take liberties like that?'

He gave a soft, low laugh, before lowering his head again, and it was only because I made a determined effort to wrench my head away that he didn't find my lips once more.

'Stop it,' My hands flew up, and burying them deep in the thickness of his black hair, I tugged with all of my might. 'Stop playing games.'

'Playing games?' He laughed harshly. 'I don't usually go in for that kind of thing. I leave it to my brother. This time, though, he went a little too far, and innocent as you may claim to be, I'm afraid you and I are going to play one, too, and I, and only I, will decide when it is over.'

I stopped tugging at his hair — he barely seemed to notice my efforts anyway. 'You said I should have my say,' I didn't hesitate to remind him, racking my brains for the suitable solution that he might just accept, but which had so far eluded me, despite the fact that I might have led him to believe otherwise.

'I changed my mind,' he stated categorically, in a tone that brooked no argument. 'Between the pair of you, you and that brother of mine have placed me in an awkward and very embarrassing situation that was not in any way of my own making, and definitely not of my choosing.' He threw me a look that brought the hot colour flooding back into my cheeks. 'You can't believe that I would tie myself to one of Nick's cast-offs, even briefly, if there were any other way.'

He made me sound like a . . . I couldn't even bring myself to form the word silently. I had never been so humiliated, and the worst of it was that I could actually see his point of view.

'I'm not willing to discuss this any further,' he continued, in a voice so grim that I wouldn't have dared to interrupt, even had I managed to come up with something reasonable to say. 'Given more time,' he went on, 'I might have come up with a better explanation for your presence, but as it is — well — we are just going to have to live with this one for a time.'

'Yes.'

'I . . . ' he paused, stared down at me, his firm grip slackening slightly and asked, 'What did you say?'

'I said yes,' I repeated meekly, hating

myself for giving in so easily, but really feeling that I had no choice but to go along with his crazy idea, at least for the time being. If Nick had only been here . . . But he hadn't been, and he obviously wasn't going to be. I hardened a heart that was going to cause me a lot of pain when I had time to consider just how badly I had been let down. Better for now, I thought, to try not to think at all.

'Well.' The hands on my arms were almost caressing now, the strength of his fingers warm and gentle through the wool of my sweater. 'That's better.' He actually smiled.

If he was surprised at my sudden capitulation, I thought he hid it very well, and there was no sign of triumph on his face, for which I was grateful.

I sighed deeply. 'What do you want me to do?'

He released me abruptly, so that I took an involuntary step backwards, before subsiding weakly on to the bed in an untidy heap. From there I watched him prowl uneasily back and forth, raking his fingers through the thick black of his hair in an uneasy gesture that belied his former confident manner.

He swung round to face me quite suddenly, his mind obviously made up. 'We'll play it by ear,' he said, with a deep nod. 'But my grandparents are not stupid people, for all their great age, so you must follow my lead, or they will see though this ridiculous sham immediately.' He thrust his face, grim once more, into mine. 'Do you think you can manage that?'

I nodded, fighting the desperate urge to lean back, away from him, and the even greater desire to yell that this was all absurd, and I was leaving that very minute, whatever he had to say on the subject. Why I didn't do just that, right now, I was unclear. Was it those harmless old people waiting downstairs? A car that refused to start? The man in front of me, who for all of his obnoxious ways, hadn't chosen to be placed in this situation? Or was it the overwhelming reality of a matter that I had not previously considered?

The truth actually was that I had burned my bridges for Nick Cable and his false promises, and for now had nowhere else to go. I looked up at the man who obviously despised me, and with good reason I was forced to admit. If everything he had said about his brother was to be believed, I knew that I really didn't want him to know every detail of the height of my folly, or the embarrassing depths of my gullibility. I was going to have to live with that knowledge myself, and for now that was quite bad enough.

5

Lex seemed satisfied at last that I wasn't going to make a run for it, and he gravely handed me the black boot he'd been withholding.

'Thank you.' I made no effort to keep the sarcasm out of my tone.

'Don't even think of leaving,' he stressed, putting out a tanned and thoroughly scratched hand to help me to my feet. 'Not until I say so. My brother might have invited you, but I'm afraid I shall be the one to insist on your staying, for as long as I think necessary.'

The man was insufferable, not only bossy but pompous too, in my opinion. Had he been different I might have gone along with his plan in a much more willing frame of mind, but as it was I did my best to ignore his hand, rising to my feet unaided, and trying not to notice again the many lacerations I'd inflicted.

In truth I was appalled at the damage I had done to the otherwise smooth skin, but then I reminded myself hardily that it was really no more than he deserved for the way he had grabbed me so unceremoniously. I resolutely refused to acknowledge that I *had* been about to scream my lungs out at that point, and he had simply been mindful of the elderly couple downstairs. After all, I couldn't possibly have known that, could I?

'I won't go anywhere,' I promised sullenly, knowing it was a promise I hadn't a hope of breaking, stuck as I was in the middle of nowhere with a car that refused to start. Turning away, I pulled the boot on. 'You have my word.'

'Good girl.'

He made me sound like child or an obedient dog. I fumed, but again did my best to ignore it. I raked my hands through the tangled blonde of my shoulder-length hair, and asked, 'Should I tidy myself up a bit, before we go down?'

Lex gave me a cursory glance, his eyes dark and disapproving, before advising tersely, 'Don't bother, they both know you've just climbed out of my bed.'

I tried, and failed, to halt the hot tide of colour that flooded my face. He wasn't going to miss a chance, I acknowledged, to remind me of the situation he had found me in, and for me always to rise to his bait was going to be both time consuming and pointless.

Ignoring the comment totally, I said, with a

calm I was far from feeling, 'Shall we go then?'

His eyes narrowed to gleaming slits as he viewed me suspiciously, obviously thrown by my acquiescence, but then he simply reminded me, 'Follow my lead,' before making for the door.

None of this is real, was my first hysterical thought, as I followed him obediently down the wide, curving staircase that I'd navigated, hours earlier and in a different frame of mind, in the pitch dark. Was I really here, in this remote house, about to be reintroduced by a complete stranger to his grandparents as his fiancée? Surely I would wake up at any minute and find that it had all been a weird and wonderful dream, after all.

I tried pinching myself, and the small pain told me I was wide awake and my flesh was real enough. As real as the tall, dark man I followed, with growing trepidation, into a situation that had all the ingredients of an old-fashioned Whitehall farce. It might have been really funny, I acknowledged ruefully, if it didn't all seem so sordid. I'd spent my whole life staying out of trouble and was far too old to be getting into scrapes like the one I now found myself in.

At the door to what must have been the

kitchen, Lex halted, glanced over his shoulder as if to reassure himself that I was still there, then with a brief, satisfied nod, he strolled into the brightly lit room.

I couldn't help but admire his confident, almost nonchalant air and I straightened my own slim shoulders almost imperceptibly. It was all for show and my legs were trembling so badly that I had to force them to carry me forward and into a charming country kitchen with a beamed ceiling and oak units lining the walls.

'There,' Lex's grandmother, looking up from the tea she was pouring, exclaimed in very evident satisfaction, 'didn't I tell you she was quite lovely?'

I blushed under the close scrutiny of two pairs of interested eyes, and felt sure the elderly couple were going to see right through me. They looked far too shrewd to be fooled for even a moment, and I could feel myself cringing as I waited to be exposed for the fraud I undoubtedly was.

The firm arm that settled about my waist was unexpected, but it was surprisingly very, very welcome, which astonished me. I seemed to draw strength from the reassuring warmth of the man who now stood close beside me. In one easy movement, I realized, Lex had transformed us from the two separate people we really were, into the couple his grandparents were expecting to see. I couldn't help but be impressed.

'Now, Grandmother, you're embarrassing my fiancée,' he chided, with a smile in his voice to soften his words. 'Come and say hello properly.'

'Anastasia, isn't it?' Lex's grandfather rose from the table and stepped forward with his hand extended, 'Aaron Cable and my wife is Eleanor.' There was a wide, welcoming smile on a face that was a very definite older and somehow kinder version of his elder grandson's.

'Stacey.' My lips curved of their own volition into a smile as my hand was taken and held in the warmth of a very firm grasp. 'Please call me Stacey. All my friends do.'

'Stacey it shall be, then, and I do believe Eleanor made you blush, my dear.' The dark blue of his eyes was infinitely approving. 'I didn't even realize that modern women knew how.'

'Now, Aaron, you're not to tease her.' His wife came to stand beside him, and she gave him a little push. 'We don't want to frighten Stacey off when it's taken Alexander so long to find her. Come and have a cup of tea, my dear, and tell me all about yourself. By the way,' she touched my sleeve, 'did you realize there were dirty marks on your pretty sweater?'

'Um, yes, a punctured tyre on the way here.' I was pleased to be able to tell the truth about something.

Eleanor tutted, and then coaxed me away from the reassuring pressure of Lex's arm. I looked back at him desperately. He must have seen the clear panic in my eyes, because he gave a slight nod as if to say I was doing just fine, and he strolled after us as if he hadn't a care in the world.

All the questions — and there were a great many — were all about me, and were quite easily answered, to my relief. I was able to talk happily enough about my job as a financial adviser in a small but up-coming company in the town of Brankstone, and of the flat nearby that I called home. All the while I was trying not to remember that I had, in fact, given both up — so determined had I been to believe I would be moving out of the area and on to another life elsewhere as Nick's wife. I went on to explain briefly that my parents had moved overseas some years before, neglecting to mention the fact of their divorce, which I felt was too much information to be providing to complete strangers.

'Surely, it must have been a wrench for them to leave you behind?' Eleanor Cable looked concerned. 'They didn't leave the country for health reasons, I hope, my dear?'

I smiled ruefully, thinking back to the assurances I'd been offered before they left to go their separate ways that they'd be much happier and healthier apart, and told her, 'Oh, nothing like that, but I think they'd both accepted by then that I was quite old enough to stand on my own two feet.' It was certainly what they'd told me at the time.

The older woman clapped her hands delightedly, 'You have a lot in common with Lex then,' she exclaimed, mystifying me. I had no idea what she was talking about.

'I assume my wife means that you both faced responsibility at a comparatively young age,' Aaron Cable put in helpfully, perhaps seeing my confusion.

'That's right, darling.' Lex came to the rescue in the nick of time. 'Remember I told you about taking over the business?'

'Oh, yes, of course,' My brow cleared, suddenly recalling that Nick had told me that much even if he had neglected to mention the fact that Lex was also family.

I dreaded finding myself faced with other facts that I should obviously know, but next time might not, and I was beginning to feel tired and fed up with the whole business. It wasn't very nice of us, I decided, to be pulling the wool over the eyes of such a sweet and obviously doting pair.

'Stacey looks worn out.' Lex came to stand behind my chair, one hand resting carelessly on my shoulder, and his fingers seemed to burn my skin even through the thick wool of my sweater. 'Our late arrival already got her out of bed once, and we should probably all be thinking of going up. We have a big day tomorrow.'

'Yes, of course . . . Good God, Alexander.' There was a sudden horrified gasp from his grandmother. 'What on earth have you done to your hand?'

I cringed, and only just resisted the futile urge to cover the offending scratches with my own fingers, knowing it was too late for that — much too late,

'A run-in with a cat,' came the smooth reply. 'It had got into the cellar, and I came into contact with the creature while I was looking for that replacement light bulb for the landing.'

'I think it actually caught your face, too, but the poor thing must have been frightened to death.' His grandmother's gentle tone was full of concern for the non-existent animal, but I wasn't really listening.

So the electric hadn't been off at all, was my first thought, and then I knew a vague annoyance with myself for not checking more than one switch when I'd first climbed into the house. My second was to be, once again, impressed with the speed and inventiveness of his easy explanation. A cat, indeed; my lips quirked and I found I had to turn and face Lex in case his grandparents thought that my humour was misplaced.

'Yes.' Lex looked thoughtful, and he only murmured his reply. His dark gaze fell to my lips, following the curve of my slight smile, and then he swooped — that was the only word I could find to describe the swift movement — and before I knew what was happening, I found myself being very thoroughly kissed again.

My immediate, and very angry instinct was to push Lex away with all the strength I possessed, but then I remembered the elderly audience and my promise to continue with the farce that Lex and I were a couple in love. Resisting the savage urge that had my hands pressing against that immovable chest, I pressed my lips firmly together, closed my eyes tightly and prepared to put on the act of my life.

There was a dry and amused cough and I was blushing hotly when I faced the smiling couple, and rushed to apologize profusely. 'I'm so sorry,' I stammered. 'I don't know what came over me — er — us. I don't normally behave — '

'Perfectly understandable.' There was a definite twinkle in Aaron Cable's navy eyes, and the thick black eyebrows twitched humorously.

'Wonderful to see a couple so much in love.' His wife's eyes were misty. 'I only wish it was your wedding we were going to tomorrow. I have my doubts . . . ' She stopped talking suddenly, as if she'd said too much already, and then hurried on, 'You'll be coming, of course, Stacey — to my other grandson, Nick's wedding.'

The shock was intense, despite the fact I had already been warned. I felt as if I'd been punched hard in the stomach. So it really was true, then? Nick was marrying someone else, which left me to question whether he had seriously intended to go straight from my bed to his bride's. I desperately turned my thoughts away, unable, as yet, to face the pain that accepting the depth of Nick's betrayal would bring.

My answer was immediate and emphatic, 'Oh, no, I . . . '

The hands on my shoulders tightened imperceptibly, and Lex's deep voice cut in silkily, 'Of course you will, darling.' He laughed softly — and cruelly, I thought. 'How remiss of me not to sort out an invitation, but I'm sure Stacey wouldn't miss it for the world,' he added for his grandparents' benefit.

There was just a hint of a threat in his light tone, but I was quite sure that I was the only one who was aware of it. The elderly couple just smiled fondly on. There was nothing I could do, but to smile myself and agree, through gritted teeth, 'I'd love it more than anything. I adore weddings,' while already looking for a valid excuse to avoid this one at all costs.

The hands lifted me now from my seat at the table, and with a concern that might have been touching if it hadn't been so false, he told me, 'It's bed for you, my love. You look all in. You can stay in my room, and I'll take the one down the hall. Goodnight, Gran, Grandfather.'

My own goodnights were obscured by a tinkling laugh, and then his grandmother said flatly, 'Oh, Alexander. Don't be so ridiculous. Do you think we were both born in the dark ages? We'd hardly expect you to sleep apart for our benefit, especially in your own house. You must think us very narrow-minded.'

I couldn't believe what I was hearing, and from a woman who must surely be in her eighties. I waited for Lex to refuse, and was absolutely horrified when he did no such thing, but laughingly, and with such a false show of gratitude, agreed.

'You're embarrassing the girl, between you,' Aaron pointed out, and I turned to him gratefully, sure that he would come to my rescue. Again, I was to be disappointed, and he merely said, 'She looks worn out. Take her on up, my boy, and your grandmother and I will see you both in the morning.'

A firm hand in the small of my back almost propelled me from the room, but the door had barely closed behind us before I turned on Lex with a ferocity that clearly took him aback.

'You must know that I have no intention of sharing a room with you,' I hissed, thrusting my face forward until it was mere inches from his. 'You are carrying this — this — damned farce too far, and I will not do it. Do you hear me?'

The sparks that lit those dark eyes should have warned me, but I was too angry to be wary. I opened my mouth to continue the tirade, only to have the breath taken right out of me by the speed and sheer force of the hand on my arm steering me along the hall to the foot of the wide stairs.

'Yes, I do hear you,' he informed me through gritted teeth. 'And so,' he jerked a thumb over his shoulder, before urging me with the same hand up the stairs in great strides, two at a time in places, to continue at the top, 'will they.'

He wasn't even out of breath, I couldn't help noticing. I was impressed in spite of myself, especially since I was having to take great gulps of air into my labouring lungs.

'There is no way we will be sleeping in the same room, never mind the same bed, and so I'm telling you.'

There, that should do it. I was pleased with my no-nonsense and decisive tone, even if I was still panting as if I'd run a mile.

Finding myself inside the bedroom we had so recently left, with the door firmly closed, and an angry Lex positioned, once again, between myself and it, I couldn't have said how it had happened so fast and entirely against my will, but I told myself I just wasn't having it.

'Either you get out of this room, or I do,' I told him furiously, 'if not I shall scream this bloody house down. Do you hear me?'

He advanced towards me, menace in the set of his grim face, and in the hands that were clenched into threatening fists on either side of his body. He moved with the grace of a panther, and looked every bit as dark, sleek, and dangerous. I gulped deep in my throat, sure in the knowledge that this time I had definitely gone too far.

'I hear you.' He towered over me. I could feel his warm breath stirring the loose tendrils of my hair — smell the faint aroma of his cologne and the sheer masculine odour of him. 'But I intend to make damn sure that my grandparents don't, even if I have to gag you.' He correctly interpreted my look, and dared me, 'Try me — go on, just try me. I'm just about at the end of my patience with you, and your belated show of maidenly outrage. I can assure you that your *virtue*,' he emphasized the word mockingly, 'is quite safe with me.'

I pressed my lips together, holding back an angry retort, and glared at him. The sparks in his eyes were awesome to see, and I was impressed in spite of myself. I did not quite have the nerve to see how far I could push him before he reached the end of his tether, and so I tried a different tack.

'Just tell me this.' I moved almost nonchalantly across the room, and he moved, with equal nonchalance, to place himself between the door and me again. I threw him a look of intense dislike before sitting in the leather chair. I tried to look relaxed, determined that he shouldn't know just how much I was still quaking inside.

'Why?' I continued, 'is it so important that your grandparents shouldn't know about Nick and me — and all his other little interests if you're to be believed? Yet you don't mind them believing that you are sleeping around?'

Lex stared at me broodingly for such long, silent minutes that I began to think he wasn't even going to bother to reply. His black brows dipped frowningly, narrowing his eyes to slits that glittered, and that disturbing gaze never left my face.

Then he prowled, that was the only way to describe his walk, three steps one way, and three steps back. Moving like a caged animal across the room, always keeping between the door and me, I realized.

He stopped, quite suddenly, and turned to face me again. I found my back was pressed hard against the chair, and wondered nervously what he was going to do next.

Lex sighed deeply and unexpectedly, then said in a weary tone, 'They know I don't sleep around, since they spend a lot of time with me here and for them to meet a female in my home is a rarity. I should explain that they *are* quite old-fashioned, despite the impression they might have given you, and letting us share a room is a huge concession on their part. I felt that refusing them would only cause them unnecessary embarrassment, but perhaps that's difficult for you to understand.'

Quite against my will, I found that I was beginning to, though I had no intention of telling him so.

With a shrug, he continued, 'I don't really know how to explain about Nick, except to say that my brother, being so much younger — and little more than a child when our parents died — has always been the blue-eyed boy of the family and has been rather spoiled by all of us.'

'He can do no wrong in their eyes, you see, and they would be mortified if they could see the way that he really behaves. Oh,' he shrugged, 'in his defence Nick lacks any self-awareness. I don't think there is any real harm in him but he has never been made to take any responsibility for his actions. He treats life as a game and chooses not to see that people get hurt. I'd rather our grandparents didn't become aware of that side to his nature. I have to believe there's no real harm in Nick, and that eventually he will just grow up and become a responsible human being.'

His mouth twisted in a rueful grimace, and I, fascinated, in spite of myself, waited for him to go on.

'I had the business to run as quite a young man, Nick being several years younger had the freedom to do as he pleased, and I suppose it went to his head. As the baby of the family he was doted on by our parents and then by our grandparents. Excuses have always been made for him and I know I'm guilty of doing that.

'When it comes to the fair sex,' he grimaced ruefully, 'he's always had a certain charm, I'll admit that much, having seen him exert it on more than one occasion, and he lets his success go to his admittedly handsome, but rather immature head. It might not be so bad if . . . ' he had been talking almost to himself, but suddenly he threw me a look of such intense dislike that it chilled me to the bone, 'if women like you didn't make it so easy for him to collect them like so many trophies, and make it so much fun for him to love them and leave them behind. All without a pang of regret on his part, as far as I can ever tell.'

'You hate him, don't you?' I asked almost wonderingly, 'and me, too, just because I was foolish enough to fall in love with him and believe his lies.'

'No, I don't hate him at all, or you either, come to that,' he denied sharply, and then went on, 'I don't know you, but I'm actually rather fond of Nick. I might go so far as to say I love him — he is my brother, after all. What I hate is the casual way he uses women, and the women for allowing themselves to be used like that. I hate the way it cheapens what love is supposed to be all about.'

He glared at me from beneath dark brows, and I knew, very surely, that he lied. Oh, not about his brother. Blood was, in fact, thicker than water, after all. But he detested me. He despised me, along with all the rest of Nick's 'weeping females'.

His opinion of me didn't matter, of course. I tried to tell myself that, and tried to believe it. Why should it, after all, when I hardly knew the man? Once I left this house I would never have to see him, or his deceitful brother, ever again, and I certainly had no intention at all of attending the wedding, despite what I might have said to the contrary. I refused to try to defend myself to him any more, and decided that since he was so determined to think badly of me, I would simply let him.

He interrupted my train of thought then, by moving across the room, and to my horror, he reached out and locked the door, before pocketing the key.

I sat up straight in the chair and, trying to ignore the frantic hammering of my heart, I croaked, 'What do you think you're doing?'

He was already removing his jacket, and he paused for just long enough to tell me, 'I'm going to bed, I don't know about you.'

'B-but you can't. What about me? Where am I going to sleep?' He couldn't mean it, I was quite certain of that, but I immediately began to have serious doubts about that certainty, and was forced to close my eyes tightly when he began to remove his trousers.

'I can. I am.'

I could hear a distinct rustle, and I wondered, hot with embarrassment, what else he was removing.

After a few minutes, he told me, with a smile in his voice, 'You can open your eyes now. Sleep in the chair, if you wish, but don't make so much as a squeak, or try to retrieve the key. If you do, I can promise you that you will be very, very sorry. Oh, and turn off the overhead light would you?'

6

I didn't really believe Lex would put himself calmly to bed. The house was enormous, so I was quite sure he hadn't really meant what he said about us spending the night in the same room. When the silence lengthened, though, I eventually risked a peep, and then my eyes flew right open and I stared in patent disbelief.

He'd done it. He had put himself to bed, and seemed quite settled for the night, if his steady breathing was anything to go by. How dare he?

My first instinct was to fly across the room, to pull the duvet from around his recumbent body, and demand that he damn well let me out of the room — and do it right now — or else. Then common sense returned, and I was forced to ask myself — or else what?

I could scream the place down, of course, just as I had threatened. It would certainly bring the old folks running, and bring me the freedom I desired, but at what cost? I could picture, all too clearly, the shock and distress on the kind faces of Lex's grandparents if I did just that, and then, too, the unsavoury truth would have to be told, because there would be nothing else for it. Once that happened, neither of their precious grandsons was going to be seen in a very good light and, if I was honest, nor was I, though I tried not to let that influence my decision.

It was *not* my problem. They were not *my* family, or even anything else at all to me. I barely knew them, so what they thought of me was neither here nor there, and yet I knew that I couldn't do it. Tears of frustration burned my eyes, but I dare not let them fall in case Lex turned over in the bed and caught me crying. I was still all too mindful of the 'weeping female' jibe, and knew that I would never willingly give him the satisfaction of being able to apply that title to me. If I had nothing else, I was determined I would try to keep what was left of my fragile pride intact.

I did my best not to think of Nick at all, lest I lose my composure altogether. There was, I knew full well, no use in dwelling on useless what-might-have-been. I should really have known better at my age and with my past experiences of plausible rogues. The handsome and oh, so charming Nick Cable always had seemed too good to be true to my friends who had wisely recommended caution — and to me if I was being totally honest — but in the end I had willingly let my foolish heart rule my head just because I had so desperately wanted him to be what he seemed.

I could only feel relief and even a smidgen of satisfaction that my own natural caution had prevented me from embarking on what would have been a disastrous affair with him. If I had done so, I knew with great certainty that I would have been feeling a whole lot worse now.

It seemed like a very long time, but eventually I fell into a fitful sleep, still huddled uncomfortably and fully clothed in the leather armchair. Once I slept however, I could no longer keep my subconscious under control, and I dreamed that I was walking down a very long aisle, radiant in white face, and eager to join the shadowy figure waiting for me there at the end of it.

The longer I walked, however, the further away Nick became. I was very tired. My legs ached unbearably, and pain seared agonizingly along my spine, until I knew I could walk no more. The dark figure was no closer at all, I realized with despair, but he turned towards me, his features indistinct, and fading more by the minute.

I heard myself cry his name, I reached out to him, and then he was there. I was gathered close into the warmth of his arms, and there was more tenderness in his embrace than I ever remembered. I knew then that everything would be all right, and drifted into a deep and satisfying sleep.

★　★　★

The sun was shining into my eyes when I woke, and I blinked a little before snuggling deeper beneath the softness of the duvet, curling into its warmth like a cat.

'Mmm.' I stretched a little, trying to ignore a tiny niggle I could not quite dismiss from my mind.

I should not be in this bed. My eyes flew open as the realization struck, and I found myself looking directly into the darkly disturbing stare of Lex Cable.

How long had he been sitting there, watching me sleep? The thought made me feel most uncomfortable, but hard on that thought came one that made me feel even worse. What was he doing in the chair, and me in the bed? And who — a quick check confirmed my worst fears — had undressed me?

'Did you ... ?' my voice cracked pathetically.

He didn't move so much as one muscle, but continued to regard me steadily in that

80

disconcerting way of his, as he finished the question for me. 'Undress you? Yes.' There was the faintest hint of a curl to his lips before he continued, 'But I didn't look, I promise you, and you do still have your underwear on.'

He was so cool, so composed, always so in control. How dare he? I fumed, while I . . . My whole body seemed to burn beneath the cover, and I suddenly felt unbearably hot.

'How dare . . . ?' I clutched the duvet to my chin, despite the added warmth, knowing that my show of modesty was futile, and rather late, since he'd actually seen me dressed in little more than the lace cami ever since he'd walked into the bedroom the night before.

'Dare I?' he finished maddeningly, in such a reasonable tone that it made me long to reach out and slap the smug look from his face. 'But as we're engaged, it didn't seem to matter. When we're married . . . ' His grin was teasing.

'Engaged? Married? Oh, very funny,' I interrupted furiously, determined to squash his attempt at humour, and sitting up in the bed the better to argue with him. It was only then that I noticed the door was standing wide open.

In one fluid movement, I was out of the bed, across the room, and through it. I was already running along the carpeted landing, before the sound of his laughter caught up with me, and then followed me in my frantic flight down the stairs.

I ran from room to room, noticing nothing of the decor or furnishings in my haste, and I had reached the sun-filled kitchen before I was forced to face the truth — his grandparents must already have left while I slept — there was no one in the house except me and . . .

Lex strolled into the room, casually dressed in black jeans and polo neck, and equally casual in his manner, I noticed crossly. He was still grinning infuriatingly. His smooth black hair was unruffled and he definitely wasn't out of breath, or even put out in any way. Leaning idly against one of the granite work-tops he asked, 'Going somewhere, were you?'

'Where are your grandparents?' I demanded, looking round foolishly, as if, as I told myself later, I expected them to be hiding in one of the many fitted cupboards.

'Oh, they left early. Stopping here was only to break their journey back from a few days in Cornwall. They've gone to London for the wedding. I was meant to be driving them but they said it was a shame to wake you, so I dropped them at the train station first thing. I did promise that I would wish you a good morning from them both.'

'Ooh, you,' I fumed, reaching to brush impatiently at the untidy strands of blonde hair that fell across my eyes. 'Well, now that they're gone, there is no reason in the world for you to keep me here. I'll be dressed and gone in half an hour.'

With as much confidence as I could muster, having realized belatedly that I was, once again, at the disadvantage of being clad only in my underwear, I stalked to the door with my head held high.

'You'll push the car to the main road will you?' His tone was very polite, with just the right note of query apparent, but it was hatefully smug, too. His words made my heart sink right to the beautifully tiled floor, as I was forced to admit that I couldn't go anywhere for the time being — and that Lex now obviously knew that as well. 'I thought you might like your things brought in from the car and I noticed you'd left the key in the ignition,' he added, by way of explanation. 'It might be just a flat battery but I'm afraid I don't have a battery charger handy,' he went on to suggest helpfully.

It was the story of my life just lately, and all too much. What I wanted, more than anything at that moment, was to find the relief that only bursting into floods of tears could bring. I bit down sharply on my lower lip as I felt the warning sting behind my eyelids, and keeping my eyes wide, I stared up at the beamed ceiling for a long moment, giving myself time to regain my composure, and to decide on what my next move might be.

When I felt able to face him again, I was almost certain that I caught a flicker of sympathy in the steady gaze of those dark eyes, but it was extinguished so quickly that a second later I was equally sure I had imagined it.

'I'll phone a garage, or a taxi,' I told him firmly, 'or I'll walk. Either way, I have no intention of staying in this house for a minute longer than I must.'

With as much dignity as I could muster, I spun on one bare heel, and with my tousled blonde head held high, I marched to the door.

'Wait.'

I should have kept right on walking. Ignored the vibrant command uttered in the deepest tone. I should have stepped through the door, and then closed it firmly behind me. I should have — and I really did want to — but in spite of myself my footsteps faltered.

'Let's talk about this.'

With my back turned towards him, and facing the comparative freedom of the hallway, I muttered, 'There's nothing to talk about.'

'Perhaps I think there is.'

I thought I heard him move, and was poised immediately for flight, dreading the grasp of a detaining hand, but still something held me there. Lex wasted no time in taking advantage of my hesitation.

'Look,' he said, and in such a reasonable tone that the bullying tyrant of the night before might never have been. 'Why don't you take a shower and get dressed, while I make us some breakfast? We can talk while we eat, and after that — well — it's up to you. At least do me the courtesy of hearing me out.'

You owe me that much, was the unspoken implication, and I allowed that he might just be right, for the way I had landed myself on him uninvited — albeit unintentionally, though I had no desire to give him the satisfaction of my saying so.

'I'll think about it,' I told him ungraciously, and could only be thankful when my feet obeyed me, carrying me quite steadily along the hall, and back up the stairs.

By the time I'd reached the bedroom, I had quite made my mind up. I would go. I would leave this house and Lex Cable and his relations far behind, and would put the whole unsavoury episode right behind me. It really was the only thing to do.

It had been kind of him to bring my luggage in, but then I reminded myself it was probably the least he could do under the circumstances. Grimly determined, I opened my suitcase to find clean and relatively uncreased clothes, trying not to notice, as I spread them on the unmade bed, the dents in the matching pillows where two heads had obviously rested, side by side.

I found it hard to dismiss the disturbing knowledge that I had spent the night with a man again, sharing a bed after years of sleeping in solitary splendour, but in far different circumstances from those I'd envisaged when I had set out eagerly looking forward to my wedding day — was it really only twenty-four hours earlier?

Damn Nick, damn him to hell, and his blasted brother, too. I wished I had never set eyes on either one of them and, after this, I would make quite sure that I never did again. On that very satisfying thought, I snatched up my clothes and headed for the bathroom.

I scrubbed my body under cascading water so hot that it almost scalded my skin. It was as if I would wash away all trace of the foolish woman who had fallen so completely under Nick's, admittedly charming spell, and emerge a wiser person for the experience.

How could I have been so blind? I blinked away the tears that had spurted from my eyes to mingle momentarily with the water that poured down cheeks that felt cold, despite the heat of the water.

Everyone seemed to have had their doubts about Nick, and they had all tried to warn me. There were the people at work, and others I socialized with. Everyone had tried to make me question the wisdom of the huge step I was taking, while knowing so little about the man who had seemed so intent on whisking me away from everything that had been of such great importance to me before he came along.

In a fit of pique at what I saw as their interference, I had walked out on the job I loved and allowed my home to be rented out to strangers, all in the space of the few days that followed Nick's 'proposal'. I had been so determined to prove them all wrong and show my complete confidence in the promises Nick had made. In doing so I had heedlessly thrown away the stable life that had always meant so much to me, until I had fallen head over heels in love with someone who had meant more, but someone — I could see clearly now — who had only been interested in playing games in an effort to get his own way.

I had been so sure of his sincerity, so very sure, and now . . . I shuddered at the thought of the predicament I found myself in, chilled to the bone despite the heat of the steaming water. Even so, jobless and homeless as I was, I could still only be heartily relieved that Nick's final plan had been scuppered by his family's untimely arrival, because his real intentions where I was concerned were now painfully clear.

★　★　★

'I'm ready to leave now, so if I might just use the phone . . . ?'

The smell of grilled bacon, as I opened the kitchen door, made my mouth water copiously, and my stomach growled in a timely reminder that I hadn't eaten a thing since the hasty sandwich that had been yesterday's lunch.

'It's all prepared now. It would be a shame to waste it.'

I watched Lex remove two generously heaped plates from the oven, and then pour freshly brewed coffee into waiting mugs, all the while telling myself that I definitely wouldn't stay, that the sooner I was miles away the better.

I could have sworn he didn't touch me, and yet I was amazed to find myself, seconds later, seated at the big kitchen table with a knife and fork poised over the delicious food on the plate.

'I really must go,' I heard myself insisting, round a mouthful of perfectly grilled bacon, and knew I must sound and look quite ridiculous. I only wondered that he didn't laugh out loud when I went on to skewer a juicy mushroom on to my fork.

'As soon as you've eaten,' he only agreed mildly, lifting a forkful of fluffy scrambled egg to his own mouth, and eating it with apparent enjoyment. 'Until then, I suggest a truce.'

It just seemed easier to agree, and it would be such a shame to waste the food, so beautifully prepared. I found myself eating with an appetite that did full justice to the meal in front of me in spite of everything.

'More coffee?'

Lex broke what could only be termed a companionable silence, and I found myself pushing the mug forward, and almost happily accepting a refill. I sipped it slowly, allowing myself time to enjoy the flavour and the warmth of the beverage before I must make a move — to where? and to what? I didn't yet know.

I almost choked when I looked up suddenly, to find that dark brooding stare resting thoughtfully on my face, and on the damp tumble of my hair. I resisted the urge to try and tidy myself, and could have wished that he didn't always look so immaculate. He must be wondering what on earth his brother had ever seen in me, even if he had intended me to be just a temporary fling.

'What will you do now?' he asked quietly. It was as if he could read my mind, and I felt most uncomfortable.

'That has . . . '

He continued as if I hadn't spoken at all. 'Will you go back to your job and friends? Pick up the pieces and forget all about the Cable family?'

I wanted to lie, to agree that I would do just that. I desperately wanted to, but the words just wouldn't come, not with those deep blue eyes studying me so steadily. It was more than I could do — and I was quite sure that he would see through any half-truth in a moment.

'Will you?' he prompted, and then he waited again for my answer, quite patiently. Leaning back in the chair as if he had all the time in the world.

'It's what I would like more than anything.'

The words formed on my tongue of their own volition, and then I didn't even try to stop them. He already knew I was a fool and was hardly going to be surprised at the depths of my stupidity.

'But . . . ? There is a but, I take it?' The sarcasm I had become so used to was missing from his tone, he merely looked, and sounded, curious.

'I probably have nothing to go back to,' I admitted after some moments, and with great reluctance. 'No job, and no home, even my friends will have washed their hands of me.' I shrugged. 'They saw through Nick even if I didn't. It's just a pity I refused to listen to them, isn't it?'

Lex stared at me in patent disbelief, and then he swore, so savagely that I flinched, knocking my mug over and spilling hot coffee on to the table. I jumped up immediately, running for a cloth, and glad to be doing something, and not to have to just sit and see the incredulity in his eyes.

I returned to dab at the spreading pool of liquid, and when he remained stubbornly silent, turned on him with all the fury that surfaced so suddenly it surprised us both.

'All right,' I yelled, red-faced, and as angry as I ever remembered being in my life before. 'You don't have to tell me. I can see it all there in the stunned look on your face. You think I've been a bloody fool — I know I've been one — and how do you think that makes me feel?'

'I don't know. Why don't you try telling me about it?'

He was so calm, so serious, and I had to fan at the flames of my resentment, remind myself that it was he who was so keen to keep his brother's precious reputation unsullied, though he obviously knew Nick better than anybody, and that he didn't deserve to be protected that way. How many other women had he treated like me, anyway? It didn't even bear thinking about.

'It makes me feel so angry — with myself more than anyone. I can't believe that I would fall for corny lines that must have been used so many times on so many women . . .' I shook my head, blinking away tears that must never be allowed to fall in front of Nick's brother. 'God, he was so practised, so polished, so bloody sincere. Why on earth does he do it? And why do you go on protecting him? He's not a bloody child.'

I walked away from him, throwing the cloth into the sink with far more force than was strictly necessary. I turned to find that Lex had followed me across the room, and I looked down at the gleaming tiled floor, quite unable to meet that dark gaze.

'Stacey?'

I kept my face stubbornly lowered, my chin touching the deep cerise pink of my sweater. I didn't want him to see how uncertain I felt, or how nervous he made me feel, despite my bravado.

After a long moment when I carefully studied the toes of his polished black shoes, he placed his hands firmly on my shoulders, and I looked up at him.

His expression was deadly serious. His eyes, I felt sure, held a plea for understanding. Whether it was for himself or that worthless brother of his, I wasn't quite sure.

'Surely you can understand my desire to protect those two old people from the tarnished reputation that Nick has managed to acquire. Wouldn't you do the same for a sister — if you had one?'

'I'm an only child,' I informed him hardily, 'but if I had a sister I hope she wouldn't ask or expect such a thing of me. Surely you can't protect him for ever.'

'I don't intend to, and again, I would like to remind you that it is not Nick whom I am so keen to shield from the results of his follies, though someone has to look out for him, and I do feel kind of responsible, being the elder. He's about to be married, as I told you. After that, well.' He shrugged. 'After that it will be up to his wife to keep him under control, and no longer any of my affair, thank God. If anyone can, it's Anthea, and I think she's fully aware of his failings.'

'Does she love him?'

'She certainly seems to adore him and she knew of his reputation before she ever went out with him.'

'Does he love her?'

'I believe he does — in his own way.'

'Then why . . . ?'

'Does he feel this need to make conquests of all the beautiful women that he meets?'

I nodded, wishing that he would take his hands from my shoulders. He seemed to have forgotten they were there, but the slight movement of his long fingers against the soft wool of my sweater was almost caressing.

'When Nick's with us — his family — he reverts to being the youngest child, the petted grandson, the adored fiancé, and does his best, I think, to live up to everyone's image of him and how he should be. When he's away from home and what he probably sees as petty restrictions, well, I can only presume he sees himself as a free agent and any woman he meets as fair game. Women do tend to throw themselves at him, you know. Though I'm sure that wasn't the case with you,' he

94

added as an unconvincing afterthought.

'Are you excusing him?' I was beginning to feel angry with the whole family, and wondered that Lex didn't resent the brother who seemed to have been made so much more of than he had been and was allowed to get away with murder in the bargain.

'I'm stating the facts as I see them. Aren't you trying to excuse yourself by putting all the blame on him? You did come here of your own free will, didn't you?'

'He lied to me.'

'You're not a child, either, to be so easily duped, and if you had allowed yourself to know him for longer, instead of rushing headlong into his bed . . . ' He didn't go on — he didn't have to — and hot colour swept my cheeks.

'I did not rush headlong into his bed. I've never actually been to bed with him, whatever you might choose to think, but I suppose that doesn't matter to you. You're quite determined that I should take the blame for all this, aren't you?' I demanded furiously, shrugging his hands from my shoulders, only to be disconcerted when they slid along my arms and took my hands into his own.

'Only for some of it.' He lifted my fingers and studied the pink nails, before he continued, 'Now, I want you to hear me out.

I'd really appreciate it if you'd listen to all I have to say, before you dismiss my suggestions out of hand.'

I didn't answer. I only just resisted the urge to snatch my hands away, and to tell him I had already listened to him, and to his brother before that, for long enough to last me several lifetimes. Only the realization that I presently had nowhere to go, no means of getting there, and a strong desire not to have to face the 'I-told-you-so' comments I so richly deserved from my friends just yet, kept me rooted to the spot, and, for the time being, silent.

'Stay here,' he invited, suddenly releasing me, and moving right away to the other side of the roomy kitchen. 'You said yourself that you have nowhere to go. Help me out, and let me help you, at least until you've decided what you want to do next.'

I eyed him suspiciously, realizing that there was no need to ask him about the catch. In return for his hospitality I would be expected to attend Nick's wedding later today, but as Lex's fiancée. Part of me felt almost inclined to do it. Why, just to see the stunned look on his deceitful face might make it worth while turning up. Another, more sensible part of me just wanted to put the whole sorry episode behind me and never set eyes on him again.

'Where else can you go?' he asked with brutal honesty. 'Back to where you came from with your tail between your legs — it might be a bit embarrassing, don't you think?'

A bit. It would be excruciating, and my face burned at the very thought. 'I can go abroad to my parents,' I told him stubbornly, though in truth the option of throwing myself on the mercy of either parent was no more appealing than looking for sympathy from friends, I was just anxious to show him he wasn't my only option.

'Are they expecting you?'

'No, but it can be a surprise visit.'

'More of a shock, I should think, if you turn up and tell them you've no home and no job to come back to.'

He was right, I acknowledged, and it was just as well he didn't know just how right he was. Damn him. Neither parent had wanted to take responsibility for me even when I was a lot younger, so they were hardly likely to be overjoyed at the prospect of bailing me out when I was certainly old enough to know better.

It was cowardly, I knew, but the thought of putting off the time when everyone would have to be told just how much of a fool I had been was tempting, to say the least.

'A few days, then,' I capitulated.

'A few days,' he agreed, and I tried not to notice the gleam of triumph that lit those dark eyes, or the faint unease that twisted my stomach into knots of tension, as I wondered what on earth I had let myself in for.

7

Once the decision to go along with the 'engagement', for at least a few more days, had been made I felt as if a weight had been lifted off my mind, and Lex did nothing to make me regret relenting. He didn't even gloat, apart from that one slightly triumphant look, or not as far as I could tell.

'Now that's been settled,' he said, sounding pleased — as well he might, having got his own way, 'we'll need to think about setting off. Time's getting on but we could stop off briefly at either Ringwood or Southampton.'

'Ringwood sounds fine,' I muttered faintly, 'but where are we going and what are we to be stopping off for exactly?'

'I thought perhaps you'd like to look for an outfit for the wedding,' he smiled. 'I know it's all a bit of a rush, but the wedding isn't until late afternoon. We did agree that you would partner me, now, didn't we?'

I tried desperately to remember exactly what we had agreed, but any such conversation eluded me. The thought of being at Nick's wedding made me feel sick and I couldn't believe I would actually have agreed to be there. Lex was surely quite mistaken. 'Oh, I don't think — '

'Perhaps you have something suitable with you?' he suggested, ignoring my weak protest, his tone quite patient. 'I must admit I hadn't thought of that . . . ' Lex paused to give me time to agree or disagree, but I remained silent.

His words had reminded me, with an extremely painful jolt, of the outfit that had been so carefully and lovingly packed in tissue paper — a rich creamy trouser suit that had cost me a chunk of my savings and was to have been my bridal outfit for whatever kind of wedding Nick had in mind for us,

I blinked rapidly and took a large gulp of coffee — to hide my confusion and give me time to deal with the unexpected surge of grief — burning my tongue on the scolding liquid, and swallowing a pained yelp along with the fiery brew,

A glass of ice-cold milk was thrust into my hand almost immediately, and a deep voice apologized, 'I should have warned you that it was very hot.'

Damn him. Was he a mind-reader? Was he always going to be one step ahead, or just one behind? I viewed him with still watering eyes, noticing the way he hovered over me in such a concerned way that I could imagine he knew everything about me, right down to a wedding outfit that only I and the shop assistant had seen.

'I have something with me.' I blinked hard as I said it and reminded myself there could never be a more appropriate occasion to wear the suit. 'But are you quite sure it's wise . . . ?'

'For you to attend the ceremony?' he finished for me, proving yet again that he was far too conversant with every thought I had. 'I'm sure that it's exactly the thing to do the more I think about it.' He looked at me, his gaze dark and unreadable. 'Shall I tell you why?'

I nodded mutely, quite sure that he intended to, whether I wanted him to or not. I wished he would move away because, as always, his close proximity made me decidedly nervous and far too aware of him for my own peace of mind. I doubted he was ever a man who could be easily ignored, and I was finding it quite impossible.

To my relief he sat down across the table from me, and began, to my surprise, with the hard statement, 'You were right, of course, that Nick should not be able to get away with his juvenile behaviour. Unfortunately, and to my shame I have always made it possible for him to do just that in my desire to protect my grandparents' feelings.'

'Yes, but . . . ' I found that I was springing to Lex's defence, but he interrupted, quite brusquely, before I could say that I did actually understand his reasons.

'What better way to teach him a short, sharp lesson,' his smile didn't quite reach those dark-blue eyes, and I suppressed a deep shudder, suddenly almost pitying Nick for some reason, 'than,' he continued, 'for him to find one of his little 'secrets' turning up at his own wedding? It just might give him enough of a shock to make him think twice before embarking on any extramarital affairs after the ceremony. It might also give Nick's bride a better than fighting chance of making the marriage work.' He gave a harsh laugh. 'A bit childish, perhaps, but then so, I think we both agree, is his own behaviour. He was, after all, quite happy for you to turn up here and leave me to send you on your way.'

'I thought you said — '

'Yes, I did,' Lex cut in swiftly, reading my mind yet again, 'I think Anthea has Nick's number, and she appears more than capable of dealing with any wayward behaviour on his part, but surely she deserves any help that we might be able to give her.' He reached across the table to touch my hand. 'I would hope she'd do the same for you if the positions were reversed. Anthea is a *very* nice person,' he told me with heavy emphasis: unfairly, I thought, believing the inference was that I was *not* a very nice person.

'I don't think it's such a good idea,' I said flatly, staring at his hand and suddenly distracted by the scarring I'd inflicted. I was thinking regretfully that he'd probably be marked for life, when he suddenly thumped the table savagely and I almost jumped out of my skin.

'Still trying to protect him?' he barked, his eyes flashing brilliant sparks. 'Still hoping that he might have a change of heart and come back? Is that it?'

The unprovoked attack left me speechless and it scattered my wits in all directions. Before I could explain that I had no wish to ever set eyes on Nick again, much less attend his wedding, those navy eyes had narrowed to accusing slits.

'That's it, isn't it?' he snarled, a sneer twisting his face. 'You want him back, don't you, and you still hold out hopes that he'll actually come.'

I stared at him. He was so angry it was quite frightening, and I wondered where on earth he could have got such an idea. He wasted no time in letting me know, though he

103

couldn't have been further from the truth if he'd tried.

'Don't bother to deny it,' he fumed, rising so suddenly that his chair tilted and then fell backwards with a clatter, though he didn't appear to even notice. 'It's there, written all over that very lovely face. Your head was so full of dreams that you weren't listening to me.'

Lex was round the table before I could move so much as a muscle. He yanked me to my feet with barely suppressed violence, his fingers biting deeply into my upper arms as he held me so close that I could feel his breath on my face.

'Let me go.' My voice came out barely above a whisper. Surprisingly, I wasn't angry, more upset that he should think so little of me.

'No way.' The heat of his anger seemed to sizzle from those punishing fingers like a strong current of electricity. He paused, and I could see a tiny pulse throbbing in the stern line of his jaw, before he continued, 'It seems that Nick's not the only one who needs a lesson. I want you there to see him married to someone else, and then you'll know, once and for all, that he just isn't coming back to you — not ever.'

'But I don't want . . . '

I tried to say I didn't want anything more to do with Nick but Lex was in no mood to listen to my protestations. He seemed quite prepared, and even eager, to accept that I would be willing, eager, even, to welcome Nick back into my arms, and it made me feel unbelievably hurt that he would have such a poor opinion of me.

'I don't expect you do,' he agreed, without, for once, having the first idea of what I'd been about to say, 'But you'll be there at my side, just as we agreed, when Nick is married. Afterwards,' he shrugged, 'well, afterwards, you just might have the sense to put it all down to experience, and find yourself someone who really loves you.'

He had changed his tune, I thought, as I went off apparently quite meekly to get ready. To begin with, he had seemed quite willing to believe that I'd been as much to blame as Nick, and that I had only got what I'd deserved. Had he changed his mind about that?

Why not go along with what he wants? I reasoned with myself, retrieving hair straighteners from my suitcase and plugging them in, before arranging the suit on a hanger in the hope any creases would drop out. You did promise that you would — and what have you got to lose that you haven't already lost?

Seeing Nick's face when you walk in might even make up in some small way for what he's put you through — and they do say that revenge is sweet.

It was a shock to realize that I had pushed him so far out of my mind that I barely remembered what he looked like. I could only suppose I'd done the same thing so many times in the past I'd become adept at it. Even after all this time I wasn't noticeably out of practice. Yet only yesterday Nick had been the man I had willingly thrown my career, home and friends away for, the man I'd wanted to spend the rest of my life with. I must have been temporarily insane — there was no other explanation.

I could only imagine that the spate of summer weddings I'd attended that year must have coloured my usually impeccable and very cautious judgement. I'd obviously allowed myself to become completely carried away by the thought of what I must be missing because I, too, hadn't found the love of my life.

There was no doubt Nick had happened along when I was feeling at my most vulnerable. The ticking of my biological clock had become a deafening clamour it was all but impossible to ignore, making me desperate to find my Prince Charming and the happy-ever-after that had eluded me thus far.

Small wonder then that all the attention he'd paid me had gone so completely to my foolish head, allowing Nick swiftly to overcome any doubts I might have had. He had seemed to be everything that I could ever have wanted in a man, clever, amusing, not to mention devastatingly attractive.

There had been no real mention of wedding arrangements, I realized, far too late, but there had been a proposal of sorts and marriage had definitely been dangled in front of me like a carrot that was carefully designed to lower my resistance. Had I been earmarked as Nick's final fling, the equivalent of a stag-night romp before he settled down — with someone else, of course?

Afterwards — I shivered — well, afterwards, he would obviously have dumped me with a speed that would have left me stunned, and then rushed off to the girl he really loved — if Nick was capable of loving anyone, which had to be seriously doubted. Or, worse, had he intended to carry on with his career of deceitful seduction, even after he had taken his vows?

That thought alone made me grimly determined to see this through. His brother was right about that, at least. Nick Cable needed to be taught a severe lesson, and I was exactly the right person to do it — with Lex's very willing assistance. I decided, there and then, not to dither or to fight Lex over attending the wedding for a minute longer.

So, you will wear your wedding finery, after all, I told my pale reflection, and it will be to watch your intended bridegroom marry someone else.

I laughed then, and I went on laughing until the tears came. I'd had a lucky escape. I knew that, and found I didn't regret the fact that this wedding would not after all be mine. What I did regret, and bitterly, was the fact that Nick's brother had met me under such circumstances that it meant that he was never going to see me in anything but an unsavoury light. It shouldn't have bothered me, but somehow it did.

Perhaps the tears helped, I didn't really know, but I certainly felt a whole lot calmer. 'Just get today over,' I told myself encouragingly, 'and then you can put all this behind you. Maybe even go back and make an effort to retrieve your career, your home and your friendships, but whatever happens plan forward and let this particular piece of the past go.'

Once I was dressed I stared at my wan

reflection, and was forced to acknowledge that the outfit that had been so perfect for the bride of a civil ceremony was completely wrong for me as a guest at a church wedding. The delicate cream of the suit took any remaining colour from my cheeks. Even with a black top under the jacket I looked totally washed out, and even ill. It wouldn't do. It wouldn't do at all.

There was a sharp rap at the door, which made me jump and spill the blusher that I had been idly playing with all over the vanity top.

'Are you almost ready?' the deep familiar voice demanded, 'Because we really should be leaving soon.'

'One more minute,' I offered and, listening to his footsteps retreating down the stairs, came to a decision.

I would just have to make the best of it. That really was all there was to it. I was going to this ceremony for one reason and one reason only, to teach Nick a lesson he might not forget in a hurry, and if Lex — or any of his family — didn't like the way I looked — well, that was just tough, wasn't it?

At least with my hair swept up I looked like the woman I was, and not the silly girl who had fallen under Nick Cable's spell. A little more blusher was deftly applied from the pile

I had spilled, a little more shadow emphasized the shape of my eyes, and mascara the length of my lashes. Finally, defining my lips with a defiant coral lipstick, I gave a brisk nod and a grim smile to my reflection.

'You'll do,' I said.

Lex was pacing the hall when I began my slow progress down the stairs. Hearing me coming, he paused, turned, and then came to stand at the foot of the stairs.

If I was made more nervous than I already was by his scrutiny, I was determined to give no sign of it. I kept my chin high, and my gaze straight ahead. When I reached the bottom, expecting criticism, I rushed to get in first.

'I know the outfit isn't right for a wedding guest,' I told him defiantly. 'But I'm afraid it's the best that I could do from the limited choice I had with me.'

He didn't speak for a long moment, but just stared at me until I was reduced to a complete bundle of nerves, and all of my bravado had vanished.

'You hate it, don't you?' I guessed, preparing to wrench away the hands he had taken into his, and to race back up the stairs, barricade myself back into the room and refuse, absolutely, to come out again.

'You look lovely.' As I stared at him in

surprise, he added, his tone hard and flat, 'I only hope that Nick appreciates all the trouble you've gone to.'

I knew then that I could never, ever, win with him or convince him that I wasn't some *femme fatale* or that Nick was just a blip in a pretty blameless past. Squaring my shoulders and smoothing the long-line jacket of the beautiful, and now hated suit, I followed Lex out to the gleaming BMW that was obviously going to be our transport to the wedding, praying as I did so that the day would soon be over.

8

Since I had so spectacularly burned my bridges for a future that obviously wasn't now going to materialize, a new start was obviously going to be in order for me — a necessity in fact.

My smile became grim as I determined that, once this was over, I would seriously rethink the rest of my life. The Cable brothers would definitely be no part of it, of that I was quite, *quite* certain. The thought was wonderfully comforting as was the realization that this was just one day and it would soon be over.

I made an effort to be pleasant and with careful handling, and patience on my part Lex unbent very gradually on the journey. My obvious admiration for the house we had just left had him unexpectedly telling me a little about himself, and his upbringing in the heart of the Cornish countryside. It was that, he explained, that had given him the desire for a country home of his own, though for practical purposes it had to be nearer to London.

I was careful to show only a very mild

curiosity, feeling quite certain that any probing questions would see him clamming up so fast that I'd never get another word out of him, apart from snarls, for the rest of the day.

'It must have been wonderful being brought up in the country,' I commented, 'with all that space to play in. I was brought up in the heart of town in a house with just a back yard.'

'But by your parents.'

I wasn't going to get into a discussion about the ins and outs of being brought up by my parents, so I simply said, 'I'm sorry, that was thoughtless of me. No matter how ideal your surroundings it would not have made up for losing your mother and father like that. You must have missed them.'

'Yes,' Lex agreed. 'My grandparents were wonderful, but they could never quite take their place, nor could they ever take away the feeling I always had that I was somehow responsible for the brother who was little more than a baby when we were orphaned. What he needed was a father's guidance, but I was too young for the role, and my grandfather too old. Can you wonder that I often blame myself for Nick's wild ways?'

A dozen questions and protestations leapt on to my tongue, but with an effort I remained silent, recognizing Lex's need just to talk, without constant and obviously unwanted interruptions. With an even greater effort I hoped that I had managed to hide the outrage I felt on his behalf. Couldn't Nick see how his brother felt? How could he let him go on taking responsibility for his own idiotic behaviour? Didn't he ever worry about upsetting the old couple when they had done so much for them both?

'He just doesn't think at all, is my guess.'

Lex had read my mind again. It was almost uncanny and made me feel quite uncomfortable. I would have said that he must have studied my expression, except that it would have been impossible since I'd been very careful not to look at him and he was driving anyway.

'I was taken into the business when I was still at school,' he went on, almost talking to himself. 'I worked beside my grandfather on building sites, when I was barely out of short trousers, after school hours, and at weekends. Such a thing wouldn't be allowed today, of course, but it was different back then. I was treated as a man from a very early age, Nick was, and always has been treated as a child.' He seemed to think that explained everything, and in a way perhaps it did.

'By the time I was sixteen I felt I knew

everything there was to know about the business. We had, and still have a marvellous workforce, and with their support my grandfather came to trust me enough to leave the running of the whole concern to me when he retired a few years later. He also trusted me to make a place for Nick in the company, and that I've certainly tried to do. He is, in fact, very good at his job — when he's there.'

Family was obviously very important to Lex, I realized, and it was no small wonder, since he had lost two of the most important members of that family at a very young age. Their untimely and tragic deaths had left him with a brother whose abysmal behaviour he felt responsible for, and grandparents he felt he had to shield from the reality of that behaviour. I couldn't find it in my heart to blame him for that any more.

'Enough about me.' A flicker of a smile twisted the grim line of his mouth, and I felt again a ripple of pity for the child who'd had to grow up too fast, and for the man he was now, who still obviously felt the weight of that responsibility many years later.

As we drove in to the city of London, where the bride's family apparently lived and where the wedding was to take place, Lex turned all of his attention to navigating the traffic, which was becoming increasingly heavy. It gave me the opportunity to look at him at last.

I'd have had to be blind not to notice that he scrubbed up rather well in the charcoal grey suit and pristine white shirt, but I immediately pulled myself up short and reminded myself crossly that how he looked was no concern of mine. However, if I was being honest, in spite of myself, I was still shallow enough to find some pleasure in the fact my 'fiancé' was handsome enough, in a rugged kind of way, to give his own brother a run for his money in the looks department.

My heart hammered painfully in my chest when we eventually pulled up into the car park of a very old church in an area that I wasn't familiar with, but I assured myself it was more from the dread of letting Lex down in front of his grandparents and the other guests, than any last-minute nerves at the thought of facing Nick again.

'You'd better wear this.' Lex had turned in his seat to face me, and I saw that he was holding out a ring.

'Oh, it's so beautiful,' I murmured, making no move at all to take it.

As if on cue the sun came out, its watery beam bringing a sparkle to the circle of diamonds and lighting fires deep in the large central emerald.

Taking my hand, Lex slipped the ring slowly on to my engagement finger, and he even smiled as he said, 'Look. It fits perfectly.'

There was a hesitant tap on the window, and there was his grandmother peering in at us, and looking like a brightly plumed bird in a royal-blue outfit. The extravagantly feathered hat made me regret my lack of headgear when I realized a wide brim, tilted just so, would have been the ideal thing to hide beneath.

'Come on, you two,' she urged. 'Plenty of time for that later.'

I felt my face flame at the implication, but Lex only laughed as he climbed from the car, coming round to open my door with an impeccable show of good manners.

'Nick has just arrived,' the older woman informed Lex and, twittering excitedly, went on, 'I can't wait to see his face when he meets Stacey. I'm sure he had all but convinced himself that you would never marry, you know.'

And why was that? I wondered indignantly. Did he really think his elder brother less attractive, less lovable than he was himself? The thought that he was capable of such arrogance — and I was quite sure that he was — suddenly filled me with a grim determination to show him that it was certainly not the case. Slipping my hand into the crook of Lex's arm, I said firmly, 'Let's go inside, shall we?' and found that all trace of any last-minute nerves had completely vanished.

Aaron Cable was waiting for his wife in the stone porch, so we were able to follow them up the aisle. There was an almost audible buzz of excitement at our appearance, much turning of heads and whispering behind hymn sheets so that, with all the colourful hats, the unsettled congregation reminded me of a field of wild flowers caught in a stiff breeze.

My grip tightened a little on Lex's sleeve, and he reached across to place a reassuring hand over my fingers. His smile when I looked up at him was infinitely approving.

I saw Nick before he saw me, and was startled that my only thought was to wonder what on earth I had ever seen in him. Which I supposed made me as shallow as he was in a way. Amazing how quickly you could fall out of love when the scales were brutally torn from your eyes and you could suddenly see a person for what they really were and not what you had wanted them to be.

Nick and his best man both saw me at the same moment, as the older couple stepped aside to speak to someone, and I could have laughed aloud as their jaws dropped in perfect unison — though why the best man should be so surprised to see me, I really had no idea. There was clear admiration in one pair of eyes, but only pure horror in the other and I knew then — as I kept my gaze steady and watched Nick squirm — that I had my revenge. I wasn't a nice enough person to say that it didn't feel good, because it did — it felt *great*.

Eleanor Cable bustled forward now, obviously thoroughly enjoying herself as she said, 'Look who I found outside.'

'A-Annie,' Nick stammered, quite unable to meet my straight look, his face was ashen and then scarlet in turn. 'What are you doing here?'

He looked so shaken that I could almost find it in me to feel sorry for him — almost — but not quite, when I remembered how willing he had been to use me, and for nothing more than his own fleeting pleasure, too. He certainly didn't deserve my misplaced sympathy, I reminded myself hardily.

'You've met already, have you?' Lex put in pleasantly, as if he had no idea, and then turning to the gawping best man, he offered smoothly, 'Harry, I'd like to introduce you to my fiancée, Anastasia Trent.'

Nick's mouth opened as if he wanted to say something, but he seemed quite unable to get

119

any more words out. Harry had no such reticence.

'You sly devil, Lex, congratulations.' He grasped Lex's hand and pumped it up and down with such enthusiasm that I was sure I saw him wince, but good-humouredly. 'Did you know about this?' He turned boyishly to Nick, who murmured something unintelligible and looked as if he could wish himself anywhere but the situation in which he presently found himself.

Rather belatedly remembering his manners, Harry told me, 'I'm thrilled to meet you, of course, but I can't deny that I'm surprised, since I'd always thought Lex here a confirmed bachelor. Work first, last, and in the middle, that's Lex. It was always Nick who had the eye for the ladies. It was lucky for Lex that he saw you first and Nick is finally out of the equation.'

He was joking, of course, but I resented deeply the implication that Nick would always be the one out of the two brothers to attract any woman he wanted.

'It would have made absolutely no difference,' I assured the smiling best man airily, 'because beside Lex no one else could hold a candle, in my opinion.'

'Oh, well said,' Harry applauded. Turning again to Lex he said, 'Now do tell us where you found her, and why you haven't married her already.'

'We met unexpectedly, quite recently, fell in love almost immediately, and haven't yet got around to making our engagement official, or setting a date for our marriage,' Lex explained very convincingly, I thought.

'Unofficial, or not,' his grandmother put in, obviously misty-eyed with the tale of love at first sight, 'I see Stacey is wearing the Cable emerald, and my, doesn't it suit her.'

'It's perfect for her,' Lex said warmly, lifting my hand, complete with ring, to his lips.

I was horrified to see that my fingers trembled in his grasp, and had to force myself not to snatch my hand away, but instead to remember that we were only behaving the way engaged couples were supposed to do.

'We'd better take our seats,' Lex said calmly, and as I took my place beside him on the long front pew next to his grandparents, I thought I really understood now just why he was so against me.

Harry had made it quite clear that the bias of opinion was that Lex was accepted as the dedicated businessman in his family, and Nick was the playboy and lover who always got the girl — which included me, of course, and though they couldn't have known that, *Lex* did.

I had a strong feeling that even the grandparents weren't as ignorant as Lex thought they were of Nick's reputation with the opposite sex. The inference was clearly that Nick was thought the more attractive and popular of the two men, however you looked at it. How that unfair comparison must have hurt Lex over the years — and it probably still did because no one likes to be labelled second best.

The sound of the organ swelled, and the congregation, as one, turned to catch the first glimpse of the bride. I stared stonily ahead, still fuming at the unfairness of it all, and I could feel that Lex was watching me.

I guessed he would be thinking that I was upset at having to stand by and watch Nick marry someone else, but it couldn't have been further from the truth. All I could wish — as the bride, stunning in her white gown and confident as only a truly beautiful woman can be, took her place beside her bridegroom at the altar — was that I had never set eyes on Nick Cable, never been swayed by his undoubted but purely surface charms, and never allowed myself to fall for his blatant lies and promises. Somehow, I couldn't find it in me to wish, after all, that I hadn't met his brother — only that it might have been in less damning circumstances.

Lex leaned towards me, and he whispered very close to my ear, 'I shouldn't have made you come, I'm sorry.'

'Don't be,' I said, and found the courage to slip my cold hand into the warmth of his. To my infinite relief, he made no move to reject me, but closed his fingers firmly around mine and kept them there.

I saw and heard the wedding service progress in a detached way, watched the bride, raven-haired and radiant, handed over by her beaming father. The bridegroom looked extremely nervous but only he and the two of us knew the exact reason why. I even had it in me to feel sorry for Nick when the vicar asked the congregation if anyone knew of any lawful impediment why the two should not be joined in holy matrimony, realizing he would be half-expecting me to step boldly forward and stake my own claim for his affections.

No one could have been more surprised than I was when a female voice suddenly rang out from the back of the church, saying in a firm tone, 'Yes, I do.'

There was total silence and Lex turned to stare at me. His expression probably mirrored my own and was a mixture of shock and disbelief.

I only had time to mouth, 'It wasn't me,' before pandemonium broke out and Lex, the best man, and the bride's father rushed to the rear of the church to find out what was going on.

Whoever she was, I had no doubt at all that she would have been known to Nick, and I also had no doubt it would have been in intimate circumstances, but the innocent act he managed to put on was convincing to say the least, though his brow was wet with perspiration and he tugged more than once at his cravat.

'I have absolutely no idea who she is,' he told his by now very blushing bride, who also managed to appear quite creditably unconcerned. 'I swear to you, my sweet. I've never seen her before in my entire life. She's probably come to the wrong church.'

He caught my eye, and I simply lifted one eyebrow, staring straight back at him. He did have the grace to flush an even deeper red than his intended before he quickly looked away.

The bride's mother, who had been dabbing away with a hanky from the time her daughter and husband had walked arm in arm up the aisle, now burst into floods of tears, wailing that her daughter's big day was ruined and who was that woman anyway?

The congregation, by contrast, were apparently taking this diversion from the service book in their stride and even appeared to be enjoying it. The noise as they reached their own conclusions rose in a crescendo, with all the hats bobbing up and down like gulls on a stormy sea.

I half-expected the bride to throw a fit and make a run for it, but she was far too poised and, to her credit, she remained dry-eyed and stoic with a firm hand on her groom's arm. I could only admire her determination and fortitude. It seemed that this was her day and nothing, but *nothing* was going to prevent the ceremony from going ahead. It did make me wonder if she had even been half expecting such an interruption and been prepared to ride out the ensuing storm. I couldn't do other but admire her sheer determination to get her man.

The organist began, quite inappropriately, to play 'Fight the good fight', and the vicar called for calm while looking considerably flustered himself. After several very long moments the three men returned to take their places, some sort of explanation was offered to the vicar, and the service continued without any further hitches. I thought the wedding party, at least, must have heaved a huge collective sigh of relief.

'We can give the reception a miss if you like,' Lex was saying as we followed the gossiping guests down the aisle. 'You played your part well, but I know now that I shouldn't have asked it of you. We might have given Nick a fright but in the end someone else has upstaged us and managed to give him a bigger one. After that, if marriage doesn't change him I doubt that anything will. Do you want to forget it?'

I listened to what he said and realized what it cost him to offer. A show of support for his brother would be expected of him, especially after what had happened. There would be endless speculation as it was, without bringing our relationship into the equation. Even so, for a moment I was tempted, but it was only for a moment and then I acknowledged that by leaving now I would be letting Lex himself down and, for all his sometimes bullying ways, he didn't deserve that.

I straightened my shoulders, and told him firmly, 'I wouldn't dream of it. I'm here now and will see it through to the end.'

For an instant there was a blaze of something in the dark depths of his eyes. Hope, relief, gratitude even, but it was extinguished almost immediately, and then I thought that I might have imagined it.

He reached out one hand to remove something from my hair, and smiling held out a small paper horseshoe, 'Confetti in your hair.'

I took it from him, tucking it superstitiously into my small clutch bag, though I was fully aware that the last thing I really needed was a souvenir to remind me of this day.

★ ★ ★

'Hello, Lex.'

The bride was tiny and of model-girl proportions, she also appeared very poised and confident. Close up she was even more beautiful, if that was possible. With flawless skin and huge dark eyes she wouldn't have been out of place on the pages of the glossy magazines, which forced me to question why on earth Nick had bothered with me. I didn't see myself as unattractive, but there really was no comparison.

There was a firm set to her pointed chin, and a determination in her eyes that made me feel that Nick had, just maybe, married his match. I've got him now, and I'm keeping him, the tight and possessive hold on his arm seemed to say loud and clear.

She obviously knew her new brother-in-law very well by the way she lifted her face readily, and with a bright smile, for his kiss. 'And who's this?' she asked.

It was almost comical, the way that Nick rushed to say, 'Oh, this is Lex's fiancée, Anthea. He's kept her quite a secret.'

Yes, I thought, without humour, and he isn't the only one, is he?

'He certainly has.' Anthea looked startled, almost put out, in fact. I found myself wondering again why the thought of Lex attracting a woman was such a surprise to everyone. Didn't they think he deserved to find someone to love and to love him?

'I'm Stacey,' I introduced myself, since the two men seemed reluctant to do it for me. Nick was obviously afraid of giving away the fact that he knew me before, and Lex was simply refusing to help him out as far as I could see.

Right, I told myself — as we moved into the large hotel room and were immediately encircled by numerous family members — you wanted a fiancée, Lex Cable, and by golly, you're going to get one.

Introduced to the various aunts, cousins and other distant relations, I kept a brilliant smile firmly in place, as I offered the beringed hand to be admired, admitted that a date for the wedding had not yet been set, and agreed with the many suggestions that the New

128

Forest would be the perfect setting for the ceremony. I clung adoringly to Lex's arm throughout this lengthy presentation and referred to him constantly.

Tomorrow isn't so far away, I reminded myself airily, and after this performance any debt — real or imagined, that I might owe to Lex Cable for putting him on the spot when I broke into his house, will be paid in full.

By the time the dancing started, I had all but convinced myself that I really was Lex's fiancée, and, in truth, he certainly seemed to be doing very little to disabuse me of the idea. Sweeping me into his arms and on to the dance floor, time and time again, and keeping me close by his side at all other times, he played the doting lover to the hilt.

'Wonderful to see Lex looking so happy and relaxed,' Eleanor Cable told me with great enthusiasm, watching as her tall elder grandson weaved his way towards us carrying replenished glasses of champagne, and wearing a smile. 'I haven't seen him dance in years.'

'He certainly doesn't seem to be out of practice.' I smiled up at Lex and, accepting the glass, I took an almost defiant sip knowing that I really should be drinking less, flirting with him less, and generally enjoying myself less — which was the last thing I might have expected.

There were mirrors around the walls and, catching sight of myself in one, I tried in vain to smooth the escaping tendrils of blonde hair that curled around my face. My make-up, I could see, was quite gone, so while Lex was talking to another guest I escaped to the powder room and made what repairs I could.

Was I really a jilted bride? It was hard, if not impossible, to see myself as such. I certainly didn't feel like one. I now admitted, with great honesty, and no little surprise, that I had not felt so much as one pang of regret when I had watched Nick marrying someone else. If I had needed reminding what a lucky escape I'd had, the interruption in the church had certainly been a timely one.

He had been nothing but a foolish mistake. A brief infatuation and the result of a sudden awareness that there was every chance I would be hitting my forties as a single woman, together with the very obvious and persuasive charm of an admittedly attractive man had been all it took to convince me Nick was the one.

I was hurrying back from the ladies' room when I ran slap into the very man in the deserted hallway. I would have passed Nick with little more than a nod, and couldn't have been more surprised when he grasped my arm and drew me to one side.

'Annie,' his smooth tone was slightly ruffled for once, and he looked decidedly uncomfortable as he tried to cajole and apologize all at once. 'How dreadful you must think me.'

I was so surprised that he would have the nerve to approach me at all, much less try to ingratiate himself, that for a moment I was speechless. As soon as I'd recovered sufficiently I told him shortly, 'To be quite honest, Nick, I don't think of you at all. You were, to put it simply, nothing more than an error on my part and one that will never be repeated, I can assure you.'

'You hate me,' he said, sounding regretful, of all things, 'and I know that I deserve that you should. I don't expect you to understand, and there's no reason that you should even try, but please believe me when I tell you that I never meant to hurt you.'

'You're right,' I agreed bitterly. 'There is no reason for me to believe you — and I certainly don't intend to try. Apparently you had no qualms about hurting others before me, so why should I be different?'

'But you were,' he insisted, 'and as soon as I realized it I tried to end it.'

I stared at him. 'You did not, Nick. Not once did you come anywhere near finishing it between us.'

'I said that I tried.'

The expression on his handsome face was rueful and regretful all at once, and I could almost believe he was telling the truth — almost, but not quite. Well, not at all actually. He was just despicable.

'I phoned to say goodbye — and ended up proposing to you.' He shook his head. 'I couldn't believe I'd done it myself.'

'Then why did you?' I cried, suddenly furiously angry. 'Why did you? And how could you? It was a contemptible thing to do, particularly with your wedding imminent.'

'You can't feel any worse about it than I do myself,' Nick muttered.

He looked just like a naughty child — but he wasn't one, and he hadn't been for some time. Adults just shouldn't behave in that way, I reminded myself furiously.

'Then, why?' I demanded.

'You so obviously expected it,' he excused himself. 'So sweet, you were, and so amazingly innocent.'

'So gullible,' I fumed, and then added bitterly, 'You never intended to turn up there at the house, did you?'

Nick shook his dark head and put a hand

lightly on my arm, murmuring, 'I'm sorry. I truly am.'

His apology sickened me and my lip curled with contempt, but before I could shake his hand off, a deep voice behind us said furiously, 'Let her go,' and the next minute Lex had thrust his brother away from me with a force that wasn't strictly necessary.

'What the hell do you think you are doing?' Lex grated, standing over his brother with his hands clenched into threatening fists. 'Your bride is waiting to leave for the honeymoon. Were you intending to start it right here — and with my fiancée?'

The younger brother faced the elder, his expression mocking. 'Ah, yes, your *fiancée*. What did you do, catch her on the rebound, Lex, and decide to keep it in the family?' He turned, the change in his manner towards me sudden and frightening, 'And you,' he sneered, 'I've heard of time being a great healer, but this is ridiculous. You were mine for the taking and we both know it, but I guess the second best man won in the end.'

I had already lifted my hand to smack the gloating smile right off his face, when a door opened behind us and a sharp and very feminine voice said, 'What's going on here?'

9

The bride looked lovely in her going-away outfit of a deep pink suit that clung to her slender figure like a second skin. However, admiration wasn't one of the emotions that flitted across the faces of the three of us standing in the hallway like a frozen tableau. I realized with a further sinking of my heart that it must have been quite evident to her that there was some sort of altercation going on. We all looked the very picture of guilt.

For several long minutes there was complete silence. Lex recovered first. Stepping forward he drew Anthea into the circle, telling her as he did so, 'We were just wishing Nick well for the future, weren't we, *darling*?' There was heavy emphasis and a hint of a threat in the endearment, as if he had his doubts about my support.

'Yes, we were,' I murmured at once, 'and we'd like to wish you all the luck in the world for the future.' I wondered, even as I said it, if the simple fact of getting married was all it was going to take to change Nick. Sadly, I couldn't help the feeling that Anthea was probably going to need all the luck she could get and more — and from the look on her beautiful face I think she was just beginning to realize it.

I watched Nick turn the full force of his charm on to his new wife, allowing her to feel its full effect, and he held out his arms, 'I have no need of luck with you by my side, Annie, darling.'

That had been his pet name for me, too, I realized with a slight shock. What a devious man he really was and how very convenient he must have found it that my name could be abbreviated in just that way. Watching as he drew Anthea close, I thanked God all over again that I wasn't the bride Nick had chosen. I felt guilty almost at once for feeling so relieved that he was never going to be my problem.

Poor brand-new Mrs Cable, I thought soberly. Then remembering the determined look on Anthea's flawlessly beautiful face earlier, I was suddenly quite sure that she probably had her new husband's measure, and wouldn't need or want my pity. I immediately felt much better.

The double doors opened then and, as a crowd of well-wishers surged forward to surround the happy couple, Lex drew me to one side to tell me coldly, 'Your lipstick is a mess, and since I wasn't the culprit, I would be excessively grateful if you would repair the damage.' Then, throwing me a look of intense dislike, he went back to join the throng, leaving me to go back to the powder room.

Bemused, I stared at my reflection and the perfectly outlined lips and wondered what on earth Lex thought he had seen. Didn't he know that never in the world would I have kissed his brother and that any feelings I might have had for him — recent though those feelings might have been — were dead, now, and buried? Yet he probably believed at that very moment that I was still Nick's for the taking. Any chance I might have had to convince him otherwise had disappeared the moment he had seen Nick standing so close to me in the hall, leaving him prepared to believe every damning word his brother uttered.

'Come along, dear,' Eleanor Cable put her bright face round the door to urge, 'they're off at last, and you must be there to see them go. You're part of the family now.'

I didn't even know how it happened, and it was the last thing I wanted, but as the bride went to step into the car, she turned and laughingly tossed her bouquet — straight into my reluctant arms.

The other guests were ecstatic, and Lex joined in their laughter. He took their high-spirited ribbing in good part, but when he looked at me, his glare, black and freezing, chilled me to the bone and I shivered.

'You're getting cold, darling.' The concern in his tone was as false as the endearment that slipped so easily from his tongue.

'Come back inside in the warm,' his grandmother urged, 'I've been looking forward to a lovely chat.'

'I'm afraid you'll have to make it some other time.' Lex's words were abrupt, but he managed the semblance of a smile, as he added, with the hint of an apology in his voice, 'We must be making a move. There have been severe weather warnings. Apparently there is quite a storm on the way,' he added by way of explanation. 'It's a long drive back, and I would like to make it back before it hits in the morning.'

'Well, that doesn't have to be a problem,' the older woman returned cheerfully. 'You can stay with us. You have a key.'

Apparently Lex relished the idea of sharing a room again even less than I did and he firmly, but kindly resisted the invitation. I was ushered to the BMW, and in seconds was seated inside with Lex in the driving seat.

'Smile, damn you,' was all he said as we drove away.

The miles were covered in a complete

silence that was so charged with a vicious electric undercurrent of bitter, unspoken words that I feared that once it was unleashed it was going to burn us both, and perhaps leave us scarred for ever. It was this awareness that kept me quiet, and the certain knowledge that this was my final chance to try and put things right with Lex. A hasty word now, and there would be nothing left to save, and I did want to salvage something, in spite of everything. After all, we were both victims of Nick's duplicity.

I desperately fought against the urge to cry, but to my horror a small pathetic sob escaped, and I turned to stare out of the window, desperately trying to hide the tears that would no longer be held back.

'Don't weep over him,' Lex advised flatly. 'I promise you that he's not worth it.'

'I'm not . . . ' I began, and then thought better of it, suddenly deciding I was done with trying to explain or excuse myself. It was unrealistic for me to have imagined that Lex and I could even be civil to one another, much less become friends. It was time to cut my losses and as far as I was concerned the sooner we could go our separate ways the better I would be pleased. Being homeless, jobless and friendless was infinitely preferable to being a guest of the Cable family for one moment longer than was necessary, I decided grimly.

'Switch the radio on,' Lex suddenly demanded abruptly, after we had travelled in silence for quite some time. Quite sure that he wouldn't have appreciated my reminding him to mind his manners at that particular moment, I reached out obediently to do as he said.

Classical music flooded the car, but I was far too strung up to appreciate it, or even to identify the piece. I saw Lex throw the radio a glance of intense dislike, and heard him tut impatiently. He had already stretched out a hand — to change channels, I assumed — when the announcer cut in with a warning that even as he spoke the severe gale-force winds that had been forecast were already sweeping inland from the coast.

Listening in growing horror, I learned that structural damage could be expected on a grand scale, and that trees might be uprooted. Everyone was being strongly advised to stay at home.

'My God,' I gasped, as comprehension began to dawn. 'So you were telling the truth.'

'I'm not in the habit of lying,' he said, adding, 'as a rule,' as an afterthought. 'I did know that strong winds were expected, but they've arrived far sooner than was forecast. Thankfully, we're almost home.'

The car practically hurtled along a slip road, and then as it joined a narrower New Forest road, I noticed that Lex slowed to a far more reasonable speed. I hoped it was his concern for the animals that had prompted the change, and released my grip on the sides of my seat just slightly.

With every mile the force of the wind that I hadn't previously noticed at all seemed to increase, and I noted nervously that the trees were already hurling themselves this way and that, and bending deeply under the onslaught. I was certain that it was only Lex's skilful driving that kept the car on the road. It was buffeted furiously from side to side, and I thanked God, most sincerely, that there was no other traffic in sight. The New Forest animals had, apparently, had the good sense to seek shelter and were also absent.

'Not long now,' Lex muttered tersely, not taking his eyes from the road, and gripping the steering wheel so fiercely that his knuckles showed white against the scratched tan of his hands.

I should have been terrified, I realized, but, unexpectedly, I found that I had every faith in Lex's ability to get us back to the house in one piece. Once there we would surely be safe, since I clearly remembered that the surrounding trees were far enough from the house not to pose any serious threat to the building.

If anyone could get us there, he could, I acknowledged, and then found myself wondering inconsequentially if I would have had the same sort of confidence in Nick. If I were honest, I rather thought not; he'd never shown signs of having a comparable strength of character, but perhaps I was being unfair to him as a result of my own experiences at his hands.

'Look out!'

The hoarse shout, and the arm thrown across my body, was just too late to stop me being thrown forward in the second before the seat belt locked. Miraculously, I was entirely unhurt as the car slewed across the road and skidded to a halt inches from the tree that I hadn't even noticed had fallen right into our path.

Lex was out of the car instantly. He raced to wrench the passenger door open and almost lifted me out on to the road. 'Follow me,' he ordered, and grasping my hand firmly in his he began to run.

The ground was uneven, and with the force of the wind blowing squalls of rain savagely into my face, I could see precious little.

Thankfully my heels were not of the killer variety, but all the same I staggered and tripped time after time, and knew I would have fallen if Lex hadn't always been there to catch me, and to urge me on.

'Not much further,' he yelled encouragingly, and the screaming wind took the words from his mouth immediately, throwing them high in the air.

The breath was labouring in my lungs, tears poured from my eyes, I was scratched and beaten by errant branches that clutched and tore at my clothes, and I suddenly knew that I couldn't go on — not for another step. I just wanted to lie down and let the storm continue around me. The effort to give in was just too great to be ignored.

'I . . . ' It was no good, I couldn't even speak, and so I just stopped abruptly. My rain-slippery hand was wrenched from Lex's, and for a moment he staggered forward without me.

The rain beat down on my unprotected head. It soaked through my flimsy suit and into impractical shoes that were designed solely for looking good. I could only gulp in much needed air, sinking to my knees with an infinite relief that was to be short-lived.

A vicelike grip seized me by the shoulders, I was lifted and shaken until I opened my eyes to meet Lex's furious glare, rain streamed down the face he thrust wrathfully into mine.

'What the *hell* do you think you're playing at?' he yelled at the top of his voice.

'I can't . . . ' I gasped, shaking my head and feeling utterly pathetic. 'I — can't.'

He shook me again, so that my head wobbled feebly and my eyes filled and spilled over with the weak tears that mingled with lashing rain.

'Yes, you bloody well can.' He hollered it so loudly that the shriek of the wind was quiet in comparison. 'Don't you *dare* give up now. We're almost there.'

On and on, I was thrust relentlessly forward, pushed and pulled by turns, and lifted at last into strong arms when I fell to my knees again, screaming at him in a language that even he would understand that I couldn't — and wouldn't — go on.

Lex stumbled, almost falling as, on reaching the house at last, he fumbled with the key before thrusting the front door open and stepping inside. Still holding me, he elbowed the door and then putting his back into it forced it to close in the vicious teeth of the gale. The comparative silence inside, after the noise of the storm, was almost deafening, until it was broken by the first spectacular crash of thunder that had me hiding my face in the soaked front of Lex's jacket.

'It's all right,' he told me, his tone gentle and not much more than a whisper. 'We're safe now.' I promptly burst into tears.

Still leaning back against the solid front door, Lex set me on to my feet.

'I'm sorry, I'm so sorry,' I wailed, crying even harder.

'You have nothing to be sorry for,' he insisted, looking grimmer than I had ever seen him. 'I'm the one who should be sorry. I should never have tried to beat the storm. I must have been mad. I could have killed you.' He lifted his face to stare despairingly at the ceiling, and repeat, 'Oh, God, I could have killed you.'

'Don't. Oh, please, don't.' I touched a hand gently to his face, forcing his dark-blue gaze to meet my own. 'You mustn't ever think of reproaching yourself. You did what you thought was best, and we're safe now. We're safe now.'

Wind screamed around the house, rain spattered on the door like relentless fingers furiously tapping, and the crash of thunder added to the confusion of sounds outside, but inside there was suddenly nothing but the two of us. The clamour of the storm faded away completely until it no longer existed as we stared at each other. All I could hear was the sound of my own heartbeat slamming nervously against my ribs — all I could feel were emotions I couldn't even begin to understand.

The strident ringing of the telephone was sudden and shockingly loud. We both literally jumped and then leapt apart. Since I was closer I lifted the receiver to my ear.

'Lex, is that you?'

I absolutely froze. There was no mistaking that voice, and I hissed, 'It's for you.'

'Well, who is it?'

'See for yourself,' I told him bitterly.

He stared at me, dark eyes narrowing, before taking the phone from my nerveless fingers and saying harshly into it, 'Alexander Cable speaking. Who is this?'

I moved away. I didn't want to hear more; I walked into the sitting room on legs that didn't quite feel as if they belonged to me, closed the door carefully behind me and went to stand in the middle of the room, shivering miserably.

Nick Cable. The man I had so fondly imagined myself desperately in love with until just a few short days ago, yet the minute his true colours emerged the scales had fallen from my eyes with a speed that belied the notion that there had ever been any real depth to my feelings after all. I'd realized that I really should have known better than to trust him so implicitly. It was difficult to accept I'd allowed myself to be fooled again and I could only begin to console myself with reminding myself that I'd been taken in by a complete, and very practised, expert in the art of seduction.

Far from being heartbroken, my biggest emotion to date had been pure relief that I had escaped his clutches relatively unscathed. In fact, what I'd fondly believed was the love of my life had turned out to be nothing more than a mid-life infatuation and the only thing dented was my foolish pride.

Lex stepped into the room behind me, thrusting the door back as he did so with such a force that it hit against something with a crash. I could almost feel the anger emanating from him from clear across the room.

'What's the matter?' he ground out. 'The mere sound of his voice put you all at sixes and sevens, did it?'

I turned slowly to face him, hardly able to believe that this harsh-toned stranger, and the man who had shown such tenderness only minutes before, could be one and the same person.

'It's not like that at all,' I denied, shivering under his disparaging glare and suddenly

146

conscious for the first time of the soaking clothes that clung to my body and chilled me right through to my bones.

'Oh, isn't it just?' he returned bitterly. 'Look at yourself. Go on, take a good hard look at yourself.'

Grasping my arm he thrust me across the room until I stood facing an antique gilt-edged mirror. I looked, tried to see what he thought he was seeing, but I saw only a bedraggled woman with blonde hair plastered flat to her head, whose bewildered blue eyes stared back at me.

'I look a mess,' I muttered, futilely dragging cold fingers through my hair, which improved my appearance not at all.

'You are a mess,' he retorted angrily, 'and so you will be, until you realize that that brother of mine is *not* for you, and forget all about him.'

I could only stare up at him uncomprehendingly, finding it difficult, if not impossible to accept that he really thought I still wanted Nick after all that had happened. He was so ludicrously wrong that I almost laughed right in his face, but what then? I could tell him that Nick had been a mistake that would not be repeated, that I had learned my lesson, but why even bother when I knew he'd never believe me?

'Oh, go on.' Lex gave me a little impatient push in the direction of the open door. 'Go and get out of those wet clothes.'

I stumbled forward, chilled now through and through, knowing the wet clothes had little to do with it. Lex despised me still, and it had taken the phone call from Nick to make me realize once and for all that he was never — not ever — going to forgive me for being one of his brother's 'little interests', and why should I care? After all, he meant nothing to me.

10

I turned over restlessly in bed, and listened to the rain outside hurling itself against the window as if it were as desperate for entry as I was to get away from the Cable house.

No, not away from the Cable house itself, I corrected ruefully and a little sadly, because it was truly a beautiful home, but the Cable family.

The brothers utterly despised me, each in their own way. I didn't really need to keep reminding myself of the fact but somehow I couldn't seem to help it. To Nick I had represented nothing more than a challenge, something of a novelty I supposed, given my maturity and with my old-fashioned dreams of love, marriage and happy ever after. I had no doubt at all now that, had I slept with him right at the start of our relationship, I'd have very soon been discarded and left without even my pride intact.

Lex, on the other hand, had quickly made the assumption that I was little more than a slut or a gold-digger and saw no reason to reconsider that view. He'd never made any secret of his low opinion, not since that first night when he'd walked in and found me in his bed, apparently waiting for Nick to join me. I wished wholeheartedly now that I had left the house right then — walked away if I'd had to — and never set eyes on either brother again.

I watched the cold light of dawn creeping across the ceiling, and came again to the decision that as soon as ever I could I was going to try and turn the clock back, I would go back to the life I had rejected with such indecent haste and very little real thought, rebuild the bridges I had blown up, if I possibly could, at least make an attempt to regain the career and the friendships that I had thrown away so carelessly, and then forget all about men in general and the Cable brothers in particular.

If all that proved impossible I was still young enough to make a fresh start elsewhere. The thought was daunting, to say the least, but I squared my shoulders and told myself I could do it. When it came down to it the cold hard fact was I might not have a choice.

'Coffee,' Lex offered, as soon as I showed my face in the kitchen, adding, 'You look tired.'

'It was the rain and the wind. I've never heard a storm like it, and it did keep me awake.' I sat down and accepted the cup he offered.

'Mmm,' Lex looked at the window, where the rain was still hitting the pane in regular and savage squalls, though the wind had obviously dropped quite considerably overnight and was no longer quite the frightening gale force it had been. 'I was hoping the local garage would send a mechanic to look at your car today. I'm pretty confident it will turn out to be something simple like replacing the battery — not that I know all that much about cars,' he admitted.

'Surely the rain won't stop him?' I stared at him, seeing my chance of escaping sooner rather than later disappearing with the torrents of rain.

'The rain, no, but the wind just might have done the trick,' he admitted, strolling to the window to peer out.

'The wind?' I was on my feet and after him in an instant. 'What's the wind got to do with it?'

Lex turned to face me, smiling almost indulgently, which was a surprise when I remembered his savage outburst after Nick's phone call the night before.

'We're in the middle of a forest,' he reminded me, 'in case you hadn't noticed. In high winds, trees are apt to get blown down, causing roads to be closed. We had a taste of it ourselves yesterday.'

The thought that we might have to remain where we were indefinitely filled me with horror, I put my fear into nervously spoken words. 'But if the mechanic can't get in, we can't get out and are probably trapped.'

With my imagination behaving in an admittedly overactive way, I could see days, or even weeks ahead of me, imprisoned in the close confines of this house with a man who despised me so much he couldn't bring himself to be civil for more than a few minutes at a stretch,

'There's plenty of food.' Lex seemed to deliberately misunderstand my fears, as he added, 'We can manage.'

Ignoring him, I suggested, 'I'll ring a local garage anyway, shall I, and see what they can do?'

He gave me a hard look before replying, 'It's not necessary and most probably don't work Sundays anyway. As it happens I phoned them myself yesterday morning. No doubt a mechanic will be here as soon as he can get through, though it might not be until tomorrow. The wind has at least dropped now, so there should be no more trees brought down. The councils will be clearing the debris already. They don't waste much time even on a weekend, and nor will the garage, I'm sure.'

I looked at the weather and then at Lex, muttering, 'I hope you're right.'

'Any plans for the day?'

'Like what?' I asked ungraciously and ungrammatically.

'Plenty of DVDs and books around, feel free to make yourself at home.'

'No, thank you,' I rejected flatly, 'though I would like to use the phone, if that's all right. I'd like to see what, if anything, can be salvaged of my former life. The sooner I can get back to it and forget about this whole unfortunate episode the better I shall be pleased.'

Lex looked as if he was about to question me, but perhaps correctly interpreting the look on my face thought better of it. 'Help yourself,' he said. 'There are phones everywhere or you can use my mobile if you prefer.'

I thought about my own, still lying useless in my bag, and wondered how the whole course of events might have changed if only I had kept it charged — because I would have phoned Nick on Friday for sure the minute I'd realized I was going to be very late whether he'd have liked it or not. Who knows, he just might have had the grace to let me down gently before any real damage was done. At that point the car was still behaving and I might just have made it back to town almost before anyone had even realized I'd left.

'Can I get you anything to eat?'

I shook my head, something I felt sure I would live to regret, because in truth I was absolutely starving.

I used a phone in the hall and, quite surprised to find the line unaffected by storm damage, dialled one of the directory enquiry services because I had no numbers with me apart from those in the useless mobile. The problem with its being a Sunday was that few people would be working, which limited my options rather.

Ideally I would have rung the letting agency, pretending to be interested in my own flat, in the hope that they hadn't found a tenant in such a short time. Next I'd have tried the office, thrown myself on my boss's mercy, apologized profusely for my own stupidity and pleaded for my job back. I was banking on the fact that Simon had always appeared to be quite fond of me — I'd even had the ridiculous notion once upon a time that we might have been more than business colleagues, but nothing had ever come of it.

The thought of going to him, cap in hand,

was pretty embarrassing but this obviously wasn't the time to be balking about eating huge slices of humble pie, and I actually felt fairly confident that he wouldn't even have got around to arranging an advertisement for a replacement yet. He might even be relieved to be saved the bother. While I was doing those things I would have been asking myself how on earth I had got myself into such a mess — and all over a bloody man.

In the end, with its being Sunday, and appreciating that Sam would be spending precious time with her baby, I phoned Valerie Winstanley, who was probably the only friend I had left. She alone had put aside her own very real concerns enough eventually to become excited with me and pleased for me when Nick had suddenly proposed — encouraging me to believe some things really were meant to be and reminding me as I left that *he who hesitates is lost* or some such thing.

I'd wondered at the time if she was speaking from bitter experience, and had missed out on love herself at some time in the past. A spinster, a few years older than I, Valerie lived with her elderly mother, a feckless brother who turned up when it suited him, and several cats. She appeared to have given up long since on the idea of finding a man to share her life. I guessed her job had become her life — she had certainly been working at Mannings almost as long as I had and was always the first one there in the morning and the last one to leave at night.

A very private person; I only knew as much as I did about her from the phone calls she received in an office where private conversation was almost impossible. Given to wearing long, gathered skirts and shapeless jumpers that probably hid a perfectly presentable figure, Valerie looked as if the cares of the world rested on her shoulders, and far older than the late forties she admitted to.

'Valerie,' I said when she answered the phone, injecting a brightness into my tone I was far from feeling, 'it's Stacey. How are you?'

'Oh, you know how it is, I've had a bad night with my mother, one of the cats has been sick and I've no idea where my brother's got to, but you don't want to hear about that. Have you and Nick set a date for the wedding yet? I've been dying to hear your news.'

It was quite weird to hear her excitement and to realize how recently I had shared it. In just a matter of hours — I couldn't believe it was actually less than two whole days — my newly formed, but so fragile dream of a new life had been swept away and along with it went the security of my old life. In fact I had nothing — unless something could be clawed back, which was the whole purpose of this phone call.

'I'm afraid it didn't work out,' I said simply, feeling my lips tremble, 'Nick wasn't quite what he appeared to be, so I was wondering . . . '

There was a stunned silence, but only for a moment, and then Valerie's voice came down the line, cold and flat. 'I *did* try to warn you.'

It was my turn to be stunned, and then I began, 'Well, yes I know you did, but then you were so encouraging — '

Valerie wasn't listening, 'I don't know *what* you expected. You'd hardly known the man for five minutes. A good-looking face and a flashy car are hardly a solid foundation for any kind of relationship. I'd have thought someone of *your* age would have known better than to have your head turned like that.'

The woman was vicious in her castigation of me, and the dreadful thing was that I knew that she was right. I *should* have known better, should have trusted my instincts and my friends and acted with far more caution. Basically, I had got exactly what I deserved and that was exactly what she was telling me in no uncertain terms.

'I hope you're not phoning for sympathy,' she continued, barely pausing for breath, 'or expecting to be welcomed back with open arms after the appalling way you've behaved. I will be stepping into your job as of tomorrow, apparently the letting agency already have someone ready to move into your flat and I can assure you that every one of your friends feels exactly as I do. After all, you chose to dismiss their concern and reject their advice. Quite simply, you've made your bed, Anastasia, and I'm afraid you are just going to have to lie in it. There is nothing left for you here.'

The click as Valerie replaced the receiver sounded very like the door closing firmly on my past, present and future and I shuddered. With the demise of the life I had lived before Nick Cable erupted into it went the stability that had been so important to me, and everything and everyone that was familiar to me. I could literally smell the acrid stench of burning bridges and taste the bitterness of my own fear.

Numbness swept over me and I stood rooted to the spot, staring at the phone in my hand as if I had no idea what it was. I just couldn't believe it had come to this, that I had lost everything just because I had put my trust in someone who, quite clearly didn't know the meaning of the word.

I didn't realize that Lex was there until he took the phone from my nerveless fingers and replaced it on the base before asking, 'Are you all right, Stacey? Is there anything I can get you?'

He couldn't have known to whom the call had been made or exactly what it was about, but he could obviously tell something was very wrong by my demeanour, I could detect concern in his voice and even a note of sympathy, and I couldn't bear to become an object of his pity. Insults and sarcasm were what I had become used to from him and those I could deal with.

I gave myself a little shake, and dredged a bright smile up from somewhere. 'I'm fine,' I insisted, 'but I think I'll go and start getting my things together so that I'll be ready to leave as soon as the car is fixed.'

I walked like an automaton towards the stairs, and was proud that I kept going, even when Lex asked, 'Are you sure I can't persuade you to stay on here for a few days more?' merely responding with a firm and emphatic, 'No, thank you.'

My back was straight and my eyes dry until I had closed the bedroom door behind me. Then, sagging against the wood, I allowed the tears to flow at last in a torrent of silent grief.

I had never felt so alone in the world, not even when my parents went their separate ways, fighting over the dog and the entertainment system but leaving me out of the equation. Then I had gained strength from the friends who had supported me — some of them since schooldays — and the fact that, young as I was, I had my life in order. I had been let down before, though never so spectacularly, but you would have thought I would have learned something from past experience.

'Stupid, stupid, stupid,' I taunted myself, knowing I could blame no one else because, quite simply, I should have known better. Standing in front of the mirror I repaired the damage my tears had caused to my make-up and asked myself, 'So, what are you going to do about the mess you're in? Because you know you're the only one who can do anything about it.'

I tried looking for a bright side, because there surely had to be one. I had a bit of money in the bank, so I wasn't without funds and there would be the income from letting out my flat. I could feel the tears welling up again at the thought of someone else living in my little home, but I furiously blinked them away knowing crying would solve absolutely nothing.

Perhaps I should cut all ties and start afresh. The idea was quite appealing and I didn't need reminding again that there was nothing to go back for — apart from the few bits I'd placed hastily in storage rather than leave them at the new tenant's mercy.

I could almost stick a pin in a map and take my pick, even go to London where anonymity was practically guaranteed and jobs might be more plentiful — even without a reference. Especially without a reference, I acknowledged ruefully, because I couldn't see one of those forthcoming with my having walked out the way I had.

I was beginning to feel better already. It was always advisable to be doing something rather than nothing, as I knew from experience, and what was needed in a situation such as this was a plan of action.

By the time I went downstairs I was feeling much better and, knowing the time spent in Lex's company would be limited, I was graciously able to accept his offer of lunch and to exchange small talk over cheese omelette and salad.

'It looks as if it's brightening up.' I waved a fork in the direction of the window, where a watery sun could be observed peeping intermittently from behind the remainder of the grey clouds.

Lex nodded, 'I thought I might venture out and see if I could retrieve the car, maybe even take a look under the bonnet of your Mini. It won't do any harm, though I'm not a mechanic, of course, but it looks pretty certain he won't get here until tomorrow.'

As if on cue there was the sound of wheels on the gravelled drive, the brisk toot of a horn and the roof of a white van became visible through the window.

'Oh, he's here.' I smiled, not even trying to hide my delight.

'Yes.' There was no answering smile from Lex, as he added, making his way outside, 'Freedom is at hand,' and I knew then he would be every bit as pleased to see the back of me, as I would be to see the back of him. I wasn't wanted anywhere, it seemed, and the sooner I accepted that and moved on the better.

After what felt like only minutes had passed Lex put his head around the door. 'Any chance of a cup of tea for the workers?'

Going to fill the kettle, I asked over my shoulder, 'What was it? Is it fixed already?'

'Well, it will be.' The boy, for he was little more, who had followed Lex in, wiped oily hands down his overalls and beamed helpfully. 'As soon as I can fit a new alternator for you.'

'Oh, dear.' I had no idea what it was, but it certainly sounded serious to me. 'How long is that going to take?'

'Pete here says they might have one in stock,' Lex put in. 'In which case, he can fit it tomorrow afternoon. It was very good of him to come by on his day off.'

I paused in the act of pouring boiling water over tea bags to smile at the lad. 'It certainly was, and I'm more than happy to pay you for your time today — double time if you like.'

So, I could even be on my way by tomorrow night. Now that freedom was within touching distance, I didn't know whether to be pleased or sorry that I was going to have to come up with a plan of action pretty damn quickly and immediately put it to the test. The thought was daunting and I despised myself for being so pathetic.

'That's OK, I was passing on my way home anyway,' Pete said cheerfully, accepting a mug of strong tea with, 'Thanks, just as I like it.'

I poured more tea, and passed round some biscuits I'd found in one of the cupboards.

'If you're thinking of going anywhere today,' Pete offered, 'you should get through OK. The main roads are pretty well clear now, and they've just moved the tree that blocked your way yesterday.' He shook his tousled head. 'It would have been a real

163

shame if it had fallen on the BMW and flattened it.'

'It would have been a bigger shame for us,' Lex retorted, without humour, 'if we'd been inside it.'

'Yeah, course.' The lad looked serious immediately. 'I shoulda thoughta that.'

'No harm done,' I insisted. 'As you can see, we lived to tell the tale.'

Pete agreed and went cheerily on his way. Lex turned on me furiously the minute the door closed behind him.

'I wish you would stop making light of a serious error of judgement on my part,' he snapped. 'If you're trying to make me feel better, then don't. We shouldn't even have been out in such a storm and you know it. It was pigheaded of me to imagine I could race the weather. We could have both been killed.'

I'd had enough, and slammed the cup I was holding down so hard on the table it was a wonder it didn't disintegrate, 'Oh, *will* you change the bloody record,' I fumed, getting louder and more angry with every word I uttered. 'Keeping on about it won't make it unhappen. It's over now, we're both in one piece and the whole episode could be forgotten about if only you didn't keep dredging it up. *I'm* doing my best to look on the bright side — but then that's obviously something you don't have a clue about.'

The look on his face was priceless. I doubt if Lex had ever been spoken to like that by a woman in the whole of his life, so now he would have something else to add to the case he was building up against me. I suddenly found I didn't even care and the relief I felt was tremendous.

11

After practically yelling at Lex like a common fishwife I was anxious to put some space between us. Taking the stairs two at a time I slammed the bedroom door hard behind me and leaned against it breathing hard.

I half-expected to hear his feet thundering up the stairs behind me, for the door to be thrust open and a swift demand that I leave the house immediately to be issued on the spot. I really wouldn't have blamed him. I was enjoying his hospitality, after all — if enjoying was the right word to use — and had no right to speak to him like that in his own home whatever the provocation.

Well, it was too late to take it back now, and he was insufferable with his volatile moods and short fuse. You never knew where you were with the bloody man and I pitied the woman who eventually ended up with him. I couldn't help grinning as I reflected that I had made pretty damn certain that it wouldn't be me — as if he hadn't been convinced enough already.

I looked around, wondering how best to pass the time now I'd placed myself under solitary confinement. I supposed I could busy myself sorting through my clothes, making a pile of several garments I had worn — like those I had shinned up over the front porch in — which should be laundered at some point. The cream suit, of course, was quite obviously beyond repair and would have to be binned along with the shoes, but the remainder were clean. It would have been helpful to be able do some washing, but I didn't relish the idea of going back down into the kitchen to ask such a favour and could just imagine the response I'd get if I did. Perhaps I would just repack the lot and sort it out wherever it was I eventually landed up.

The case I'd brought was a reasonable size and had been packed to capacity. It had been a struggle to get the piece of luggage into the Mini, but I was glad now that I'd succeeded because it did mean I wasn't going to run out of things to wear.

I supposed it was inevitable I would come across my mobile phone charger eventually. I retrieved it from a corner of the suitcase and stared at it ruefully. There was no point at all in belatedly accessing messages that just might have saved me from going through a humiliating and painful ordeal at the hands of Lex Cable.

I would have liked to think there would

have been at least one from Nick cancelling our meeting, our engagement and our future together. An explanation might have been good and an apology would have been even better, but either one was probably too much to ask and I was too much of a coward to check.

I didn't expect there to be any messages from my friends either, Valerie had made it crystal clear they'd all washed their hands of me, and who could really blame them? No one likes to be told to take their opinions and their concern and shove them where the sun doesn't shine and, basically, it was pretty much what I had done.

Even as I reached into my handbag for the phone, the decision not to recharge it was reached with comparative ease. Discovering what messages it might or might not hold would serve no useful purpose at this late stage and I had no wish to be hurt any more than I already had been. I had learned my lesson, once and for all, and could very well do without hearing the inevitable 'I told you so' I probably richly deserved once Valerie had shared my latest news — which I had no doubt she would rush to do at her earliest convenience.

When I'd tidied everything that could possibly be tidied I pulled on my jacket and made my way downstairs. I wasn't sure whether to be relieved or worried when there was no sign of Lex, but surmised he couldn't be far away since the back door was unlocked and the radio was playing.

From the upstairs window I'd caught a glimpse of water through the trees and I headed in that direction. What was probably normally a pretty little lake had obviously overflowed, and the ground as I drew closer was boggy to say the least. Finding a little hillock to stand on, I reached into my pocket and drew out both mobile phone and charger and without a second thought I threw them as hard as I could out into the water. Barely waiting for the splash, I turned and made my way back to the house.

There was still no sign of Lex, but the house phone was ringing as I walked in the back door. I almost ignored it. It was hardly going to be for me, and there was every chance it might be Nick again. Clearly we had nothing to say to each other. Then, realizing it might be a call about the part for the Mini I reached for the receiver.

It was Aaron Cable, but he sounded so unlike himself that it took me a moment or two, first of all to identify that it was indeed him, and then a little longer to make sense of what he was saying.

Was Lex there? he asked, sounding desperate, only Eleanor had fallen, he continued, and he couldn't get her up or even make any sense of what she was trying to say. A chill swept through me, but I knew I had to remain calm in order to encourage Aaron to get Eleanor the help she so obviously needed and quickly.

'I would dial 999, Aaron, if I were you,' I advised, doing my best to sound unruffled.

I must have made too good a job of sounding unconcerned, because he seemed to want to argue, saying, 'But she's only slipped and I've made her comfortable with a cushion and a rug. If Lex could pop up and give me a hand or perhaps I should call the surgery.'

'Just phone for an ambulance,' I urged. 'Anything else will take too long and she may have broken a bone or be concussed or something and require urgent treatment. It's best to be on the safe side. *Don't* try to lift her yourself whatever you do. Lex would tell you the same. I'm going to find him now, he's around here somewhere.'

'We wouldn't want to be a nuisance.' Aaron sounded close to tears. 'It might be a false alarm and she'll be fine in a minute or two.'

'Just phone for the ambulance for Eleanor's sake.' My tone remained calm but inside I was screaming with sheer frustration. 'If it's a false alarm no one will mind in the least, I promise you. It's always best to be safe rather than sorry.'

'Well, if you're sure.'

'I'm quite sure. Do it right now, Aaron. It's the best thing for Eleanor.'

I was out through the door before the phone had landed on the base, and was running down the drive before I realized I had no idea where Lex was or which direction he'd be coming back from. I could be going in entirely the wrong direction but the fact that I had to do *something* kept me going.

The relief was enormous when I rounded the first bend at full pelt and saw the BMW coming towards me with Lex at the wheel. He slammed on the brakes, though there was no real danger of his hitting me.

He was out of the car in a minute, looking furious, and I waited for him to stride across and confront me in his usual fashion, before berating me. Instead, lounging against the open door, he demanded, 'Going somewhere in a hurry, were you? It must be bad if you prefer to run all the way home rather than to spend another minute in my company. Just take my car, there you go.' He held the door wide and urged, 'The keys are in the ignition, get in and take yourself off back where you came from — if they'll have you.'

Bloody, *bloody* man. He never missed a chance to vent his spleen at my expense and probably never would. If it weren't for the circumstances, I knew I'd have willingly jumped into the damned car and roared off into the wide blue yonder.

Still trying to catch my breath, I puffed, 'You. Are. Insufferable. No time to argue. Emergency.'

His mouth was open, ready to launch another attack, no doubt, and then the last word must have caught his attention and in a stride he was in front of me, his hands gripping my arms.

'What is it? What's happened?'

I heaved a great breath into my labouring lungs, and managed, 'Your grandmother has had a fall, I told Aaron to phone an ambulance right away. It may be serious. You must go. They will need you.'

To his credit Lex didn't hesitate or stop to ask questions, but leapt back into the car and spun it around, scattering gravel far and wide. He paused only long enough to lower the window and ask, 'You'll still be here when I get back?'

I nodded, and he was gone, leaving me to stare after him, until the car disappeared from

172

sight. I turned then and trailed back to the house wondering why, on the one hand he seemed hell bent on making me leave, and the next was as good as requesting me to stay.

I shivered in my thin jacket and was glad to get back inside to the warmth of the house. It looked as if once more I would be spending a night alone in this isolated place. But this time there would be no intruder to disturb my sleep, I decided, as I locked and bolted both front and back doors so that even those with a key would have to wait to be invited in.

The house seemed much bigger without Lex in it, and I wandered round for a while admiring the tasteful furnishings and marvelling that my tiny flat would have sat quite comfortably in just a quarter of the ground floor. The telephone remained stubbornly silent and it was barely dark outside when I took myself off to bed and tried not to think too much about what might be happening in London.

I slept only fitfully and daylight had barely broken before I was up, showered, dressed and ready — ready for what I wasn't quite sure. I was sitting at the kitchen table nursing a cup of tea when there was a sharp rap at the back door. I opened it to find Lex standing on the step, his expression grim and his face grey with fatigue.

Swallowing all my questions I stood back to allow him inside and fought the urge to give him a big hug. He looked as if he could really use one. Instead I hurried to pour him a cup of tea, adding sugar though I was well aware he didn't take it.

'I don't take . . . ' he began when he took the first sip,

'Just drink it,' I said bossily, seeming to have lost some of the natural reserve I always felt around him, 'it will do you good. Could you eat something?'

He shook his head wearily, but I ignored him and bustled about grilling bacon, frying eggs and buttering bread. Neither of us said anything until I put the loaded plates on the table and I began to dread what he was eventually going to tell me. The silence was becoming ominous to say the least.

'Is your grandmother' — I began hesitantly, and finished in a rush — 'all right?'

'She will be,' he said solemnly. 'My grandmother almost certainly *hasn't* had a stroke — which is a mercy — but it could easily have been a different story. I would guess that that possibility was your first thought, as it would have been mine, and you would also have known speed is of the essence in those cases. Thanks to you the ambulance was there within minutes.'

I did the only thing I could do, and promptly burst into tears of relief. It was so silly, she wasn't my grandmother, but I had felt so responsible because I was the one who'd answered the phone to Aaron.

Lex was beside me in a minute, kneeling beside my chair and taking my cold hands into his, 'She will be all right, I promise you, and once all the tests have been carried out, we shall know what caused her to fall. I do thank you for keeping a cool head and yet managing to impress upon my grandfather the need to get expert help quickly.' His dark gaze rested unwavering on my face and I stared back at him, almost mesmerized, for what seemed like a very long time. Then I stood up and broke the spell.

'Nothing to thank me for.' I became brisk, and dried my eyes on a piece of kitchen towel. The moment passed as I urged, 'Eat up, eat up. Can I get you more tea?'

'Thank you.' Lex passed his cup over. 'I'll finish this, get showered and changed, and make my way back.'

'You'll have a sleep,' I told him, in what I hoped was a firm tone that showed I would brook no argument, 'even if it's only for an hour.' I could tell he was about to protest and went on, 'It's either that, Lex, or I will drive you up to town myself. It's very dangerous to

175

get behind the wheel of a car when you're as tired as you must be, which is something you must know very well.'

'But what about your car?' he said, adding, 'The mechanic is due today.'

'We can ring him and leave the keys somewhere for him to find, can't we?'

'You'd do that for me and delay your departure?'

'It's nothing, and I would do the same for anyone,' I insisted, making quite sure he didn't get the idea that he was a special case. 'We might not get on that well, but I wouldn't like to see you have an accident. Just think what something like that would do to your grandmother.'

In less than an hour we were both ready and seated in the BMW. I'd never driven a brand new car, much less a top of the range model such as I took this one to be and my hand shook as I reached out to turn the key. Even before we had reached the end of the long driveway Lex was fast asleep, but with the satnav already programmed all I had to do was to follow the directions it gave. The car was a joy to drive and it literally ate up the miles. It felt as if no time had passed before I was entering the capital and being swallowed up by the morning's heavy traffic.

For long moments after I'd parked in the

grounds of a London hospital I wasn't familiar with I sat quietly watching Lex sleep, loath to wake him when sleep was so clearly what he needed. He looked years younger in repose, I thought, the harsh planes of his face were smoothed and softened as if the cares of the world had dropped from his shoulders — if only temporarily,

I felt the strongest urge to reach out and smooth the hair back from his brow and had to clench my hands into my lap and remind myself that any kind of familiarity wasn't appropriate and would not be welcomed.

'Are we there yet?'

The childlike query made us both smile and lightened the moment.

'Safe and sound.' I nodded, adding, 'Nice car.'

'Will you . . . ?'

'I won't come inside,' I said firmly, forestalling the question I knew was coming. 'This is a time for family and I am not part of your family — whatever your grandmother believes. Take your time.'

'You can't wait here,' Lex insisted, 'and if you go wandering off, how will I find you? Do you have your mobile with you?'

'I don't have one,' I answered truthfully, 'but I'll go and find the canteen, and you can look for me there. Give Eleanor my love.'

'Tha — '

'Don't thank me,' I forestalled him again. 'I'm happy I could help.'

I bought a newspaper and sat down to read it with a cup of coffee and a toasted teacake, marvelling at the things that had been going on in the world. For others, life obviously went on as usual, while I barely recognized mine. The life I'd been living since entering the house in the forest seemed as far removed from reality as it could get. I found it unbelievable that so much could have happened in such a short time.

I wasn't destitute but I was suddenly feeling despondent to say the least and found it necessary to remind myself, quite forcefully, that I was young and healthy, which was surely half the battle. There were millions of people in the world having to deal with far worse calamities than the results of their own stupid actions and I should seriously stop feeling so sorry for myself and start making plans.

I poked around in my bag for the notebook I always carried and I made a start on what seemed like a reasonable plan of action. I'd become so engrossed that I was taken completely by surprise when I eventually looked up to find that Lex had taken the chair opposite and was stirring a black coffee.

I was even more surprised when he smiled in a friendly way and said, 'Is your tea all right or can I go and get you a fresh cup?'

I looked at him suspiciously, then said, 'It depends why you're here so quickly and what you're about to ask me to do, because you are going to ask me to do something, aren't you?'

He laughed and shrugged, 'I'm that transparent, am I?'

'I've noticed you can come up with a certain amount of charm when you're about to try and get your own way. Mind you,' I hastened to add, 'when you don't get it, you soon go back to bullying tactics, but I'm getting used to that, too, so I can tell you beforehand that it won't work.'

He stood up. 'I think I'd better go and get that tea.'

I stared after him, tall and muscular in black leather jacket and jeans, and noticed how female heads turned his way as he walked by. A couple of nurses looked back at me enviously and I felt like telling them that I had absolutely no claim to him and they were very welcome to him anyway.

'How is Eleanor?' I asked as soon as he placed the steaming cup in front of me.

'They're pretty sure it's an inner ear problem, which isn't great but is still something of a relief. The symptoms are highly unpleasant and incapacitating and can be similar to those of a stroke, apparently, as both can leave a patient challenged with vertigo.' He smiled ruefully. 'Of course, I actually knew none of that. I'm just repeating, parrot-fashion, some of what the doctor just said to us, for your benefit.'

'Thank you, but will your grandmother be all right and can it be treated?'

Lex nodded. 'With medication, physical therapy, or both.'

I smiled back at him for the first time then. 'Oh, I am pleased,' I said, and then queried, 'So, what were you going to ask me?'

'She wants to see you, and I know you don't want to play this game any more, but she is old and also very sick . . . '

'And you'll do anything to keep her happy. But how long can this — this charade go on for. Lex? When is it going to end so that I can go back to living my own life?' Not that it was going to be as simple as that, as I knew only too well, but that was my business, I felt.

'Please.'

I was totally and unexpectedly disarmed by what was obviously a genuine plea, issued without threats or bad humour, and I knew instinctively that if I refused he would accept my decision without an argument.

I opened my mouth, but before I could say a word an all too familiar voice behind me said, 'My, my, what have we here?' and I froze.

12

Lex rose to his feet, and without a hint of annoyance at the sarcastic tone, greeted his brother levelly. 'Nick, it was good of you to cut your honeymoon short — and you, too, Anthea.'

'I suppose it was the least we could do under the circumstances.' It was Nick's new wife who replied in a less than happy tone, adding, 'How is Eleanor?'

While Lex repeated the information he had already shared with me, I went off to purchase refreshments for the newcomers, returning with great reluctance to the table where they were all sitting now and talking earnestly.

'Thank you, darling.' Lex pulled a chair up close beside him and once I was seated he took my hand in a seemingly casual fashion. A sign of ownership, perhaps, or just a big act, but I found I didn't really care and instead gained comfort from the strength and warmth of his fingers.

I doubted I was ever going to be at ease in Nick's company, though it had nothing to do with any left-over feelings for him. I found I couldn't have cared less about him and his tawdry reputation. I knew I was well rid of him, but I did have concerns about his wife and any suspicions she might still be harbouring about the two of us after the little scene at the wedding reception.

'You must go up first,' Lex encouraged the other couple, 'after coming all that way home.'

'Well, to be honest, we wouldn't have bloody bothered if we'd realized it was only an ear infection,' Nick said shortly, any concern he might have had for his grand-mother appeared to be evaporating by the minute. 'I do think you might have waited for a few tests to be carried out before summoning us home, Lex, It's hardly the emergency you led us to believe, is it?'

To give Anthea her due, she did protest. 'Oh, that's hardly fair, Nick. Given your grandmother's age I'm sure Lex did what he thought was best.'

The disparaging look on Nick's face left us all in no doubt of his opinion of Lex's best and without another word, he stalked off, taking Anthea with him.

'He's insufferable. It was hardly *only* an ear infection,' I said indignantly, 'And he would have been the first one to object — and vehemently no doubt, if you hadn't told him what was happening.'

'Don't let it worry you.' Lex shrugged. 'That's Nick all over and it really doesn't bother me.'

'Well, it should,' I said roundly. 'His attitude stinks, yet you continually excuse his bad behaviour and let him get away with it. Why?' Then I continued bitterly, 'Oh, don't tell me — it's because he was so young when your parents died that he must be forever shielded from the harsh realities of life. But, Lex, he's a man now and it's time you all stopped making excuses for him.'

I suddenly realized he was just looking at me, and I stopped, shrugged and said, 'I know, I know, it's none of my business, but where is the concern for you, Lex? Tell me that. You lost your parents, too, and yet had to take on responsibility for the whole family — a young boy and an elderly couple — at a very early age, which is something no one appears to give you credit for.'

'Have you finished?'

I nodded, waiting for the fireworks, the fierce demands that I keep my nose out of the Cable business and my opinions to myself.

Lex still held my hand and now he looked down at it. Tracing a pattern on my palm and up and down my fingers, he said, without looking up, 'Do you know what? I think that's

184

the first time anyone has ever looked at things from my point of view. Thank you for that, Stacey.'

'You can go up now.' It was Anthea and she hesitated beside the table for a moment before adding in a brittle tone, 'He doesn't really mean it, you know,' but for once I noticed Lex didn't agree or offer an excuse for his brother's behaviour. Neither did he apologize for calling them home.

We watched her hurry away, and I worried about what her life would be, but then consoled myself that she must surely have had some indication of what she was getting into before she married Nick — if not, the interruption to the wedding service itself should have set alarm bells ringing loud and clear, but she'd still chosen to go ahead.

Suddenly tired of thinking of them when my thoughts should have been on Eleanor I came to a decision, stood up, collected my bag and coat and said to Lex, 'I won't be a moment and will catch up with you by the lifts.' I had seen just what I wanted in the shop right beside the front doors of the hospital and I made my way there.

It was lovely to see the way Lex's face, normally so serious, broke into a huge grin when I appeared round the corner holding the string of a huge helium-filled balloon with a bright 'get well' greeting emblazoned across it.

'To cheer her up,' I told him, 'and I got her these flowers, too.'

'I should have thought of that,' he said ruefully, putting his hand in his pocket, 'and I'll certainly pay for them.'

'You will not, it was *my* idea. You think of your own.'

Lex laughed and ushered me into the lift. He was still smiling, watching my struggle to control the floating object and prevent it making an escape, when we entered the side ward with Eleanor's name on the door.

She looked frail, frightened and pale against the pillows, but still brightened perceptibly when we walked through the door and even raised a smile at the sight of the balloon and flowers.

'Oh, you shouldn't have, dear,' she protested, but not very convincingly.

'How are you, darling?' I sat beside the bed and took her hand into mine.

'I fear I'm being a dreadful nuisance,' she began, but I cut in even before Lex got the chance, insisting, 'Indeed you are *not*, Eleanor. You can't help being poorly. It could happen to anyone.'

'But poor Nick and Anthea cutting short their honeymoon like that and coming all the way home.' She looked close to tears and added, 'I've told them they shouldn't have flown back to England on my account. I feel so bad about it.'

'Well, you shouldn't, my love.' Lex came to stand behind me and put his hands on my shoulders. 'They both assured me it was no trouble at all,' he went on, not altogether truthfully, given Nick's uncaring attitude earlier, 'and they will resume their holiday as soon as they're sure you are on the road to recovery.'

'Oh, yes.' She looked relieved and, holding tightly on to my hand, Eleanor said, 'I told them that's what they should do, after all I still have both of you and my dear Aaron. I will be fine once the doctors have decided on the right course of action.'

'Of course you will,' I said firmly, 'and you will get the very best of treatment here.' I'd never seen the inside of a private hospital before and couldn't fail to be impressed by an interior that mirrored that of a four- or five-star hotel. 'That, with plenty of rest, will soon put you back on the road to recovery.'

'That's what I told her,' Aaron chipped in heartily, but not heartily enough to hide the hint of fear in his tone and I felt so sorry for them both.

'I've already told the doctor, the best place for me is at home with my family,' Eleanor smiled up at us, and I felt my own smile freeze on my face as I anticipated correctly what was coming next. 'I was sure the two of you wouldn't mind having me stay for a little while, just until I'm back on my feet. That would be all right, wouldn't it?'

Lex's grip on my shoulders tightened until it hurt. I looked up at him and he looked helplessly back. If I hadn't known better I would have said he was doing all of this on purpose, but then what would have been the point? He had no more desire than I did to prolong a situation that was becoming impossible for us both.

I could say no. Eleanor would still have Lex and Aaron to care for her and they were the ones who mattered. No one, least of all Lex, who had got us into this mess in the first place, would think any the less of me for bowing out right now.

My mind was made up and I'd already opened my mouth to make my excuses when the pleading look in Eleanor's eyes stopped me stone dead. I had the strangest feeling that she knew — knew everything — and yet she wanted me to stay anyway.

It was ridiculous. It was impossible, but I still found myself saying, 'Darling Eleanor, you must come and stay with us for as long as you want.'

'I can't explain,' I told Lex in the car on the way home, realizing with a start that I was thinking of the house as home, even though it wasn't and never would be.

'You don't have to.'

'I know you don't want me there, and I don't want to be there, but I found myself agreeing anyway.'

'I said you don't have to explain. Not to me. I know it's an intolerable situation for you to find yourself in, but I can understand why you did it, and I really do thank you and I shall, of course, make it worth your while,'

I was horrified, 'Pay me, you mean?' I stared at him. 'You'll do no such thing, Lex Cable. It's not always about money, you know.'

'I'm so sorry. You seem to be paying dearly for getting mixed up with the Cable family.'

I just thought that he didn't know the half of it and then could have wept when we reached the house, to find my car had been fixed and that now it was far too late to be of any use, it started first time.

'I know what you're thinking,' Lex said, with a rueful smile.

'No,' I said, refusing to smile back, 'I don't think you do.'

'Perhaps we should start again,' he said, 'from the beginning.'

'What?' I followed him into the house and closed the door reluctantly behind me. 'Pretend we just met.'

'If you like,' he agreed, 'and this time we cut Nick right out of the equation.'

'I would like nothing better,' I assured him, 'and we need to put things between us on a proper footing, before your grandmother gets here. Set out a few ground rules.'

'Good idea,' he said, 'but can we do it while we eat, because I'm absolutely starving? I've no idea why we didn't stop for something on the way home, but it's a bit late for that now. Steak and chips?'

'Only if we get mushrooms, too.'

'Done.'

We tucked in fairly companionably and, once replete, cleared the table and Lex set down a tray of freshly made tea.

'You can be mother,' I told him.

His lips quirked. 'Thank you,' he said.

'I will continue to wear your ring,' I said.

'Thank you.' He sounded really quite pleased about it, which I thought was a bit strange.

'But,' I continued, 'I will not continue to share your room under any circumstances. Not that we have been doing,' I added hastily, 'but I mean for your grandmother's benefit. You can tell her what you like to explain it, tell her you're fed up with my junk cluttering up your room or something, tell her I snore.' I shrugged. 'I don't care. Actually,' I went on, 'I've been meaning to say that I will move out of your room, I only took it over by default and you can have it back. There are plenty of other bedrooms I can move into.'

'You don't have . . . ' Lex shrugged. 'Oh, OK then.'

'Also,' I continued, gaining courage as I spoke, 'I don't want you giving me a hard time over Nick any more. I made a mistake and a complete idiot of myself over him — I accept that. However,' I put up my hand when Lex seemed about to interrupt, 'I didn't sleep with him, and whether you believe it or not it is still the truth, and anything I might have felt — or thought I felt for him, is quite gone. The man I believed he was doesn't exist and never did. The man he is means nothing to me and I have already paid dearly for ever putting my faith in him. I was a fool, but I don't need you reminding me of the fact every time we have a disagreement. Is that clear?'

'As crystal,' Lex said, quite humbly.

'Now it's your turn.'

'Thank you, that's very kind,' he said, with

no trace of sarcasm that I could hear, though I stared at him suspiciously. 'If we could just behave like a normal engaged couple would during the day, that's all I will ask of you, and it would make things much more pleasant if we could get along even when my grandparents aren't around.'

'We can but try.' I didn't mean to sound doubtful, but it was there in my voice all the same. 'And when your grandparents go back to their life, I go back to mine, and this farce ends once and for all — agreed?'

'Agreed.'

I pushed back my chair and stood up. 'I'd better start getting things ready. Perhaps a downstairs room would be best for your grandparents?'

'There's really no need, I normally have help when I'm staying here.' He laughed at the expression on my face and asked, 'You didn't think I kept the place spotless by myself, did you? I wish I could take the credit, but I'm not that domesticated and I have a business to run.'

'But what am I supposed to do?' I almost wailed, 'I've never been a lady of leisure in my life and I've no intention of starting now.'

He shrugged and put out his hands, palms up as if lost for words, then he offered, 'You could pretend this is for real and do exactly what you would do if it was.'

I stared at him for a minute, then said, 'All right, I will then.'

'I have some calls to make, so will you be . . . ?'

'I'll be fine.'

The first thing I did was find the utility room and deal with the pile of washing in my room. I didn't quite have the nerve to ask Lex if he had any dirty laundry because handling his unmentionables just seemed like far too intimate a task to take on and I quailed at the thought.

I chose a room upstairs as far away from his as possible and set about transferring my clothes and toiletries. This time I hung everything away properly and arranged the room as if I was staying. Well, I had been invited to make myself at home and that was just what I was going to do.

The bed, I had already noticed, was made up in the new room, but I stripped the linen from the one in Lex's room and remade it with fresh sheets that I found in a huge old airing-cupboard on the landing. I tuned into a music station on the clock radio by the bed and I sang as I worked. I felt happier than I had since the day I threw my life away for Nick Cable's fake promises of happy ever after. It all seemed a very long time ago — though in fact surprisingly little had actually passed — and I suddenly felt more confident of a future I now had time to contemplate. After all, a change was as good as a rest, or so the old saying went.

Whirling around with an armful of bed linen, I crashed into Lex who was standing in the doorway with a bemused expression on his face.

'Christ, you gave me a fright,' I said cheerfully, as I pushed past. Making my way to the stairs I said over my shoulder, 'I'll soon have your room shipshape and Bristol fashion again.'

'I can see that,' he commented, 'but you didn't have — '

'You said I could do what I like, and I am. At least when Mrs whoever-she-is comes in she won't have to start from scratch.'

'I thought you said you worked in an office dishing out financial advice.' Lex stood watching me unload and reload the washing machine, as if he couldn't believe his eyes.

'Well, I do, but I don't have 'help' coming in at home. I do my own dirty work and I quite enjoy it,' I said, transferring the clean washing to the tumble dryer and setting the dial. 'Of course,' I added, trying to be fair, 'my place isn't a fraction of the size of this one, and I'm not the best cook in the world either.'

'Cooking is something I do enjoy,' lie admitted, surprising me, even though I'd seen and tasted some of the evidence. 'Not that I get the time or opportunity very often. However,' Lex rubbed his hands together, 'that's something that could be about to change. I might just make us a light snack if you have no objection.'

'Who, me? Why on earth should I object? I'll just finish off upstairs and get a shower before I join you, shall I?'

You would have thought we were two different people, I thought, as I hung various garments back into Lex's wardrobe and successfully resisted the urge to tidy the numerous drawers. We had become so civilized it would have been easy to believe all the snarling and sniping comments we'd previously hurled at each other were simply figments of an overactive imagination.

Mind you, I thought ruefully, how long it was going to last would be anybody's guess.

Things changed again once the 'help' Lex had mentioned returned to her duties mid-week. Mary — an efficient, well-rounded fifty something, who seemed to set her own hours — was very respectful but also very possessive of what she obviously viewed as 'her' territory and, as a consequence, I was left with far too much time on my hands

— especially when Lex suddenly took himself off to oversee his various building projects.

I had the car, but nowhere particular to go, and who knew when Eleanor would be released from hospital? What I should have been doing was looking around the nearby towns for somewhere suitable to make a new start. What I actually did was find myself driving back to the place I had used to call home, and even my knowing without a doubt that going there was a very stupid idea wasn't enough to make me to turn the car around and go back the way I had come.

13

Of course, I wouldn't actually go anywhere near the office, or my flat either, come to that. I had already made up my mind about that before I arrived in the town. If I were seen by anyone I knew, I just couldn't face the questions and the humiliation — so how I came to be out of the car and skulking around streets that were far too close for comfort, I had no idea.

In the past, I was fully aware, I would have breezily stated that I could happily have lived anywhere in the UK; after all I had no family in the country to tie me to any one place, but now I was beginning to realize that I had actually been wrong in that assumption.

Continuing to live in Brankstone after my parents' final separation had, I could see belatedly, given me settled status and a safe haven after the turmoil and insecurity of my childhood. Both the area and the people were familiar, providing the solid foundation I had been so much in need of at that time and, I realized far too late, it was exactly what I presently needed, too.

It had been a mistake to come back. Filled

with a sense of loss, close to tears and with my head down, I made my way back to the car, crossing the local park where I used to eat my lunchtime sandwiches and feed the birds on a sunny day.

'Stacey?'

Oh, God, I should have known I would be spotted. At the sound of my name my immediate instinct was to tuck my head down lower and walk faster, but it soon became clear I wasn't going to get away that easily, as my name was called again much louder and with an urgency that was impossible to ignore.

'Stacey? It is you, isn't it?'

Of all people, it had to be my boss — ex-boss — I'd practically bumped right into. Running away was no longer an option, not if I didn't want to look even more of a fool than I already did. I could do nothing other than stop and turn to face him. To my utter amazement he was smiling the same kind smile that I had been used to seeing in the office every day.

'Simon, how are you?'

A tall man, he was in his forties, pleasant-looking and known for his equally pleasant nature. I found myself staring up at him quite unable to believe that even someone as placid as Simon could find it in him to be so nice towards an employee who had — let's face it — dumped on him ruthlessly from a great height by walking out at a moment's notice.

'Missing you,' he said simply, and it took me all of my time and willpower not to just stand there and cry like a baby.

'I'm sorry,' I said. 'I'm so sorry for just going off and leaving you in the lurch like that.'

The smile didn't waver, though he replied ruefully, 'Well, I can't say I was entirely happy about it, but you were right — everyone is entitled to a holiday.'

'A holiday?' I tried and failed to grasp what on earth he was talking about.

'Well, yes. I know you didn't give me much notice, but it was obviously very important for you to have the time off right away and I should have respected that.'

I couldn't actually recall anything much of that particular conversation, apart from the fact that Simon had told me in no uncertain terms that it wasn't a great time for me to decide on a last-minute holiday and he would like me to rethink.

What I *could* recall — only too clearly — was the hasty letter of resignation I had then written in an absolute fury. Choosing a time when Simon was elsewhere, I had simply left the angry missive on his desk for him to find on his return. I had then walked out of the door without a thought or a backward glance, eager to start the future with Nick that I had so foolishly imagined awaited me.

I cringed as I recalled with awful clarity scribbling black words on white paper and using pretty blunt language as I'd spelled out exactly what Simon could do with his job. How on earth that could have become interpreted as me taking an impromptu 'holiday' I really had no idea — unless . . .

Only one thing would account for the conversation we were currently having. Someone had removed the letter before Simon's return — because it was becoming increasingly obvious that he had never set eyes on it. The question was, who would have done it — and why?

'I shouldn't have walked out like that,' I said honestly and speaking carefully in an effort not to drop myself — or my rescuer — in it, 'but yes, it was important to me at the time. I hear that Valerie has been managing my workload very well while I've been away, though.'

'Valerie?' Simon looked at me quizzically. 'Valerie is an assistant and, even with her years of experience is not capable of taking on the level of your work, neither does she have the rapport with the clients that you enjoy. No, Samantha has taken on the lion's share. She's been working full-time to try and keep on top and says she's glad of the extra money to put by for the holiday she and her husband have planned for later in the year.'

I had my answer. Obviously Sam had intercepted the letter and in doing so — and taking on my work — had managed to keep my job open for me to return. Relief flooded through me, quickly followed by enormous guilt at the level of her sacrifice.

Sam worked part-time because she had a baby. Little Poppy wasn't even a year old, yet Sam had given up precious time with her child on my account. She wasn't that desperate for money, either, holiday or not, because her husband Ian earned a very good living as a plumbing and heating engineer. Even in my vulnerable state I was aware that all of this didn't amount to the behaviour of a friend who had washed her hands of me, and I wondered what the hell Valerie had been playing at.

'That's so good of Sam,' I told Simon, and only I knew what a massive understatement that was. 'I shall have to make it up to her.'

'Were you on your way back to work?' he asked hopefully, though he must have known that that wasn't so, since I'd been heading away from the office and not towards it.

'Sorry,' I said, and he could never have guessed how heartfelt the apology was, 'but I still need a little longer. There's something I just can't get out of. If you would rather replace me . . . ' I made the offer with my heart in my mouth, because it would just be too cruel to find my old life was still within my reach — only to have it snatched away again.

'You must know,' Simon said, surprising me, 'that no one could take your place — and I don't just mean at work.'

I couldn't begin to work out what he meant by that, so I didn't even try. I just turned to go, saying over my shoulder, 'I really appreciate your patience. I'll keep in touch and let you know the minute I can come back to work.'

'Do that.' He nodded, adding, 'And give Sam a ring, would you? I know she's been trying to get hold of you.'

'Oh, has she?' I wasn't as surprised as I might have been before the enlightening conversation I'd just had with Simon. 'Perhaps you wouldn't mind explaining to her that I've lost my mobile and with it all my numbers.' I ignored the fact I could have phoned a landline with the help of directory enquiries and he didn't appear to pick up on it. 'Please thank her for everything she's done for me anyway, would you? Tell her I'll see her soon.'

I practically flew back to the Mini — wings on my feet didn't even begin to describe the euphoric lightness in my step. I still had a job, despite what Valerie had said — and I couldn't even begin to contemplate the level of her spite, so I wasn't going to try — and I still had at least one friend. Two if I counted Simon, who appeared to be suddenly wanting more than friendship if his unsubtle hint was anything to go by.

I frowned, and then common sense came to my rescue, reminding me quite firmly that Simon was a confirmed bachelor who saw me as nothing more than a valued employee. He'd never so much as invited me out to lunch in all the years I'd worked for him unless it was work-related. He'd missed me, that was all, and I would do well to keep my overactive imagination in check.

The car drove like a dream — as it always did when it was regularly serviced and cared for — and I found my way back to the house in the forest with ease, grateful for the time the journey gave me to think about my options.

By the time I turned into the driveway I had made up my mind to lay my cards on the table and tell Lex that — amazingly — I *was* going to be able to go back and pick up the pieces of my life, starting with my job. However, I would make it clear that it was going to have to be sooner rather than later, so it was crucial we told his family the truth or, at least, an acceptable version of it. I was quite sure he would understand because, unlike his brother, Lex was a decent man. There was no doubt about that or the fact that I was beginning to warm towards him — even if only slightly.

He met me at the door, but before I could say a word he began, 'Darling, wonderful news . . . ' as he drew me inside.

For a moment I thought he knew about my job and understood what it must mean to me, then I saw Aaron standing in the hallway behind him and realized that they were both smiling, which could only mean one thing.

'Eleanor?' I guessed.

'Yes, we've been allowed to bring her home.' Aaron looked so thrilled and relieved that I could do no other than be happy for him — even if it did mean my own plans must be placed on hold for a little longer.

This, I realized, wasn't the time or the place to be putting myself first. I had made a promise and for the time being I was going to be held to it.

Pinning a bright smile to my own face, I said, 'That's wonderful. How is she?'

'Come and see for yourself,' Lex urged. 'She's been dying to see you. Where have you been?'

The question was casually asked, but somehow I knew Lex had been concerned by my absence and I wondered why. Surely he didn't still think I would take off with no warning and leave him in the lurch? I thought he had come to know me better than that these past few days.

I replied with a bit more than a hint of the truth, 'Oh, I've been checking on the job prospects around the region.'

'Oh,' he said. 'Any luck?'

'One or two things that might suit,' I said vaguely.

'I'd have thought you'd have enough to do, what with planning a wedding and running a home once you're married,' Aaron put in, 'but I suppose I'm old-fashioned. Eleanor never worked a day in her life, but she always found plenty to keep her busy.'

'A bit of a contradiction in terms, Granddad.' Lex laughed easily and, throwing a careless arm around my shoulders, he added, 'whatever makes Stacey happy is fine by me.'

I could almost have believed he really

meant it. He was obviously becoming as accomplished an actor as I was.

'Come along and see Eleanor,' Aaron urged. 'And thank you for arranging a downstairs room. It will make life so much easier and she won't feel so cut off.'

'Oh, you know, it was mostly Mary's doing.'

I thought I heard Lex say, 'My eye,' but I could have been mistaken. I was sure he had no idea of the tussle I'd had with Mary about the rearrangement of what had been a rather charming drawing-room, and, still with his arm around me, we walked side by side in to see Eleanor.

To my mind she still looked pale and tired, but her eyes were brighter and certainly not as sunken as they'd appeared to me when I saw her in the hospital.

'Darling Stacey.' She held out her hand to me and the warmth of her welcome really surprised me. 'I've been looking forward to seeing you most of all. Men's talk is all very well but, you know, it's not the same as a good chat to another woman. Come and sit beside me and tell me what you've been up to.'

I had little chance from then on to mull over what I had discovered earlier in the day and what it might mean for my future. I still couldn't believe how fortunate I was. The thought that my job was at least safe for the time being was a tremendous boost, and even as I concentrated on Eleanor and her needs, I could feel a smile curling my lips and threatening to turn into a full-blown beam.

'It's good news about the treatment, Eleanor,' I enthused, resignedly putting the welcome news I had been given to one side in order to concentrate my energy on her immediate future. 'I hear they've decided on a combination of medication and physical therapy.'

'Yes, because Lex heard somewhere that people unable to move because of vertigo can be up and walking a few minutes after therapy. Something called vestibular therapy can be extremely effective apparently.'

'Oh, that sounds excellent.'

'Yes,' Eleanor agreed, nodding with evident care, 'but it all requires specially trained physiotherapists and there aren't too many of those around, unfortunately. However . . . '

'Go on,' I encouraged, leaning forward.

'Lex just got right on the case, and has found one who is prepared to work with me without delay. Isn't that wonderful?'

'It's marvellous,' I agreed without reservation, knowing that — despite Lex's having the means to pay for such treatment, which would undoubtedly have helped, he would also have moved heaven and earth to get the help his grandmother needed, spending his last penny if he had to without a thought.

While his brother was away enjoying his honeymoon, still muttering about it being 'only an ear infection' and worrying about how his grandmother's illness would affect his own plans, Lex had dealt with the whole thing in his usual capable manner. My respect for him as a genuinely good person could not but grow daily and I knew without a doubt which brother I would always prefer to have on my side.

'Tea, ladies?' The man himself put his head around the door. Then, pushing it wide open he walked through carrying a laden tea tray. He set it down and offered, 'I'll be mother, shall I?'

'I'd love to see you try.' I grinned and, reaching for a scone, obviously freshly baked, added, 'Mary's been busy.'

'Oh, yes.' Lex nodded. 'She's definitely upped her game since she discovered you ensconced in what's always been her domain. The competition is obviously doing her good — and us, since we get the benefit of the results.'

'How long will it be, I wonder, until she discovers I'm no competition at all?'

I laughed out loud and then suddenly realized that no one was laughing with me. Lex obviously thought I was referring to my temporary role in the household and was looking meaningfully at his grandmother who merely looked confused.

'Because I can't cook anything more complicated than a fry-up to save my life,' I hurried to add and explained, 'Not much point to fancy cooking when there's only one of you.'

'But surely your mother . . . ?' Eleanor began, with a little frown pinching her brow.

'She wasn't much of a cook herself.'

'Oh, dear, and Lex does so enjoy his food. I know,' the wrinkled face brightened, 'I shall make it my project to teach you the basics the moment I am able. It will give me something to work towards.'

'Sounds good to me,' Lex said approvingly, and I felt a twinge of unease at what sounded to me suspiciously like long-term plans. I could have slapped him when he added, 'I hadn't quite pictured you in the role of domestic goddess, my love, but it certainly appeals to me.'

'And there's me thinking you were marrying me for my brain,' I said smartly. 'Life is full of surprises, but then so am I, *my love.*'

Eleanor looked from one to the other of us and then her laugh tinkled out. Lex looked at her fondly, then he took my hand and, squeezing it, he said, 'Thank you for being here, Stacey, you're a real tonic.'

'Why would you thank her, Lex?' Eleanor stared at him. 'Surely her place is here with you? However, I do agree, she *is* a breath of fresh air and just what this family needed. Not to mention being just what *you* needed in your life.'

Oh dear, this was all becoming a bit serious for me and I searched frantically for something to say to lighten the moment but, for once, words failed me. I almost found myself wishing I were really the person Eleanor still believed me to be and that I was just what this family — and Lex — needed. That was plainly ridiculous, of course, and a very uncomfortable line of thought for me to pursue. My old life was waiting and that was what I should be focusing on. Beginning with letting Lex know exactly how things stood as soon as it was possible.

This, I found was easier said than done because when we were together it was either in Eleanor's company, Aaron's or both, and one day drifted into another with me no nearer making specific plans to return to work.

In the end I purposefully sought Lex out in his study, telling myself the interruption was warranted. He was obviously dealing with his business affairs from home as best he could, but the same option was not available to me and if I didn't act soon Simon was going to run out of both goodwill and patience. I hadn't even had a minute to speak to Sam, either, and I felt really bad about that.

The deep, familiar voice invited me to 'Come in.' Lex motioned me to a chair, indicating the telephone receiver in his hand and mouthing, 'Sorry,' before continuing with a conversation that seemed to revolve around the depth of a particular set of footings and the delivery of building materials that hadn't arrived.

Losing interest in the one-sided dialogue quite quickly, I looked around nosily. I was impressed that everything seemed to have its place, particularly because Simon's office was such a forest of lofty piles of paperwork and files that I was always surprised anything could ever be found when it was wanted.

On the walls there were pictures of Lex, and some of Nick, too, suited and booted and shaking the hands of various dignitaries. I had just turned my attention to the various framed awards when Lex terminated the conversation. He replaced the receiver and turned to me with the warm smile I had come to expect and to appreciate.

'Before I ask what I can do for you, can I thank you again for all you have done for us, Stacey? I know this hasn't been easy for you, but you've made the very best of a bad job — and I do totally accept it was one that I got us both into and then cajoled you into continuing both by fair means and foul long after we should have called it a day and come clean. Just, thank you, you've gone way beyond anything I could have expected of you — especially since my grandmother's illness.'

I managed a light laugh, though in truth I had never felt less like laughing, and said ruefully, 'As we speak she's perusing bridal magazines, Lex, and having the time of her life. I have to say I do feel a total fraud and wonder how long we can allow it all to continue with a clear conscience.'

'My excuse,' he began to explain, 'is that keeping my grandmother's spirits up is definitely aiding her recovery. This has been confirmed by her therapist, who believes a goal to focus on — such as the drive to be well enough for the wedding — will encourage the huge effort necessary on my grandmother's part. I know it's a lot to ask of you, but if you could look on it as a job . . . '

'And that,' I said, forestalling yet another

offer to pay me for my time, 'is what I came to talk to you about. You know I told you on the day Eleanor came home, that I had been checking job prospects around the area?'

Lex nodded, but the smile was missing and he looked his usual serious self. I wondered why I felt so guilty for being the cause.

'Well, I found out on that day my old job is being held open for me. For some reason my letter of resignation never reached my boss and he believes me to be on an extended holiday break. Having said that, however, he isn't going to keep my post open for ever and, in fairness to the colleague who is covering most of my work, I should return sooner rather than later.'

'I see.'

I felt terrible and worse by the minute. Lex looked crushed. It was almost as if I had slapped him and I found myself rushing to add, 'There's no reason why I shouldn't commute from here, if you agree; it shouldn't take too long using the Wessex Way, and at least I would still be around *some* of the time.' It wasn't what I had meant to say at all and even I could see how ridiculous an idea it was, so I hurried to apologize. 'Sorry, stupid idea, forget I even mentioned it.'

Lex just stared at me in a way that made me feel most uncomfortable, and I wanted to protest that I had only been trying to help.

'You would do that — for me?' he said at last, when I was just about ready to rush for the door and leave him to brood on my stupidity.

'Well, it would be for your grandmother, really, wouldn't it?' I pointed out firmly. 'I wouldn't want to be the one to hinder her recovery in any way.'

'It would mean carrying on with the engagement.'

'I realize that.' I glanced down at the beautiful ring and recognized how used to wearing it I had become and how naked my hand would seem without it. 'I suppose I don't mind, if you don't.'

Lex smiled suddenly, and surprised me by saying, 'It will be a pleasure to enjoy your company for a while longer.'

'Ha,' I harrumphed. 'That's not what you said when you found me in your bed on that first night.'

He gave a bark of laughter. 'Don't remind me. Talk about getting off on the wrong foot, but you more than fought your corner, as I recall. I don't think I've met a feistier woman in the whole of my life. Had I really been an intruder, I think I would have taken to my heels.'

'I take it I've made a lasting impression, then?'

I was joking, but Lex looked very solemn when he said, 'You can be sure I won't forget *you* in a hurry.'

I stood up quickly, suddenly lost for words, and Lex rose to his feet also. Reaching out, he took both of my hands in his and the look in his eyes was quite unreadable as he said simply, 'Thank you, Stacey, I know I have asked a lot of you on too many occasions now, and I will be forever in your debt.'

I laughed and said abruptly, just to lighten the moment, 'Just as long as you don't forget it.'

I would have turned to go, but couldn't quite bring myself to wrench my hands from his. The moment lengthened and the silence deepened as we stared into each other's eyes. Lex leaned forward and for one heart-stopping moment his lips were mere inches from my own. I could swear he was going to kiss my mouth and then he seemed to think better of it and kissed my cheek instead.

In my room later I couldn't honestly decide whether I was relieved or sorry, and I spent far too much time wondering how it would make me feel to be kissed for real by Alexander Cable.

14

It was eventually decided I would return to work on the following Monday, and I had extra reason to be glad the decision had been made when a message came advising us of the imminent arrival of the newly-weds.

It was perfectly reasonable that they would want to visit Eleanor, but the thought of having to endure Nick's obnoxious company once again wasn't something I relished.

Ridiculous as it may seem I had truthfully all but forgotten Nick's part in this whole scenario, which I realized probably made me seem very shallow. When I did think about it — which wasn't often — I still couldn't believe the way I had behaved like an inexperienced teenager around him, believing him to be 'the one', falling for his lies and throwing caution to the wind.

Allowing any man, especially him, to capture my heart even for so short a time, had been a huge error of judgement on my part, but in the end I was sensible enough to accept I had escaped with little more than dented pride, and Nick was just another lesson learned.

It was difficult not to have regrets, but I found I could not regret the unconventional circumstances that had brought me into the Cable household — even given my undignified entrance through the landing window — because there had truly never been a dull moment since. Sparks had flown between Lex and me from the moment we met. They still did from time to time despite the recent truce, and even the web of deceit we had woven — though regrettable — brought an element of excitement into a life that had become dull in recent years, to say the least.

'Oh, my dear, I *am* going to miss you.' Eleanor looked so upset that I couldn't help but become extremely concerned about how she was going to take it when it eventually became apparent that it wouldn't only be my job that I'd be returning to, but to take up the life I had left behind. I only hoped Lex knew what he was doing by continuing with this deception indefinitely.

'Where are you off to then, Anastasia?' said a familiar voice from the doorway and I was still cringing as he continued. 'It must be nice for you to be a lady of leisure and, of course, planning a wedding takes so much time doesn't it? Remind me again, where is it you plan to hold the ceremony? Westminster Abbey, was it?'

'Oh, Nicholas, don't be so foolish.' I had never heard Eleanor speak in such a tone before and stared at her. 'Anyone would think it was a crime for a woman to spend her time in the home these days. There's far too much emphasis on women 'having it all', or whatever it is they say these days, in my opinion.'

Nick put his hands out as if to fend off his grandmother's fury and pulled a comical face, which cut no ice at all, as she continued to put him in his place by saying, 'Stacey has just told me she's returning to work on Monday — which, of course, she is quite entitled to do — though how we are to plan a wedding with the bride absent for most of every day, I have no idea.'

I laughed lightly, ignoring Nick as I told her rashly, 'I thought I would leave most of it in your capable hands — as long as you're not finding it too much. I've liked every suggestion you've come up with so far.'

Eleanor flushed with pleasure. 'Really?' She beamed. 'You would put that much faith in me?'

'Really,' I assured her. 'You have impeccable taste and I trust you totally.'

'Well,' she was almost puffed up with pride, her blue eyes bright with excitement, 'if I say it myself the events Aaron and I organized in our younger days were talked about for weeks afterwards.'

Turning to Nick she asked him, 'Do you remember that spring ball we held, back in . . . ?'

I left them to their reminiscences and went in search of Lex, fully intending to tell him that pretty soon, enough was going to be enough, and we were going to have to pull the plug on this bogus engagement. If we didn't call a halt soon, we were going to find ourselves married for real, and that was what I intended to tell him.

Rounding a corner silently I came across him deep in conversation with Anthea in a corner of the hallway. It was clear they hadn't heard me approaching and they were speaking softly and earnestly, their dark heads so close they were almost touching. The sight of them stopped me in my tracks and, feeling like an intruder, I was about to turn on my heel and walk the other way when Lex spotted me.

For the briefest moment he looked as though he had been caught with his hand in the till, but he recovered so swiftly that the next moment I thought I must have imagined what looked suspiciously like a guilty expression.

'Darling.' He stepped around Anthea and

reached out to draw me into the circle of his arm. 'I was just telling Annie that she's arrived in the nick of time with you returning to work at the beginning of next week.'

'Not that I'm going to be here myself for that long,' Anthea was very swift to put the record straight, adding, 'fond as I am of Eleanor, running your own business doesn't allow for lengthy breaks and I've already been away for too long.'

'I've just told Eleanor she can have free rein with the wedding arrangements,' I confessed, wondering what Lex's reaction was going to be to that, 'and she was so excited that I don't think she will notice even if no one is at home. A pile of bridal magazines and the telephone to hand, I would say she'd be happily occupied for hours.'

'That was generous of you.' Anthea was looking at me curiously and with a hint of disbelief in her expression, if I was interpreting it correctly. 'I wouldn't have wanted anyone interfering with my wedding. It *is* the biggest day of your life, after all.'

'Well, that's Stacey all over. Generous to a fault, aren't you, darling? There's nothing guaranteed to get the invalid back on her feet quicker than giving her something to get her teeth into.'

Lex's warm approval rather took me aback, but if he had no objections, who was I to argue? I presumed he realized this would make the task of eventually telling his grandmother the whole thing was off that much harder, but that was entirely his problem, not mine. Weddings were called off every day of the week, after all, often over nothing more than some minor disagreement.

'I'd better go and say hello.' Anthea looked from Lex to me and back again. 'At least the wedding will give me something to talk about.'

'Why would she need something to talk about?' I wondered out loud. 'I always thought she and Eleanor got along famously.'

Lex shrugged and then said vaguely, 'They've had their differences in the past. You came along then just in the nick of time — if you'll excuse the pun — because Anthea's definitely suspicious about the reality of our relationship and I don't think Nick has entirely convinced her that there was never anything between the two of you either. I think the talk of our wedding plans has her fooled — at least for now.'

'You should have let me leave right at the beginning.' I shook my head. 'I can't help thinking it's all getting out of hand. We should have confessed or called the whole thing off long before this.' I gave Lex a hard look and added, 'Before you know it we'll be married for real and that really will be a step too far as far as I'm concerned.'

'Oh really? I thought becoming Mrs Cable was exactly what you wanted.'

I was shocked; the sarcastic tone that had been missing of late was back with a vengeance and I didn't like the words or the tone used one little bit.

'Just when,' I hissed furiously, 'will you get it into your thick skull that I don't want your *brother* — and I don't want *you*? Marrying into this family is the last thing I want and the sooner this bloody farce is over, the better as far as I'm concerned.'

I spun round, intent on getting away from Lex before I said something I might regret or someone might overhear. He put his hand on my arm as if to stay me and said my name, softly, urgently, but by then I was far too angry to listen to anything more he might have to say.

I stared down at his hand, the fingers clasped lightly around my elbow, and I shook it off easily. 'Don't touch me, Lex. Don't you ever touch me again.'

I was fuming, but by the time I reached my room I was surprised to realize that I was also very hurt. I'd thought we were better than that, had reached an understanding and even begun to like each other just a bit. All the furious sniping and petty digs had seemed to be a thing of the past — until now.

I busied myself checking through the wardrobe for an outfit for work on Monday — I wanted to make a bit of an effort to show I was serious in my commitment to the firm and to the boss who had given me a second chance. I also meant to make up to Samantha for the extra time she had put in on my behalf and for saving my job in the first place, because I'd fully accepted that she was the only one who could have removed my letter of resignation from Simon's desk.

Choosing the suit and blouse I would wear took no time at all, given the limited choice available, and I was soon back wondering what had rattled Lex's cage. He hadn't been that touchy since . . . I was suddenly still when it came to me that he hadn't been that touchy since the last time Nick was around. Did he seriously think that, despite my continued insistence to the contrary, I was still interested in his brother, to the point at which I might even be a threat to his marriage? Was his opinion of me so poor that he believed I would stoop so low? Though it wounded me deeply I had no choice but to accept that the answer to that question was obviously a resounding yes.

★ ★ ★

Over a very short time I had come to love the house in the forest, but my return to work was well-timed, and I was actually glad to be getting away from it. The atmosphere inside was tense to say the least and, though I couldn't believe it was because of anything I had done, Anthea seemed particularly brittle. I wasn't sure if I was the one whom she was specifically avoiding or whether it was just company in general.

The scene when I came across her whispering with Lex in a corner of the hallway came back to me time and again, and I couldn't help but wonder if there was something going on between the two of them. I dismissed the idea as completely ridiculous since Anthea was clearly besotted with Nick, but the cosy image stayed with me and led to endless speculation on my part.

Why should I care? I asked myself that question time after time, and the answer was that I didn't, not at all. I certainly wasn't jealous; for one thing Lex wasn't mine to be jealous over and our relationship, if you could call it that, was temporary to say the least.

However, I didn't have him down as a philanderer and that image of him and his brother's wife made me feel uncomfortable and, yes, a little disappointed in him. I didn't accept his explanation that she was becoming suspicious about our relationship, because why would she even care?

In the end Lex and I called an uneasy truce and he even very kindly offered me the use of his BMW for work, saying, 'You'll need something reliable to travel that distance every day, and I do also have a four by four at my disposal.'

I flew swiftly to the defence of my beloved Mini, pointing out that it had only broken down in the first place because of my own negligence, and turned down his second offer which was to fill the car up on his fuel account.

'You're an independent soul, aren't you?' he said, and I tried and failed to find a trace of sarcasm in his tone.

'I'm already living here rent free,' I pointed out, 'and even if we were really a couple, I wouldn't expect you to subsidize me. I'm quite capable of paying my own way.'

'It would be different if we were married with children, of course.'

I stared at him, and could feel myself pulling a frowning face, 'That's a very strange thing to say. There's absolutely no point, Lex, in speculating about a happy ever after to this story, because you know as well as I do that it's never going to happen and neither would we want it to. What you should be doing is looking for a way out for both of us, and probably sooner rather than later. I know I'm in danger of repeating myself but this can't go on indefinitely, you know.'

Suddenly Lex was grinning, and he said, 'Oh, I don't know, Stacey. I find I quite enjoy being one half of a couple when the other half is you. It's a bit like having a sparring partner and I have to keep my wits about me to make sure you don't always win. I think the score is pretty even at the moment.'

'Oh, don't be so bloody ridiculous,' I snapped, but I was smiling in spite of myself as I walked away. At least one Cable brother could confess to enjoying my company, even if it was only for a limited time, and only when he was in a good mood.

I thought that at some point in the future I might look back on this interlude with a certain fondness and that worried me. I should be recognizing that the whole thing was a complete mess from start to what was probably going to be a very uncomfortable finish and looking forward to the day I could put it all behind me — to the day I finally got my life back.

I was off to a good start that first day because I hadn't been back in the office for much more than two minutes before it felt as if I had never been away. Samantha gave a shriek and leapt up from my desk with a show of relief that wasn't put on at all. She had stood in for me before and managed perfectly well whenever I'd taken my annual leave in the past, but I guessed this time she'd also had to face the fact that I might never come back.

She pressed the intercom button and said in a tone of authority, 'We'll have two coffees in here, please, Valerie. One white, no sugar, one black, two sugars.'

'How many times do I have to tell you, Sam,' I said fondly, 'that the two sugars you have more than make up for the milk you do without.'

'Humour me,' she said with a grin. 'Black coffee and walking to work is at least a nod in the right direction. I keep reminding myself that I can't expect to lose baby fat overnight and, yes, I do know Poppy is a year old now. Wait until you have kids and then you'll know what I'm talking about.'

'But you hate black coffee and you look fabulous exactly as you are.'

'I used to be a size ten,' Sam reminded me ruefully.

Valerie came through then with the coffee, thumped the tray down and said without looking at me, 'There's been a delivery — of flowers. Should I bring them through?' So far she had managed not to acknowledge my presence in any way, not even when I walked through the front door.

'I should think so, Valerie,' Sam rolled her eyes in my direction, 'unless they're for you. I expect they're for you from Simon,' she said with a grin, as Valerie stalked out of the room. 'He's over the moon to have you back — and so am I.'

'I wanted to thank you,' I told her, 'so much, for everything you did for me — especially for ditching the resignation letter — and to say I'm so sorry for leaving you in the lurch, I will make it up to you in every way I can. Two-hour lunch breaks, leaving early every day, anything you want basically is yours, you only have to ask.'

'Did I hear babysitting mentioned?' Sam asked in a hopeful tone and I laughingly agreed.

Valerie's expression was even more sour and disapproving when she crashed through the door carrying a massive bouquet of assorted blooms. She dumped them unceremoniously on my desk with a sniff and then left without a word to either of us.

'Crumbs, I've really blotted my copybook with her.' I grimaced as the door slammed. 'Did you know she told me she'd been promoted up to my job? It's one of the reasons I didn't get in touch.'

Sam's mouth dropped comically open and stayed open, pointing at the door and then at me, 'She didn't,' she managed eventually.

'Mmm.' I nodded. 'And told me you'd all washed your hands of me.'

'Oh, well, that's it,' Sam fumed, walking to the door, 'I'm not having that and I shall have it out with her right now.'

'No, don't do that, Sam. You know she has problems at home and she probably doesn't mean any harm. I just wanted you to know why I never got in touch.' I giggled, and added with a shrug, 'I threw my phone into a lake in case I got any 'I told you so' messages.'

'It didn't work out with Nick, then?'

I shook my head, 'But I'm over it and absolutely fine.'

'So where have you been? There's someone else living in your flat — I know because I went round there looking for you.' Sam stared at me suspiciously, and then at the flowers, 'Who are those from if they're not from Nick?'

'Well, Simon obviously, just as you said.

Who else could they be from?'

Right on cue Simon walked through the door, beamed all over his face, and said enthusiastically, 'Well, you're a sight for sore eyes, Stacey. Welcome back. Who are the flowers from?'

'No idea.' I was completely mystified. I reached for the card and slid it from the envelope bearing my name.

I would have slid it right back in, but Sam was too quick for me. Snatching the card from my hand, she demanded, 'Exactly *who* is this Lex sending you love on your first day back?'

They were both staring at me, waiting for me to divulge the identity of my apparent admirer. Then Sam caught sight of the engagement ring I foolishly hadn't even given a thought to removing and it was all too late.

'My God,' she squealed. 'I don't believe it. You went off fully intending to marry one man and in little more than a couple of weeks you've come back engaged to another.'

'It's not exactly like that,' I protested.

'How is it, then?' Simon spoke at last. He was looking at me quizzically and I have to say he didn't look very happy. In fact, he looked thoroughly put out.

What could I say? It was an arrangement? It was a convenience? Both were true, and neither sounded particularly savoury, even to me.

Backed into a corner, I heard myself say reluctantly, 'It was all very confusing. I ended up going to Nick's wedding — he was marrying someone else, of course, not me. I met his brother, Alexander or Lex . . . '

'And it was love at first sight,' Sam finished in a statement that couldn't have been further from the truth. Clasping her hands to her chest she heaved a blissful sigh. 'Oh, Stacey, I'm so happy for you.'

'When we've all finished discussing Stacey's extremely complicated love-life, perhaps we could get some work done around here,' Simon's voice cut in, his tone suddenly cold and businesslike. 'And,' he went on, glaring at me, 'I hope you weren't thinking of taking off on honeymoon any time soon. You have quite a bit of catching up to do, since your protracted break means the work has been piling up, despite Samantha's and Valerie's best efforts.'

I didn't get a chance to reply to that because he marched into his own office and, while he didn't exactly slam his door — such behaviour not being at all his style — he shut it with a very decisive snap that left us in no doubt of his disapproval.

There was nothing more for it but to get

our heads down and concentrate on the work in hand. I was relieved not to have the opportunity for further discussion, but I could tell that Sam was gagging to get every last detail out of me.

Bloody Lex and his bloody flowers — what on earth had made him send them? Thanks to him I had dug myself into an even bigger hole and now it wasn't only his family who thought we were getting married, but my friends, too.

15

I had whipped myself up into a frenzy of self-righteous anger by the time I got back to the house in the forest and then had to bite my tongue for the whole of the evening.

Eleanor, it soon became apparent, had woken that morning feeling so much better that she'd insisted that as long as she rested all day she would be well enough to join everyone in the dining room for a proper family supper. It was a case of each of us being on our best behaviour, though the tension around the table, even as we took our places, must have been as obvious to everybody else as it was to me. I couldn't believe Eleanor and Aaron didn't notice the minute they came into the room, but they just beamed at each of us in turn as they took their places at the table.

'How did your first day back at work go, dear?' After the general but fairly stilted chit-chat as we helped ourselves to Mary's roast beef and all the trimmings, Eleanor's question ensured that every eye was turned on me. Each person was apparently waiting for my reply with an undisguised interest that was difficult to explain.

I couldn't even begin to tell Eleanor the truth and so I made do with a feeble, 'Fine,' and then, realizing how pathetic and vague that sounded, I forced myself to elaborate. 'Actually, a couple of hours back at my desk and it felt as it I'd never been away. My closest colleague had kept on top of my work as much as she was able, and now I will be returning the favour and putting in extra hours while she has her break.'

'It must be a very small firm if staff can take breaks just when they feel like it,' Anthea said in the disparaging tone she seemed so fond of using.

Any sympathy I had once felt towards her was disappearing fast. Indeed with each barbed comment I was closer to reaching the conclusion that she and Nick actually deserved each other. I ignored her, but she wasn't finished yet.

'I expect to be working *very* long hours while I play catch-up, and I can assure you that no one will be taking a break until I'm satisfied that nothing has been overlooked or left outstanding, but then,' she gave a little self-satisfied smirk and continued, 'it *is* my own business. I am the force at the helm and the staff always struggle to cope in my absence.'

'I'm happy to say there are no such concerns at Cable Construction. We have a great work force and I have every faith in them and their capabilities,' Lex put in, adding, 'they don't need either Nick or me to be there continually cracking the whip and telling them what to do. The majority of the staff have been with CC for at least as long as I have and know the business inside and out.'

'Unfortunately, most of them ought to have been drawing their pensions and put out to grass years ago,' Nick said scathingly, looking annoyed at his brother's words. 'New blood and new ideas is what every firm needs.'

'Youth and enthusiasm doesn't make up for age and experience, particularly in the building industry,' Aaron pointed out mildly enough, but I thought he sounded upset. 'Even I can still put in a full day's work on site when I've a mind to.'

'So you always say,' Nick responded, 'but we have to look to the future or we shall lose out to the competition from newer and trendier companies in the end.'

'Do we have to talk business round the table?' Eleanor asked plaintively, and I wondered whether she was now beginning to notice the tension in the room. It would be difficult not to, I thought.

'What would *you* like to talk about,

darling?' Lex's tone was both kind and encouraging and I momentarily warmed to him, despite my annoyance over the flowers he'd thoughtlessly sent to me.

'The wedding,' she answered immediately, and my heart sank as I wondered when I was ever going to get away from it — *and* how I was ever going to get out of it.

It soon became apparent that Eleanor had quite literally taken my word for it when I'd foolishly given her *carte blanche* over the arrangements for a wedding that was never going to take place, thinking only that it would keep her amused while she was laid up. To make matters worse, Lex seemed to go out of his way to encourage his grandmother, and as Eleanor got more and more enthusiastic, I got more and more angry.

By the end of a meal that seemed interminable, it was clear that the whole thing had already been planned on paper with meticulous precision, and everything was pretty much decided, as far as I could tell, apart from the date.

'And that can't be left for very much longer.' Even Aaron was joining in, 'Or any dates you might have in mind will already be booked. Where had you thought of honey-mooning?'

I sat and seethed as the merits of the

Seychelles were compared to those of Jamaica, Mexico and almost every other far flung destination.

In the end, I couldn't sit and listen for another minute. Pushing back my chair, I managed a huge yawn and said, 'I hope you won't mind excusing me, only my bed has been beckoning for some time and I can hardly keep my eyes open.'

'You do look a bit jaded,' Anthea offered in a tone that couldn't have been less sympathetic or more critical if she had tried.

'I hope you're not going to find working and planning a wedding too much, my dear,' Eleanor fretted.

'I can see you have everything under control, Eleanor,' I said with a smile that I was well aware didn't reach my eyes, 'so it will be a breeze. All I will have to do is to turn up fashionably late on the day — whenever that is.'

I was sick of it — sick of it all — and if I didn't get out of that room pretty damn quickly I had a feeling I was going to say something I would bitterly regret. I almost ran into the hall and up the stairs and was on the landing when Lex caught up with me.

Staying me with a hand on my arm, the simple remark, 'Are you all right?' coming from him, unleashed a fury on to his head that he obviously hadn't been expecting. He actually took a step back away from the onslaught.

'Am I *all right*? What do you bloody well think? We're being married off here, Lex, for richer for poorer, in sickness and in health, until death us do part — and you ask me if I'm *all right*.'

'Keep your voice down,' he urged in a stage whisper. 'Someone will hear.'

'It would be a *relief* — do you hear me? A relief, if someone did hear, so that we can put a stop to this ridiculous bloody charade. This has been going on for too long and it has gone way too far. That old lady is putting her heart and soul into making this wedding into the stuff that dreams are made of. A day to remember for the two of us, so just when, Lex, are you going to tell her it's all a huge bloody joke?'

'Shhh,' he urged.

'I will *not* be shushed,' I yelled, stamping my foot into the carpet, aware I was behaving like a child in my frustration.

I couldn't believe it when a hand was clamped over my mouth and I was lifted bodily and carried into the nearest bedroom, which just happened to be his. Lex closed the door behind him with a well-aimed kick, keeping his arm around me, and the hand firmly in place to ensure my silence.

I did the only thing I could in the circumstances and bit down on his fingers, releasing a strong sense of *déjà vu* as I did so. Turning me in his arms he laughed down at me, as if he, too, remembered and our eyes locked and held for a long endless moment during which I clearly heard Nick and Anthea's raised voices as they passed the door on their way to their own room. It would appear we weren't the only ones in the middle of an argument, I thought fleetingly.

Then they were gone and there was no longer any need for Lex to guarantee my compliance. I couldn't explain why the fight went out of me, why Lex stopped laughing or why neither of us moved to put some distance between us. When he did move it was to take his hand from my mouth only to capture my lips with his own seconds later.

Had I pushed him away, I was well aware Lex would have released me immediately, but I was also aware that that wasn't what I wanted at all, though winding my arms around his neck and pulling his head closer wasn't my intention either. It was as if all self-control had gone and sanity and self-preservation had flown out of the window — it was as if this moment was exactly what I had been waiting for.

Gathered close until I felt as though all the breath had been crushed out of me, I felt his body hard and demanding against mine, immediately eliciting an answering need in me. It had been so long since I had been held in that way, so long since I had known a passion that swept common sense away and very soon it was far to late to be having second thoughts.

I couldn't deny that Lex was everything a lover should be — and more, much more. I was too honest to pretend it shouldn't have happened or that it wasn't what I had wanted, and I was quite sure Lex would have laughed in my face, since any enthusiasm on his part was more than matched by my own.

'Wow,' he said later, pulling a sheet over the nakedness of our entwined bodies, 'a vixen both in and out of bed.'

Past caring, I smirked, 'Shocked you, huh? Well, it has been a very long time.'

'I only followed you to see if you were OK,' he said with a wry grin. 'You seemed upset downstairs. I know the situation isn't ideal, but it won't be for ever — I *will* sort this out, I promise you.'

I sighed deeply, feeling the last vestige of desire disappear in a cloud of concern, and tried not to stare at his bare chest, or to be distracted by what had just happened between us. 'Lex, it can't go on.'

His smile slipped and then faded entirely. 'I know,' he agreed, 'but it's just not that easy.'

'You're telling me,' I said ruefully. 'The whole tale is growing and spreading like bindweed in an untended garden. The flowers you sent with your name on the card were a kind thought, but not a great idea, because along with the ring I'd forgotten I was wearing I felt I had no choice but to explain that Nick was history and you were the new man in my life.'

Did I imagine it, or did he look *pleased*? I stared hard at him, but his expression appeared to be only rueful as he apologized and admitted he hadn't really been thinking about any consequences the flowers might have.

'What are we doing, Lex?' I indicated the compromising position we were in, and added, 'and what are we going to do?'

He stared back at me, his blue eyes darkening, as he queried softly, 'Do you mean right now? Because I do have a few ideas.'

We were consenting adults, I soothed myself, giving myself up to sheer unadulterated pleasure and throwing away the thought that what we were doing was very probably only going to make matters far worse and certainly extremely complicated.

I was awake at dawn, feeling more alive that I had for a very long time. I stretched like a cat and, probably feeling the movement, Lex reached for me in his sleep. Resisting the urge to give in and relish the closeness, to simply enjoy the feeling of being held, I slipped out of his arms. I headed for the shower and reluctantly soaped away the scent of him on my skin. A feeling of a slight soreness reminded me vividly of the enthusiasm and inventiveness in our lovemaking that had left me gasping and begging for more.

Wrapped in a fluffy towel and ready to make my way back to my own room to get ready for work, I stopped by the bed and stared down at a sleeping Lex. He looked more youthful somehow, with his skin smooth and all the lines of care erased. I wasted long moments, lost in thought and unable to bring myself to move away and get on with the day ahead.

Shocked, I found myself wishing that it was for real, this thing between us, because I wasn't going to try and kid myself that one night spent together was the start of a beautiful and meaningful relationship between us. Circumstances had thrown us together, one thing leading, almost inevitably, to another, culminating in a moment when passion over-whelmed us. There was nothing more to it than that.

I was lying to myself, of course, and the room tilted and swayed as at last it came to me that I had fallen in love with Lex. Head over heels and with all my heart I loved him and I had no idea what I was going to do about it.

I suddenly found myself looking into his blue eyes and my heart gave a great lurch that told me without a doubt that I had been kidding myself all along and had probably had feelings for him almost from the start. Obnoxious and arrogant he might be at times, but he was all too easy to love — as I had found to my cost.

He smiled a slow, lazy smile, looking me up and down, along the length of my bare legs to the top of my tousled and shower-damp hair. Holding out his hand, he said, 'Come here.'

It took me all of my willpower and more to turn away, to say lightly and coquettishly over my shoulder, 'Maybe later. Things to do, places to go and people to see right now.'

'Stacey.' He spoke my name huskily, and I stopped with my hand on the door handle and looked back at him. 'You look absolutely beautiful,' he said, and in such a way I found it hard to believe that he didn't mean it.

In my own room, I told myself quite forcefully not to read too much into what had happened. By any stretch of the imagination, attraction wasn't the same thing as love, and wishing that it were wasn't going to be of any help at all. Just because I had been suddenly struck by Cupid's arrow, it didn't mean that Lex felt the same way.

He obviously desired me, was evidently up for an affair, but nothing more than that. We both knew where we stood and I shouldn't build my hopes up for a future with him that was never going to exist except in my imagination.

So here I was again, embarking on the dead-end affair that I had managed to avoid with Nick, for all his machinations, and I was going into this one with my eyes wide open. It was my choice, no promises had been made, and I was free to walk away any time I chose or take what was on offer and enjoy it while it lasted.

I didn't have to think for very long. I knew it would have to be the latter. I couldn't walk away this time, even if the love on offer was only mine and unlikely to be returned.

I'd imagined myself in love many times, especially when I was younger, it was only now that I realized the true meaning of being 'in love'. What it meant, as far as I was concerned was to love the whole person, and every single thing about them, and for the first time in my life I knew that I did.

I dressed, made up my face and did my hair in a daze, and wondered at how everything could change in one startling moment of realization. I also wondered how I was going to keep my feelings from showing, because the last thing Lex would want would be his make-believe fiancée looking for a real happy ever after with him.

There was an atmosphere you could cut with a knife in the kitchen when I walked in, and it quickly became apparent that whatever Anthea and Nick had been quarrelling about the night before had not been resolved and was still on-going over the breakfast table.

However, I had my own problems to deal with and theirs, thank goodness, had nothing to do with me. I poured coffee from the cafetière, adding cream and sugar under Anthea's horrified gaze and began helping myself to scrambled eggs and grilled bacon left warming by Mary, who was obviously already working elsewhere in the house.

Lex walked in then, and ignoring the other two, took me in his arms and kissed me soundly. I swear it was all I could do to stay on my feet. Fresh from the shower he smelled and tasted wonderful and seemed full of *joi de vivre*. He really was everything a man should be and I could only wonder why it had taken me as long as it had to realize it.

Releasing me, he took a smiling glance at my heaped plate and said approvingly, 'That looks good. I think I'll join you. Is there any toast?'

'Good morning,' I said pleasantly as I took my breakfast and joined the others at the table.

'For some,' Nick replied morosely, pointedly burying his head back into the newspaper he was holding.

'Sleep well, did you?' Anthea glared at me, her tone sarcastic. It was quite obvious she knew where I had spent the night and probably what we had been up to, though why on earth it should matter to her I had absolutely no idea.

Annoyingly, I flushed rosily and was immediately irritated with myself. As far as everyone in the house was concerned Lex and I were engaged and planning a wedding, surely, given our respective ages, it would have been more unusual had we *not* shared a room, at least occasionally.

'Well, I certainly did,' Lex put in, taking the seat next to mine and tucking into his food with a great show of enthusiasm. 'Got anything planned for today, you two?'

'I find myself at a loose end, since my lovely wife insists on returning to work before the ink is even dry on the marriage certificate.' Nick didn't sound impressed at all and he wouldn't even look at his wife as he spoke.

'That's not fair,' she began. 'Something important has come up and — '

'And the staff can't cope without you, my love,' Nick's tone was bitter, 'so I believe you told us at great length over dinner last night, but I still didn't expect you to go careering back before the honeymoon was even over.'

Lex made a brave attempt to calm things down. 'I thought I'd pop into Bournemouth this morning, Nick, see how building work on the new bank is progressing. They should be close to removing the scaffolding by my reckoning. Do you fancy coming along?'

Nick laughed a little too heartily and shifted in his seat. 'You don't need my company or assistance, and anyway I have a couple of meetings set up now.'

I thought Lex gave him a questioning look, but it was Anthea who came right out and said sharply, 'Already? But you only knew about me going back to town last night.'

He threw her a look of dislike. 'You're not the only one in demand,' he said with a distinct edge to his voice, 'and Lex isn't the only one who can bring new business in for Cable Construction, either, whatever any of you might think.'

With that Nick rose from the table, almost toppling the chair in his haste and, leaving his breakfast half-finished, he threw the newspaper down quite savagely and stalked from the room.

For a long moment we, all three, stared after him, and then Lex said wryly, 'Well, someone certainly got out of the wrong side of the bed.' Then turning to me he changed the subject swiftly with an offer to drop me at work and pick me up later.

I was so inordinately pleased at this indication that his interest extended beyond the bedroom that I had to remind myself not to read too much into his offer or to accept it too eagerly.

As for Nick and his over-the-top reaction to a simple query, my immediate thought was to wonder what he was trying to hide, but I quickly reminded myself that his behaviour had absolutely nothing to do with me and I was extremely thankful for it.

16

'About last night,' Lex began, before we had even reached the end of the driveway.

Oh, God, as soon as he spoke I knew instinctively he was about to say the night we had spent together was a huge mistake and should never have happened.

I rushed to get in first, forcing myself to laugh lightly and say, 'Yes, I know. Talk about getting carried away in the heat of the moment.'

It was a monumental understatement, but was all I could come up with in a split second and would have to do. I continued quickly, 'I guess it's hardly surprising, the way circumstances have continually thrown us together — we're only human, after all.

'Think no more of it, Lex, what happened between us was my fault as much as yours. No harm done at all. We're both consenting adults. It was just a moment of madness.' I carefully ignored the fact the 'moment' had lasted all night and hurried on, eager to show there were no hard feelings or blame to be apportioned, 'And putting all that aside I'm actually finding I do quite enjoy your company *when* we stop fighting.'

I felt pleased with the way that sounded and Lex looked quite taken aback. I suspected he was as relieved as hell at my relaxed attitude to our night of passion, and that he'd probably been dreading the thought that I might start planning a wedding for real. I couldn't have made it clearer that I expected nothing from him.

'Will it put you out, waiting around until I finish work?' I carried on talking, since he remained silent. 'Your business isn't going to take all day is it?'

'Nick isn't the only one with meetings set up,' Lex said then, 'so I can easily fill the day and I thought we could eat out tonight instead of going straight home.' He smiled then, adding, '*I*'ve discovered I enjoy *your* company, even when we are fighting.'

It was ridiculous to read too much into it, but his words put me in a good mood for the rest of the day. Even Valerie's sour expression and her abrupt to the point of rudeness responses every time I made the smallest request, made little impression on my frame of mind.

'Something — or someone — has put a smile on your face and kept it there all day,' Sam said grinning, when we were packing up and closing the computers down at the end of the day. 'I haven't seen you this happy since — '

'Nick.' I turned from dropping a file into the cabinet and helped her out when she stumbled to a halt.

'Sorry,' she said ruefully. 'That was thoughtless of me.'

'No worries.' I smiled to show I wasn't bothered, and I truly wasn't. 'He was an error of judgement on my part, a mere blip on my radar, because they may be brothers but Lex is worth ten of him.'

I suddenly realized that Sam was no longer listening to me and was instead looking over my shoulder to the open doorway. I spun on my heels, expecting Valerie to be standing there earwigging, as she was prone to do, and came face to face with Lex.

We all started talking at once to cover our embarrassment, though I'm sure Sam wouldn't have thought my comment was unusual given that Lex was apparently my preferred choice of man.

'The receptionist told me it was all right to come on through,' Lex said by way of explanation for his unannounced entrance. 'Sorry, I should have knocked.'

In spite of my embarrassment I couldn't help thinking how much Valerie would hate being labelled a mere receptionist.

'You must be Lex.' Sam was all pink in the face and as flustered as I'd ever seen her. There was much fluttering of eyelashes and flicking of her bobbed hair, which really wasn't like her. She'd obviously fallen for the undeniably tall, dark and ruggedly handsome package that was my 'fiancé' — and she a happily married woman, too. Then she giggled and added, 'They do say listeners never hear good about themselves, but on this occasion 'they' must be wrong because Stacey was just singing your praises.'

I could have smacked her for pointing out the bleeding obvious. 'I'm just about ready to leave,' I blustered, feeling the heat burning my cheeks, and hoping Lex wouldn't read too much into either Sam's comments or mine.

Having already charmed Sam, Lex then succeeded in winning even the disapproving Valerie over on the way out with little apparent difficulty. However, when Simon appeared, he was a different kettle of fish entirely and quickly made it clear he was not about to be won over. He viewed Lex with very evident suspicion and was stand-offish, to say the least. His manner must have put Lex's back up because the two men skirted each other like a pair of tomcats spoiling for a fight.

'He fancies you,' Lex said the minute we were in the car.

I stared at him. 'Who? Simon?' I scoffed. 'Don't be so ridiculous, we've been friends and colleagues for years without so much as a hint that he's ever viewed me as anything more.'

'I bet he's regretting he didn't make his move before this,' Lex said, in what sounded like a very satisfied voice, 'because now he's missed the boat.'

'Oh?' I said coolly, giving him a straight look. 'How do you make that out? To all intents and purposes I am still a free woman, actually.'

'He doesn't know that, though, does he?'

'He will as soon as we put an end to this ridiculous charade,' I pointed out, adding firmly, 'and at the risk of repeating myself, *yet again*, it has to be done, Lex, sooner rather than later. Simon has nothing to do with this, but we can't possibly go on letting Eleanor throw all of her energy into a wedding that's never going to happen, it's just too cruel. She's going to be absolutely devastated as it is and the longer it goes on the worse it's going to be.'

Lex opened his mouth as if to reply, then seemed to change his mind and remained silent. Instead he turned the steering wheel of the car deftly, made a sweeping turn across the road, and drew up with a flourish in front of a rather grand country house hotel.

'Will this do for you?' he asked, as if finding somewhere to eat was the only thing of any importance at that moment, 'I haven't been here myself for quite some time, but it does have an excellent reputation and the added benefit of being fairly close to home.'

I sighed, but decided to let the subject of the wedding drop at least until we were seated. Between courses there would be ample time to come up with a reasonable solution to a very sticky problem that had been allowed to drift on endlessly. Though had I really thought about it I would have known it was never going to be that simple — nothing to do with the Cable family ever was.

The minute we walked through the door we seemed to be besieged by people who knew Lex in one guise or another. There was even a local vicar, keen to shake him by the hand and tell him what a marvellous job his company had made of the renovations to the church. A job for which, it became apparent during the course of the conversation, there had been no charge.

'But then,' the vicar smiled knowingly at us both, 'a little bird has been telling me that there will soon be a way I can return the favour and do something for you. I hear congratulations are the order of the day.'

I stiffened and felt the smile freeze on my face. Bloody hell, Eleanor and the wedding plans I had fondly supposed were confined to paper were moving along even more swiftly than I had imagined and she hadn't even left the house.

Hot on the heels of that revelation we had someone called George offering his horse and carriage to take me to church and then, to top that little gem, on our way to a table — set discreetly in an alcove away from prying eyes, I noticed — the *maître d'* sincerely hoped the hotel would have the honour of providing the venue and catering for our reception. This whole thing was swiftly turning into a nightmare of gigantic proportions.

I managed to stay silent while we were seated and drinks were ordered, but the minute we were alone I turned furiously to Lex — only to find that he was laughing. Not just smiling, but practically laughing his bloody head off.

I drew myself up in the chair and, narrowing my eyes, managed to keep my voice down as I demanded, 'You're finding this all very funny, aren't you?'

'Sorry.' Lex immediately sounded and looked contrite — and serious — but then he ruined it all by failing to hide the quirk to his lips as he added, 'If you could have seen your face.'

I tried to stay angry — well, I was very angry — but even I managed to find the funny side and a slight giggle escaped, 'I think it was the horse and cart that did it.'

'Ooh, George won't like his carriage being referred to as a cart, I can tell you.' He looked scandalized and went on to explain, 'That carriage has been used by royalty, let me tell you.'

I sobered suddenly and said firmly and with no remaining trace of humour, 'It really isn't funny, you know. The whole thing has taken on a life of its own and it really has to be stopped, Lex. I would say before it all gets out of control but I think it already has.'

The waiter brought the first course then, and we were silent apart from saying yes or no to the various items we were offered to accompany our meal. In fact I left Lex to accept or decline for us both as he pleased, because, quite clearly, I had other more pressing matters on my mind.

As soon as the waiter left Lex switched right back to the conversation in the car. 'So, this Simon, then?' he began.

I sighed deeply and tried to hold my temper. 'Why are you doing this, Lex?'

'Doing what?' he asked as if it was a perfectly reasonable question.

I began to get annoyed then. 'Changing the bloody subject every single time I try to sort out the mess we're in.'

'Humour me,' he requested, forking up a succulent mushroom from his starter. Chewing thoughtfully, he appeared to give all his attention to enjoying the flavour, then eventually he added, 'I do have my reasons for asking whether he is of any importance in your life — apart from being your boss, of course.'

'There isn't and never has been anything between us,' I replied impatiently, 'and before you ask again about Nick, he was a mistake, pure and simple and one that won't be repeated. I'm sure you've made a few of those in your time, but I'm respectful enough to realize that your past is none of my business. I wish you would also respect that mine is none of yours.'

'Now,' I continued briskly, 'can we get back to discussing just exactly how we are going to get around breaking off this farcical engagement and putting an end to this nonsense once and for all?'

'You can ask me, you know. You have every right.'

'Pardon?' I wasn't sure if I was being particularly dense, but Lex seemed to be talking in riddles.

'About my past.'

I was just about to tell him in no uncertain terms that I had absolutely no bloody interest in his past — even if it wasn't exactly strictly true because I confess to being as nosy as the next person — when the waiter appeared again to clear away the first course. His timing, I marvelled, was impeccable.

I'd barely touched my melon starter, but I indicated that he should take it away, at the same time assuring him it was absolutely delicious and my appetite was at fault.

'Pre-wedding nerves,' Lex said flippantly, and I itched to pour my untouched glass of Pinot Grigio right over his head, but somehow managed to laugh lightly and take a sip instead.

'This,' I said severely, once the waiter had left again, 'is no laughing matter, Lex. It might be vaguely funny if it only involved the two of us, a few friends, and your brother and sister-in-law, because, in the scheme of things whether we eventually marry or not is scarcely going to matter to them.'

'The hard fact is your grandparents

— especially Eleanor — are going to be absolutely shattered, no matter how gently or diplomatically we break the news that we are no longer an item, but we both know it has to be done — and I really don't think it can be put off any longer.'

In spite of myself, I flinched at the thought, and I hadn't even begun to think about how I was going to feel about going back to a life without Lex in it, though I knew that that, too, was going to have to be done.

I couldn't look at Lex, fearing he would be able to read something of what I was feeling in my eyes. When he reached for my hand, I was surprised into glancing up and found myself staring at him, hoping against hope he wasn't going to use his very persuasive charm to allow the situation to continue indefinitely. I would have to remind him that if we allowed that to happen there was a very real possibility we would find ourselves not only engaged, but actually married for real.

I was sure I hadn't spoken those words out loud, but it sounded as if Lex was echoing them when he made some remark, probably flippantly since he was smiling broadly, about doing it for real.

I wasn't sure whether to ask him to repeat himself or berate him for making a joke about a serious situation, before the waiter appeared with the main courses. I could have screamed in sheer frustration as he fussed around straightening cutlery, placing vegetable dishes just so and making sure that everything was to our liking. It didn't go unnoticed that Lex was irritably abrupt in his responses.

For a few moments we ate in silence, though I had real difficulty in chewing or swallowing. What was probably delicious food was entirely wasted on me.

'What do you think then?' Lex put down his knife and fork, focusing all of his attention on me.

'What about? I didn't quite catch what you said, with the waiter arriving with the food.' It was no more than the truth, but it also gave me a few moments to compose myself before Lex spelled out what was on his mind.

He laughed, though the sound was harsh, strained rather than light-hearted, 'Thank goodness for that, at least you haven't dismissed the notion as being too ridiculous for words.'

'What notion? You're not making any sense, Lex.'

'The notion of making our make-believe relationship into a real one.'

The room — in fact the whole restaurant seemed to slip sideways taking all of the other diners with it. Where was the bloody waiter when you really needed him?

'Stop joking, Lex,' I pleaded, concentrating on my plate, quite unable to meet his gaze, 'because it's just not funny any more.'

'Who said I was joking?'

My heart began beating heavily in my chest and I found it hard to catch my breath. I had heard somewhere that heart attacks could be brought on by shock and wondered if this was what that felt like.

'You look terrible,' Lex said, adding, 'Is the thought of being engaged to me really so very dreadful?'

'I don't know what to say,' I said, which was no more than the absolute truth at that moment. 'I can't understand what on earth brought you to that idea?'

He shrugged, thought for a moment, and then said, 'I've been thinking about it for a while.'

In a moment of sudden clarity, I looked him right in the eye and demanded, 'How long a while — since last night? You think we have to get married because we slept together, Lex? How very old-fashioned is that?'

We both gave up on any pretence at eating and the food began to cool and congeal on our plates.

'That isn't the reason,' he protested,

'although,' he added, obviously trying to be honest, 'that might have been one of the deciding factors for me. I think we get on famously, both in and out of bed.'

I stared at him in disbelief, 'You do? But what about all the times we end up arguing?'

'I wouldn't want to be with someone who didn't have their own opinions,' he told me simply, 'or someone who didn't care about my grandparents' feelings either, because they are very important to me.'

I pushed my plate away, and leaned on the table towards Lex. 'Is that what this is all about?' I asked incredulously, 'Because you know we can't get engaged for real just to please your grandparents. You're clearly living in cloud-cuckoo-land if you think that's going to work. Do you know what, Lex? I think this has gone far enough.' I pushed my chair back and stood up. 'Someone has to call a halt to this farce, and it looks as if it will have to be me.'

The waiter came rushing over, asking anxiously, 'Is everything all right?'

'Everything,' I told him bitterly, 'is just perfect — and anyway, where were you when I needed you?'

I was out of the restaurant, and out of the hotel before Lex caught up with me. I presumed he would have stayed behind to pay the bill. I had no choice but to wait for him, since I had absolutely no idea where we were, except it was obviously in the middle of nowhere. I stood with my back to him, waiting for him to release the door locks on the car.

'Is the idea of being with me in a real relationship so repulsive?' he said softly. I hadn't realized he had come to stand right behind me but he was so close I could feel his warm breath on my neck.

Repulsive? If only he knew it was taking me all my time not to twist around, throw myself into his arms and accept everything he offered — however much, however little.

'I don't know what you want from me,' I said stubbornly refusing to answer his question in case I gave myself away.

'A chance,' he said, turning me slowly to face him. 'A chance to see if we can make things work out for real.'

'Why?'

'Because I think we can be really good together if we forget everything that's gone before — well, not *everything* obviously — but the circumstances, and the fact that you were with Nick first.'

'I never was *with* Nick, not in the sense you mean.'

'I know,' he agreed, 'and I can accept that

now, but no one likes to feel they are second best.'

Especially after a lifetime of feeling just that, I realized, with a pang.

'So,' he pulled me slowly towards him and smiled down into my eyes, 'what do you think? You've seen the worst of me, are you willing to hang around and see if you can also bring out the best in me?'

Despite my reservations, or perhaps even because of them, I found myself agreeing and I knew exactly why. Lex was everything I wanted, everything I'd ever dreamed of, and if there was the smallest chance he might return my feelings one day, I had no choice but to take it.

Lex's motivations weren't nearly so clear. He was rich, successful, good looking and could have any woman he wanted. So, why had he chosen me?

17

'We'll take it slowly,' Lex promised me that night as we drove home from the hotel after an out-of-the-blue proposal that had left me reeling, 'pretend we just met and start afresh.'

I wasn't sure how that was going to be possible when so much water had gone under the bridge since we met, but he was as good as his word.

Perhaps courtship is too old-fashioned a word. Certainly it was not one that sprang to mind when it came to any of my previous relationships, but that's what ours became in essence and it suited me perfectly — was perhaps exactly what I had been looking for all of my adult life. It really was almost as if we had only just become a couple, which of course we had, even though nobody else was aware of it.

Lex made it clear to Eleanor, in a kind but firm manner, that we had no intention of being rushed into an early marriage, but would agree to a date in our own good time. She seemed incredibly meek in her acceptance of this decision, which surprised me, given the way she had forged ahead with the arrangements previously, as if haste in getting us to tie the knot were imperative.

With the pressure off I became relaxed enough around Lex to really begin to enjoy his company for the first time. He in turn seemed to enjoy mine and went out of his way to be amusing, charming and thoughtful in all kinds of ways. A fluffy teddy bear appeared on my pillow out of the blue after I told Eleanor I'd never owned one, wellingtons in my size appeared by the back door after a few days of rain and it got to the point where I couldn't mention a favourite food or it would be on the table when I arrived home. For the first time in my life I felt as if I really mattered.

By sharp contrast to our blossoming relationship, that of the newly-weds seemed to be deteriorating at a speed that was distinctly worrying. I couldn't help wondering why they chose to play out the drama under the embarrassed gaze of Nick's family, never mind me, a comparative stranger, especially when I realized that they did actually have a brand-new and very expensive home of their own waiting for them in London.

Heaven knows what made it imperative for Nick to remain in the Hampshire area, but to my surprise Anthea went to the trouble of commuting back and forth between Brocken-hurst and Waterloo station each day, often to find when she arrived home that her husband was either absent 'on business', or barely speaking.

On those occasions, she was careful to give the impression that she couldn't have cared less and either went to bed early with the latest bestseller, or sat up until all hours working on her laptop.

I did have some sympathy for Anthea, knowing that if things had turned out differently I might have been the one in her shoes. However, I doubted I was the best person to become involved in their affairs, added to which I found Anthea brittle and unapproachable in the extreme.

On a cold, crisp Saturday morning I suggested that Eleanor and I might try a slow walk down to the lake, more in an effort to get us both away from what threatened to be yet another furious argument between the newly-weds than for any other reason.

'Yes,' she said when I mentioned it, 'I think I can manage that easily. The vestibular therapy has been particularly effective in speeding up my recovery, for which I'm very grateful.' A telling glance in the direction of the warring couple gave me the distinct impression that the constant sniping and backbiting was having the opposite effect on her health.

'I don't understand it,' she confided as, coated and booted, we made our way at a leisurely pace away from the house, taking with us an air of relief. 'They were so definite about wanting to be together, no matter who got hurt in the process and now they can hardly bear to be in the same room together.'

That sounded intriguing, but when I glanced at Eleanor hoping for enlightenment, it was obvious that she thought she had already said too much and her expression became closed and almost secretive.

'You're not too upset about Lex and me dragging our heels when it comes to setting a date for our wedding, are you?' I think I asked the question more as a way of changing the subject than anything else.

'Oh, no dear.' She smiled up at me sweetly and squeezed my arm. 'I'm just surprised — and pleased, I confess — that you've decided to get married at all.'

I stopped and turned to look straight into her face. 'Why, Eleanor Cable, what do you mean?'

'You might have fooled Aaron.' She nodded knowingly. 'He's very trusting, but it's not so easy to pull the wool over my eyes. I've known Lex all his life, remember, and I can tell when he's lying. Fiancée indeed.'

'You know,' I gasped, shocked. 'How long?'

'I've always known.' Her laugh tinkled in the morning air. 'Lex didn't have a clue who you were, did he, when he discovered you in his bedroom?'

I shook my head and waited for the next question, which was bound to be the one about what I was doing there — but it wasn't forthcoming.

'I'm not going to ask what you were doing there, but I have my own ideas on that. At the time it amused me,' Eleanor said with a wry smile, 'to go along with the charade and see what happened. 'Oh, what a tangled web we weave when first we practise to deceive'. Are you familiar with that saying?'

We had reached the lake by this time and sat side by side on a wooden bench set at the water's edge. The day being cold and still, without even the benefit of a slight breeze, the surface lay smooth as glass reflecting the blue of the cloudless sky above and hiding heaven knew what in its depths. Was anything ever what it seemed? I wondered.

I nodded, feeling extremely foolish now that I knew the big deception had all been for nothing.

'It was all very silly and honestly not my idea.' I felt I should make that clear at least, adding in Lex's defence, 'I think Lex thought it would offend your sensitive nature to find him in such a compromising position, and you have to remember he was thinking on his feet at the time.'

'Obviously the best explanation he could come up with at a moment's notice.' Eleanor nodded, then gave me a sharp look, 'But that doesn't explain why you went along with it.'

'I was in the wrong,' I admitted with a shrug. 'In my defence I didn't know it was Lex's bed I was in — I didn't know who it belonged to — but quite simply, I shouldn't have been there.'

'Well,' she patted my hand, 'I'm very glad you were. It didn't take me long to see you were just what Lex needed in his life. I am usually a very good judge of character and I took to you straight away. You love him, don't you, my dear?'

I stared at her. 'Is there anything you *don't* know, Eleanor?'

'Nothing much escapes my attention. Old age leaves you with far too much time on your hands, gives you time to pick up on things that would normally pass you by. Does he love you?'

'I was hoping you would be able to tell me that.' I tried to smile, but it took a big effort. 'I'm pretty sure he at least *likes* me.'

'Oh, so am I,' she said emphatically, and nodding. 'Enough not to want to let you go. Give it time, Stacey. Men are not normally as swift on the uptake as we women. I knew I would marry Aaron the day I met him, it took a while longer for him to see what was staring him in the face, and then he thought it was all his idea. That's the behaviour of a typical man for you. Be patient, my dear, because Lex is yours if you want him, and I think you do. He's a wonderful man and will be well worth a little wait.'

'I know,' I said simply.

The house was silent when we got back, and we raised our eyebrows at each other at the unaccustomed peace.

'Nice walk?' Lex came out of his study and smiled as he watched me help Eleanor out of her coat.

'I think the fresh air did me the world of good.' She smiled at her grandson and then at me. 'And it was lovely to chat, but I think I would like a little lie down before lunch.'

'Mary's left everything ready for us.' Lex offered his arm, and I heard him say, as he walked Eleanor towards her room, 'Cold meat and salad, and it will just be the four of us.'

'Aaron?' she queried, looking around, always anxious when he wasn't close by

— especially since her illness.

'Driven to the library in Ringwood . . . ' I didn't hear the end of the sentence as Lex's voice trailed away when they turned the corner and disappeared from my sight.

'Driven out of the house by the sound of raised voices more like,' I muttered under my breath and went to put the kettle on, relishing the sound of silence.

I didn't realize that Lex had come in behind me until his arms snaked around my waist and I jumped almost out of my skin.

'Sorry.' His voice was very close to my ear. 'I didn't mean to scare you.'

I hoped he wasn't aware of how fast my heart was beating, or how much I wanted him to turn me around in his arms and kiss me soundly. In fact, I didn't think I had wanted anything so much in all my life as I wanted him in that moment.

Somehow I kept my voice steady. 'You don't scare me, Lex. You never have.'

He laughed softly, 'You've sure scared the hell out of me a few times, I can tell you.' He kissed the top of my head. 'You're quite a woman, Anastasia Trent, but I know next to nothing about you, and I think that's something we should remedy, sooner rather than later.'

'An inquisition? That sounds ominous.' I

272

wasn't sure I was ready to bare my soul to this man. It might ruin any illusions he had and change his mind entirely about wanting me for his wife. I was still all too aware of how tenuous our engagement was.

'Not at all.' He did turn me around then, and smiled down at me, his blue eyes dark and warm with approval, 'But we've never really talked about ourselves in any depth, have we? There must be things you would like to know about me, surely?'

'One or two,' I admitted, keeping my tone light. 'Now are we going to drink this coffee before it gets cold and am I imagining it, or is it very quiet in here?'

'Yes, to both questions.' Lex let go of me, and picked up the cups and carried them across to the table. 'I had to have a word,' he said, ruefully. 'Suggest they tone it down a bit because it wasn't fair on the grandparents. I think they've taken themselves off elsewhere for crisis talks — hopefully in the middle of the New Forest where no one can hear them. I'm sure they can sort things out. The trouble is, they're both a bit too used to getting their own way and have obviously never heard of the word compromise.'

'Which brings us to the question of where we hold our summit meeting.' I set a plate of biscuits in the middle of the table, warning,

'Don't eat too many of those or it will spoil your lunch.'

Lex looked at me. 'You sounded just the way my mother used to when you said that.'

'Oh, I'm sorry.'

'Please don't be.' He smiled. 'It's kind of nice to hear it again.'

'Hello.' The back door opened and Aaron poked his head in. 'Is it safe to come in?' He came in anyway, waving a book in his hand. 'The library got this in for me especially. Take a look, Lex, at some of the old methods they used to use in the building trade. Nick might scoff, but you have to admit they've stood the test of time. Look at this place, for instance. Turn of the eighteenth century. They certainly built to last in those days.'

I went to pour a cup of coffee for Aaron, and smiled over my shoulder at the dark head and the white close together as they pored over the pages of the book lying open on the table. The peace lasted for far too short a time and was shattered by the slamming of the front door and heavy footsteps coming our way.

'That's it then,' Nick said, almost carelessly, flinging his car keys down on the table beside the book. 'It's all over between Annie and me.'

The silence in the room was deafening as

we all stared at him. He certainly gave the impression of being unconcerned but I wasn't convinced, and neither was Lex if his next words were anything to go by.

'Are you sure?'

'I don't know why you're even asking that.' Nick turned on his brother, annoyance written all over a face that was far too good looking. 'We can't agree on anything. Don't tell me you haven't noticed — and spare me the lectures and the I-told-you-so I probably richly deserve, because I can very well do without them.'

Aaron looked upset and very confused. 'But you only just got married. I don't know what Eleanor will say.'

Nick gave his grandfather an impatient look. 'No offence, Granddad, but basically it's no one else's bloody business. I just thought you should know. The marriage is over, by mutual consent. I wish I could say it was fun while it lasted, but I would be lying. Time to move on and all that. I don't intend to hang around moping, and I have places to go and people to see, so I'll see you all later.'

With that he picked up his car keys again and was gone, with a 'Sorry, Lex,' that made no sense at all, thrown over his shoulder, almost as an afterthought as he left.

We stared after him, then I asked, 'Why is

he apologizing to you?' and Lex simply shrugged his shoulders in reply.

I thought Aaron looked distinctly uncomfortable, but then I could understand how someone of a very different era would view the abrupt dismissal of such recently made marriage vows as upsetting in the extreme.

Lunch was a quiet affair and the mood around the table was sombre. Both Eleanor and Aaron showed a quite touching concern for Lex, who seemed fine to me but I supposed what affected his brother would also affect him. I did have the thought that they might imagine that now the brief marriage was over, Nick and I might resurrect our relationship, but then I realized that that was ridiculous because they didn't even know that I had been seeing Nick first.

However, Lex did, and that began to bother me as I wondered what he was thinking. I was determined to set the record straight at the first opportunity, just in case he was harbouring any thoughts in that direction. Given that he had been made to feel second-best to his brother through most of his life it would hardly have been surprising.

Lex hadn't booked a restaurant for us that evening but allowed me to choose where we would go. We ended up walking on Poole

Quay, muffled up in thick coats against the cold November air. Neither of us had worn gloves and Lex took one of my hands and placed it with his into the depths of his coat pocket as we walked along.

I was very conscious of the warmth and strength of his fingers wrapped around mine, and very conscious that with every glance and every touch I was falling more deeply in love with him. I couldn't help but wonder where it was all leading and where it was going to end.

'So,' he said, suddenly stopping, 'tell me something about yourself. Anything you like.'

'Such as?' I suddenly felt very boring and wondered what I could say to make myself sound more interesting and appealing to someone like Lex, who had grown up in a different world from the one I was familiar with.

'What about family?'

We walked on again and it felt easier to talk on the move. I found it hard to concentrate when all of his attention was on me.

'Just me and my parents, who probably thought they had more than done their duty by staying together until I had completed my education and was settled in a job — pretty much the job I'm still doing now but with more responsibility and more money thrown in over the years. They then divorced in double-quick time and moved abroad to live in separate countries, so you could say I have no family.' I stumbled to a halt, glad to have got the worst over.

The break-up of my family was something I never talked about and I rarely allowed myself to think about it either. It was done, and dwelling on it wasn't going to help or even change a thing as far as I could see.

'Christ, that must have been bloody hard to deal with.' Lex sounded shocked.

Hard to deal with didn't even touch it — I had been in shock for months, clinging to familiar surroundings and developing a fear of change that was to stay with me for years to come. I tried to explain some of this to Lex and to his credit he did appear to understand.

'You would have craved stability.' He nodded as if he knew how it had been and his next words showed that he did. 'That's exactly how Nick and I were after our parents died. When your world has been rocked on its foundations, it helps if it can settle back into a similar and recognizable pattern, I suppose. We were lucky enough to still live in the same house and go to the same schools, because our grandparents moved in with us. I'm guessing your home was sold out from under you.'

'I did get a share of the divorce settlement,'

I explained with some irony. 'Money towards a roof over my head and a little to put by for a rainy day. I think my parents felt that absolved them from any further responsibility. As far as they were concerned, by then I was big enough to stand on my own two feet, and they were right, of course. They could have done a lot less.'

'They could also have done a bloody sight more.' Lex sounded incensed, adding, 'My grandparents, even at their great age still look on Nick and me as their responsibility.'

'But you were children when your parents died, and anyway, I can take care of myself,' I said a trifle defensively. 'I was just trying to explain to you why I never moved from where I grew up and why I settled for being a medium-sized fish in a little pond, when I could have gone to London, swum among all the sharks and probably made a killing in my line of work. Though I give financial advice for a living, money doesn't matter to me — I thought I should mention that just in case you're wondering.'

'I'm not,' he said decisively, 'and I'm sure that was never the attraction with Nick. But — if you don't mind me saying — I can't help wondering what was — aside from his admitted good looks — when it must have been clear, even to you in the relatively short time you knew him, that he's not the most reliable of characters.'

'A couple of months of madness.' I shrugged. 'I don't know, it's hard to explain, but he brought a big exhilarating breath of fresh air into a life that was desperately lacking any form of excitement and had been for years. I'd been hurt in the past, more than once, and it made me cautious to the point of paranoia about any kind of involvement. But everyone around me was falling in love, getting married and having kids, while I . . . '

I stumbled to a halt and then continued, 'Nick came along when I was finally ripe for change and just about ready to throw caution to the wind. He told me he loved me and I wanted to believe it, so I did. It was as simple as that. He told me we would be married and I believed that, too, but it was all part of the plan to get me into bed, I know that now — perhaps I did all along. If you hadn't turned up that night with your grandparents it would probably have succeeded and a lot more than my pride would have been damaged.'

'Did you love him?'

I wasn't sure if I imagined that Lex was holding his breath but I knew that if I didn't set the record straight now, he might forever feel second best. Were we ever to have a future together the time for the truth had arrived.

I took a deep breath myself, kept putting one foot in front of the other and, without looking at Lex, I said firmly, 'No, I did not. I didn't know what love was until I met you.'

18

It was a few minutes before I realized that I was walking on alone. Turning, I discovered Lex rooted to the spot and staring after me with a stunned look on his face.

'What?' he said. 'What did you say?'

I managed a laugh, highly embarrassed, and pleaded, 'Lex, don't make me say it all over again. I just wanted you to know that, whatever silly game began this whole thing, whatever my previous involvement with your brother, you are not and never will be, second best for me.'

Lex moved towards me then, and with a huge smile on his face swept me into his arms and whirled me round until I was dizzy, both with the movement and with my love for him. When at last he finally put me down we were both breathless.

'It stopped being a game to me a long time ago.' His expression was suddenly serious. 'I love you Stacey. I think I fell in love with you the minute I set eyes on you.'

I blushed hotly, light-headed, practically delirious and absolutely overwhelmed, but still trying not to show it. 'I suppose the fact that I was wearing next to nothing at the time had little to do with it,' I joked.

Lex crushed me to him, growling, 'God, I was so angry when I discovered you were waiting for Nick — and him about to be married, too. I was furious with you both, even though I soon accepted you were the innocent party, whatever impression I gave to the contrary. I was jealous — as jealous as hell, if I'm truthful — and sometimes, I admit, I still am.'

'Nick was a mistake,' I shushed him, 'just a mistake and we all make those, don't we?'

'Are you sure?'

I could have become annoyed that he would continue to question me, but, all too aware of his family history, I did try my best to understand.

'I'm not on the rebound,' I insisted, 'because there's nothing to be on the rebound from. It was no more than a schoolgirl crush — women do have those, you know, often long after they should have grown out of them. Nick seemed too good to be true and he was. As soon as I discovered he had feet of solid clay I lost interest in him so quickly even I was shocked — but you, I have to admit, were the perfect antidote.'

'I was afraid you agreed to become

engaged to me to pay Nick back. I wouldn't have blamed you.'

'You were quite forceful and highly persuasive in equal measures,' I reminded him; then, reaching up, I pulled his head down to mine and just before our lips met, I whispered, 'But, Lex, can't we forget, once and for all, how we got together and just enjoy the fact that we are?'

We kissed, at first lightly and then with more urgency, Lex unbuttoned my coat and ran his hands over my unresisting body until I was weak and pliant in his arms. I moaned against his mouth and he laughed softly and dragged me hard against him so that I was left in no doubt of his desire for me. I couldn't believe that this was it, and all my unrequited dreams of finding real love had finally come true. The circumstances were still quite unbelievable.

'Home?' he asked, holding me at arm's length for a moment.

'Mmmm.' I nodded, knowing that what was in my heart was there in my eyes for him to see.

Tenderly Lex buttoned my coat, lifting the collar up around my throat, and looking down at me, he said, 'I do love you, Stacey, more than I have ever loved anyone or anything. You're what I've been waiting for all my life and I will always love you.'

'And I love you,' I told him, without hesitation.

It was only then we became conscious that we were the focus of attention for all the hardy drinkers and smokers congregated in the cold night air outside of the row of quayside public houses. It was quite possible they'd heard every last word.

'Did the lady say yes?' one wag hollered, loud enough for everyone to hear, and there was a lot of hooting and laughter.

I felt my face grow hot, and would have hurried away, but Lex was having none of it. Slipping his arms around my shoulders he replied firmly with a great deal of pride in his tone, 'She most certainly did.'

The roar of approval rang out into the night and across the black water of the quay itself, and a good few raised a glass and offered a cheerful, 'Good health and long life to you both.'

'Come on,' Lex urged, 'let's go and join them.'

I was reluctant, they looked a bit of a motley bunch, but he was so happy and proud that I soon gave in, and hand in hand we walked to the nearest pub, the Lord Nelson, and went inside.

'The drinks are on me,' he said loudly

enough for the well-wishers outside to hear, and we were soon surrounded by a laughing and cheering crowd.

'What are we celebrating?' I turned to find a smiling Sam standing behind me. 'Don't tell me you're actually setting the date?'

'What are you . . . ?'

'Doing here,' she finished for me. 'It's practically my local, Stacey, don't you remember? Or it was until Poppy was born. It's where Ian and I met. Look here he is.'

'Hi, Stacey.' Ian swept me into his arms and kissed me on both cheeks. 'Lovely to see you, but what's all the fuss about? Don't tell me this is the Lex Sam's been telling me all about?' He turned to shake Lex's hand and to assure him that he was getting one of the very best with me.

Sam and Ian stood close together with Ian's arm draped casually round her shoulders, chatting away to Lex, explaining that they were enjoying a rare night out while Sam's mother baby-sat. Watching them, I realized that they were the example I'd had for a long time in my mind of the perfect relationship.

Probably it had been the birth of their first child that had started me thinking, first making me aware of my own biological clock ticking, perhaps making me slightly desperate as the months went on and all too ready to fall for Nick's very slick patter. I still couldn't quite believe what a fool I had been or how it had all turned out in the end.

I watched Lex admire a photo of the beautiful Poppy, ask how old she was and listen with apparent interest to the list of her many accomplishments.

'She must be well above average intelligence for a year-old child,' he said, more than willing to be impressed, and I knew he couldn't have said anything to endear him more to the doting parents.

All the while drinks had been dished out across the bar, including champagne for those who wanted it — mostly the women present, I noticed, including Sam and myself. The majority of the men preferred what they probably saw as a more manly pint of beer.

Lex probably won the approval of the men by lifting a pint and toasting the whole pub, including the staff, with a hearty, 'Your very good health,' and drinking with every appearance of enjoyment, though I noticed it was little more than a mouthful and remembered that he was driving.

'When's the wedding, then?' asked a young man with close cropped hair, who was wearing a vest despite the chilly night, perhaps to show his tattoos to the best advantage.

'Not soon enough,' Lex told him ruefully, then asked, 'Are you married yourself?'

'Divorced,' said the young man to my surprise, because he just didn't look old enough to be married, let alone already divorced. 'It didn't work out, but I'd give it another go. That's my girlfriend over there.'

I turned to see a sweet-faced girl barely out of her teens. She smiled and lifted her champagne glass in a wordless toast. I raised mine back and silently wished her better luck than the first wife, if she made it to the altar.

'What about a Christmas wedding?' Sam suggested, with a twinkle in her eye.

'But that's only weeks away,' I protested, imagining the flap Eleanor would get into. Efficient as she had been, even she wouldn't manage to pull that one off without being placed under a huge amount of pressure, which was something we couldn't allow given the delicate state of her health.

Lex must have realized all that; he still looked at me hopefully, but seemed to accept with good grace my emphatic, 'No,' especially when I added, 'Eleanor couldn't be expected to cope. It wouldn't be fair and I refuse to pass the responsibility to anyone else when she will get so much enjoyment from being in control.'

'You're right, of course,' Lex said when we left the pub, with the good wishes of the drinkers — some of them fairly inebriated by then — ringing in our ears, to begin walking back the way we had come. 'But I still regret telling my grandmother that we're in no hurry to be married. At this moment tomorrow doesn't feel soon enough and a wedding at Gretna Green by special licence seems particularly inviting. Have you ever been to Scotland?'

I shook my head, laughing. 'We can't do that to Eleanor. It will be all the more special for waiting,' I added, though I didn't believe it for a minute and wondered why we both felt the need to marry immediately. Surely we weren't worried that something could go wrong? I shivered at the thought,

'You're cold,' Lex said, slipping his arm round my waist and pulling me close, 'and probably starving hungry, too. I can't believe we forgot about eating.'

'Who needs food?' I smiled up at him, and then sniffing the air, I said, 'Can I smell fish and chips? I need food.' We both laughed out loud.

'Out of the paper?' Lex's eyes lit up, and without any further discussion we crossed the road to the chip shop where an eager queue was already forming.

★　★　★

'Fish and chips, Lex.' Nick looked faintly disgusted as he helped himself to a breakfast of poached eggs and wholemeal toast. 'Is that the best you could do for your bride-to-be?'

'He couldn't have chosen anything that would have pleased me more,' I was quick to insist. 'Though in fact they were my choice and absolutely delicious. I haven't had fish and chips out of the paper for years.'

Ignoring Nick's sarcastic, 'I should bloody well think not,' Aaron licked his lips and said, 'I can't think of anything nicer. You were down on the quay at Poole, were you? I can recall fishing from there as a boy a time or two if I try hard.'

'I didn't know you had an interest in fishing, Granddad,' Lex commented. 'I'm surprised you didn't keep it up, especially when you and Grandma moved to Cornwall to take care of us.'

'I suppose there was never the time,' Aaron sounded vaguely regretful, 'with the business and family commitments. Anyway, your grandma always hated boats and I'm quite certain she wouldn't have eaten anything I

290

might have caught.'

'Why?' Even Nick was curious enough to ask the question all of us were thinking.

'She's verging on vegetarian, in case you hadn't noticed, and would have felt sorry for the bait, never mind the fish.'

'But she's always cooked meat for us and shared it with us,' Lex pointed out.

Aaron shrugged his slightly stooped shoulders. 'She didn't think it right to foist her views on to you two — or on to me, either, come to that — and given that she has the appetite of a bird at the best of times you probably wouldn't have noticed how little of the meat she actually ate. Anyway, she thought growing boys should probably have meat as part of a healthy diet — though I've no doubt there is evidence out there somewhere to the contrary.'

'Anyone got any plans for the day?' Nick asked suddenly, and we all stared at him. It was most unusual for him to show any interest in what anyone else was doing and we were well aware of that. 'I only ask,' he went on in an unconcerned tone, 'because Annie is probably coming by to collect some of her stuff. I won't be around, but I thought it would be nicer for her if someone were here, rather than her coming into an empty house. Although she does have a key,' he said, 'so it's not really a problem.'

My first thought was how very selfish he was and then almost straightaway, unbidden, I saw myself arriving, as I had, at the dark and deserted house at his invitation with no one to welcome me and without the benefit of a key to let myself in.

'I'll wait for Anthea,' I said shortly, 'so don't even worry your head about it.'

Nick gave me a look that I had no difficulty interpreting as him wondering why on earth I would think that he would even give the matter a second thought. Nick had his list of priorities and he, not Anthea or her thoughts and feelings, was obviously right at the very top.

He pushed his empty plate to one side, swallowed the rest of his coffee, and was gone, leaving someone else to clear away his dirty breakfast dishes. I realized that that was Nick all over: leaving someone else to clear up behind him was exactly what he had always done.

Eleanor came wandering in and while she was eating and discussing the contents of the Sunday paper with Aaron, I managed to pull Lex to one side and suggest that he might take his grandparents out to lunch.

'If we're all sitting here we might look like a welcoming committee,' I pointed out, 'and your grandparents — especially Eleanor — might find it all very upsetting, as I'm sure they're very fond of Anthea.'

He looked disappointed. 'I had hoped we might spend the day together,' he said.

'So had I.' I reached out to touch his hand, and reminded him, 'There will be other days for us — lots of them.'

'Of course there will.' He smiled, caught both of my hands and pulling me towards him, kissed the tip of my nose.

In the guise of kissing him back on the cheek, I whispered, 'You might want to take them into Burley afterwards. Eleanor loves the shops there — and the cream teas — because we have no idea what time Anthea will be here, do we? Even if Nick knew, you will have noticed that he didn't see fit to share that little detail with us.'

When we turned round Eleanor and Aaron were looking at us fondly. Probably pleased to see at least one of their grandsons happy in a relationship, I guessed, and smiled across at them.

We explained that I was staying at home as we had decided to share a room, something Lex's grandparents had already stated they were perfectly fine about. I said that I would spend the time moving my things into Lex's room because it was so much bigger than mine.

'But surely Lex should stay and help you?' Eleanor was most concerned that I was being left with all the work to do.

'Nonsense.' I smiled at her. 'It won't take two of us and, anyway, he will probably just get in my way.'

'Well, that's me told,' Lex said, equally lightly, 'and just as I was about to offer, too.'

By late morning they had set off, but not before Lex had apologized over and over again that I had been left to do Nick's dirty work.

'It doesn't seem right,' he said, 'and yet letting her come back to an empty house is a pretty heartless thing to do. A pity Nick didn't see it that way and take on the responsibility. Why don't I stay and you go out for the day?'

'It's all arranged now and the explanations for my absence have been made,' I pointed out. 'I really don't mind. Perhaps, with me being a woman, Anthea will feel she can talk to me, and she'll definitely be more likely to accept help from me than you to pack up her smalls.'

'I suppose you have a point,' he conceded, still looking a bit glum.

I could understand how he felt because it did seem a bit of a sorry state of affairs that our first day as a real live bona fide engaged couple should be spent apart.

'We'll make up for lost time tonight,' I promised, with a suggestive wink. 'Now go.' With that I turned him round and sent him on his way with a saucy pat on what was, I thought, a very attractive bottom in close fitting denims.

I waved until the car disappeared round a bend in the drive, then went back inside. The house seemed very quiet and I felt quite unsettled. I spent some time wandering round in a desultory fashion, tidying this and picking up that, but Mary was too good at her job for me to find much that really needed doing.

At last, when an hour or so had passed with no sign of Anthea, I went upstairs rather than waste any more time. I emptied the wardrobe and the drawers of clothes on to the bed, piling them neatly, finding that preferable to removing them piecemeal along the landing. That way I could decide what was going where before I even got to the other bedroom and carry it there accordingly.

Pleased with such forward planning, unusual in someone usually fairly disorganized, I spent time separating trousers and skirts and was marvelling about how much time it would save me when I was getting ready for work each morning, when I heard a sound in the doorway behind me. I jumped almost out of my skin, turned quickly and found Anthea standing there.

'Sorry,' she said abruptly. 'Didn't mean to scare you. I didn't realize anyone was at home and I let myself in. I still have a key,' she added by way of explanation, and I didn't tell her that Nick had already mentioned it.

'You've had enough, too,' she went on, indicating the piles of clothes, and I could see it must have looked to her as if I were packing to leave, too.

Before I had the chance to tell her that wasn't what I was doing, she was speaking again, her tone so harsh it hurt to listen to her. After a short while I wished with all my heart I hadn't.

'Bloody brothers,' she said bitterly, 'always in competition. I suppose you knew that I was originally seeing Lex?'

I froze, but somehow I managed to nod and not make it apparent that I had known no such thing and therefore look an even bigger fool that I apparently was.

'Nick always gets what he wants, though, and taking me from his brother was like taking candy from a baby. I doubt I was the first, and I doubt I'll be the last, so you want to watch out for Nick. I'm surprised he hasn't tried it on with you already. He had me believing every word he said, especially when he proposed. Telling me he'd had too many meaningless affairs in the past and was ready to settle down, that I was the one for him and he'd never met anyone like me. The surprise is that he actually got round to marrying me. I'm still not entirely sure why he did.'

It all sounded too sickeningly familiar and I felt as if I wanted to die. To be duped by one brother was bad enough, but to be made a fool of by both was almost more than I could bear. I had recovered from the first blow because my heart was still intact, but I had a feeling it was going to take me a very long time to get over the way Lex had been using me to get back at his brother.

19

How ironic it seemed that, in the end, it was Anthea helping me to pack my things. We left the house in the forest together, closing the front door firmly behind us, and then turning to face one another.

'There are better men out there,' Anthea said firmly and with a defiant nod.

I just stared at her, wishing with all of my bruised and battered heart that I could believe she was right. It was made all the more difficult to accept such a thing as the truth because, despite her insistence, I could tell she wasn't anywhere close to convincing herself and, unfortunately, bitter experience told me she couldn't be more wrong.

We kissed each other awkwardly on the cheek, and wished each other well, all the time knowing that, though we finally appeared to have so much in common we could never really be friends and would probably never meet again.

We climbed into our separate cars to go our own ways. I couldn't speak for Anthea but I felt older and a whole lot wiser than when I had first come there late at night with such high and completely false hopes of a lasting relationship with Nick Cable.

My eyes were dry as I drove away and I refused to look back, fully accepting that the part of my life in which the Cable brothers had played a part was well and truly over.

I had no idea where I was going, but the Mini seemed to find its own route along the Wessex Way and back to the familiar streets of Brankstone. I drove aimlessly around, debating the merits of bed and breakfast versus hotel accommodation, eventually finding myself walking up the steps of a hotel in the centre of town like someone in a daze.

A drink suddenly seemed like an extremely good idea, perhaps even more than one. There was nothing stopping me, I didn't intend to drive any more that night. Once I'd booked a room for the night, the car could remain safely in the car park.

'Gin and tonic, please — a large one,' I mumbled, fumbling for my purse. I never drank gin, but that didn't seem to matter; perhaps it was time to try something new.

'Stacey?' The voice was familiar and I jerked my head up to come face to face with Valerie Winstanley — of all people — serving behind the bar of a hotel of all things.

'Valerie?' I was shocked out of my stupor. 'What are you doing here?'

'This is my way of supplementing my income,' she said, without a trace of embarrassment, 'and it gets me out of the house and gives me a bit of a social life at the same time. I could ask you the same thing, but I'll get you that drink first — you look as if you could use it. Look,' she added, pointing, 'there's an empty table over there. I'll bring it across. I can even join you for a bit, if you would like, as I'm due a break, but you can tell me to get lost if you like. I would actually quite understand if you did.'

Only when she came and set down the drinks did I remember I hadn't paid even for mine and I reached for my bag.

'Put your money away,' she insisted, flapping a hand at me. 'I owe you a lot more than a measly drink and I would like the chance to explain my appalling behaviour if you would give me the chance.'

I would let her talk, I decided, positively uncaring. It would be easier than talking myself or even simply telling her to shut up, and anyway I didn't have to listen.

'I've been a bitch,' she began, putting a hand up as if I might be about to contradict her — which was actually the furthest thing from my mind to do, 'and I've been so embarrassed. I couldn't even begin to justify to myself all the stupid lies I told you that time over the phone to myself, never mind to you. I've always liked you.'

Interpreting the disbelieving look I gave her correctly, Valerie hurried on, repeating, 'I *have* always liked you — and admired you too.'

That was too much to swallow and I choked on my drink. I coughed and put the glass down, now giving her my full attention and wondering how many more lies I was going to be expected to believe. I quite obviously had mug written all over me and yet I didn't even have the energy to get up and walk away.

'You had everything,' she began as if that explained things, and perhaps to her it did. 'A good job with regular opportunities for promotion — which I can accept were always well deserved because you've always worked hard if nothing else. You had a life and a home of your own, and even a good man sitting waiting, right under your nose for you to notice him.'

I stared at her, wondering what on earth she was talking about — especially the bit about the man.

'Yes,' she went on, obviously getting into her stride, 'you had everything *I* ever wanted, but it wasn't enough for *you*, was it? You fell for looks, money and a line in bullshit that stank to high heaven and willingly threw everything away in the hope of what? If it was a fairy tale ending straight out of a Mills and Boon novel you were looking for you failed dismally, didn't you?'

'I thought Nick loved me.' It sounded like a poor excuse even to my ears, because I had acted with indecent haste, there was no doubt about that and then proceeded to do exactly the same thing all over again with his brother. I could hardly wait to see what Valerie would have to say when she got to that bit.

'Love,' she scoffed. 'What could either of you have known about love in the very short time you were together? I admit it, I was glad, yes, glad, when I got your phone call and realized it had all fallen apart. I felt you had got no more than you richly deserved. That's why I said the things I did, because I didn't see why you should just come waltzing back and pick up the pieces of your life as if nothing had happened.'

Valerie sat back, took a deep breath and a long swallow of her drink, before continuing relentlessly — as if she had to get it all said now that she had begun. 'I did it because I was full of jealousy and resentment. I admit it. I hate my life and would give anything to be able to live yours, but you just go from one disaster to another, don't you? I would imagine the fact you're here means it's all gone wrong again for you. I'm right, aren't I?'

I nodded miserably, still trying to take in even half of what she had been saying. I could admit I had never given a thought to the life she lived, even though I knew about the elderly and, by all accounts, extremely demanding mother who shared her home, and the feckless brother who turned up from time to time when he had nowhere else to go — stole from her unashamedly to feed his gambling habit until he eventually won enough to disappear again, until the next time.

It wasn't that Valerie had ever complained, or even discussed her home life, but I had inadvertently overheard Valerie's side of many a conversation she'd had with her mother, and had seen for myself the brother come into the office with his hand out.

Even knowing all of that I felt I still had to say, in my own defence, 'My life isn't so great, you know. Yes, I have — had — a nice home and a good job, but I should have done even better with my qualifications and would have if I'd only had the nerve to go out in the world and try. None of that would have mattered, though, if I could have had the one thing I've always longed for — a family of my own. It's what I've wanted most ever since my parents made themselves scarce, but everyone I've ever loved has let me down.'

'I had given up and was prepared to settle for the life I had, Valerie, and then Nick came along, convinced me it would be different with him and I believed him — probably because I so badly wanted to. I should have known he was too good to be true and now his brother has turned out to be exactly the same.'

'Then I'm sorry,' Valerie said, and she actually sounded as if she meant it. She smiled wryly. 'My nicer nature — and I do have one despite recent evidence to the contrary — knows full well that you do deserve better. I suppose the truth is that none of us necessarily gets what we think we deserve in life.'

I sighed deeply and took another sip of my drink.

Valerie leaned forward and looked right into my face. 'It doesn't make you worthless, you know, just because you're not married with a family. It's not the be all and end all. Some of the married women I know are even lonelier than I am, now that their kids have grown up and have left home, because they've suddenly realized that they have absolutely nothing in common with the man they married. You can be a long time married to the wrong person.'

I stared at her, unable to quite dismiss the ring of truth about what she said. 'Didn't you ever want to be married?' I asked.

'Of course I did — once — but I always had other commitments that had to come first.' She smiled wryly and went on, 'These days I would happily settle for a quiet life with no one to be responsible for but myself.'

Someone called her name then, and she said, 'Oh — oh, I've got to go.' She got up, took a step or two away from the table and then came back to say, 'If you're looking for a bed for the night you're very welcome to stay with me, Stacey. My brother isn't around, so I have a spare room. It's not quite the Central but it is clean and tidy.'

I was surprised by her offer and didn't quite have the heart to say no, even though I badly wanted to. I really couldn't think of anything worse than being beholden to Valerie, never mind having to put up with her mother.

However, she'd apologized for her behaviour and even tried to explain it, offering an olive branch that I felt I should be big enough to take. She'd also made me realize that I'd spent far too long thinking about my own life to the point at which I had never given a thought to anyone else's. There were people worse off. Life was a challenge and it was about time I rose to meet it.

★ ★ ★

'Come in,' Valerie opened the blue-painted front door wide.

No sooner had we stepped inside than a voice quavered, 'Is that you, dear?'

'Yes, Mum, won't be a minute,' Valerie said loudly. 'I'm not sure who she expects it to be as I'm the only one with a key,' she murmured just loud enough for me to hear, 'but she says the same thing every time I come through the door.'

The brick-built bungalow was as neat as a new pin inside and spotlessly clean, but almost spartan, minimalist without the intention to follow current trends. It was clear that there was little money to spare for fripperies in this household.

'Through here.' Valerie led the way and opened the door of a bedroom, sparsely furnished with the bare necessities, a narrow bed, bedside table, single wardrobe and chest of drawers. 'Make yourself at home,' she invited, 'and feel free to stay as long as you like.'

I slept very little, though the bed was reasonably comfortable. I heard Valerie go into her mother's room at least twice during the night, and then she was up first thing. It made me wonder how on earth she managed to hold down two jobs on such a limited amount of sleep.

She was swift to assure me over breakfast, when I said as much, that her mother was quite able-bodied, and it was more in the way of reassurance that she was looking for from Valerie with her demands for attention.

'Mum doesn't need a full-time carer and she attends a day care centre most days, so she doesn't lack for company and loves her TV programmes when she's at home. Won't miss *Big Brother* for anything, you know.'

'I'd vote 'em all out,' came a sharp voice from the doorway. 'Two faced load of back-stabbing b— '

'That's enough of that.' Valerie shushed the old woman, who came tapping across the room to the table to join us, relying heavily on a walking-stick. 'We have a guest.'

I stood up, feeling I should, especially as there were only two chairs. 'I'm Stacey. Very pleased to meet you, Mrs Winstanley.'

'My name's not Winstanley.' The face, deeply wrinkled already, shrivelled even further with very obvious distaste. 'That's *her* name, or the name of that creature she married.'

I felt as if I'd been suddenly thrown into a life I didn't even recognize any more, with people I didn't recognize either. Was anyone actually what or who they appeared to be? Given my recent experiences it would appear not.

Valerie's face flamed scarlet as her mother went on with cruel satisfaction, 'I told her it wouldn't last five minutes and I was right, wasn't I?'

Valerie didn't answer and I wondered how often she'd been taunted in this way and why she didn't defend herself.

'How long were you married, Valerie?' I asked, more out of curiosity than any real desire to know.

I was well aware it was none of my business and it went through my mind that at least she had been married once, which was more than I could say. At the very least my question gave Valerie the chance to speak for herself.

'Ten years.'

I gave her mother a straight look. 'Hardly the five minutes you predicted, is it?'

The woman blustered, but I could tell she wasn't used to anyone contradicting her, and she didn't quite know how to deal with it. I felt I could take a good guess that Valerie's mother's taking up residence in the marital home was very probably what had spelled the beginning of the end for the Winstanley marriage. I didn't think I'd be far wrong.

'Is is all right to take a shower?' I made for the door as Valerie nodded. 'I can give you a lift to work this morning,' I said brightly, 'because you usually take the bus, don't you? Nice to have met you, Mrs . . . I'm sure we'll get the chance to talk later.' I didn't add that I would look forward to it. I thought that would be stretching the truth a bit too far.

The old woman had made me think of Eleanor, and now I wept the tears I'd been holding back for so long in the shower, imagining her bewilderment at losing one grandson's wife and the other's fiancée in the space of just a few days. I refused to allow myself to cry over Lex and his duplicity, reminding myself that he was just like the others had been over the years and was not worth a single one of my tears. I couldn't believe I was still such a poor judge of character that I could put myself through the same thing time after time. It was obvious to me now that I was destined to live my life alone and the sooner I accepted it the better it would be for me. As Valerie had so rightly said, there were worse things.

'About my marriage,' Valerie said as soon as we got into the car.

'You don't owe me any explanations,' I

assured her quickly. 'Your marriage has absolutely nothing to do with me.'

She smiled, just slightly. 'I'll just say that he was a very decent man, who doesn't deserve to be labelled as anything else by my mother.'

'I believe you,' I said. Then, to change the subject and also because it had been bugging me since the night before, I asked, 'What did you mean when you said to me I had, 'a good man waiting right under my nose for me to notice him'?'

'Oh, dear, me and my big mouth — I shouldn't have said anything.'

'Well, you did,' I reminded her, 'and we can't pretend it was unsaid now.'

Valerie was silent for a minute, then she muttered, 'He'll kill me for opening my mouth, but surely you've noticed the way Simon looks at you.'

'*Simon?*' I turned to stare at her and then had to brake sharply to avoid a car in front that had stopped without me noticing.

'Careful,' Valerie said.

'It's you who should be careful,' I said it with a slight laugh, to take the sting out of my words. 'Isn't it perjury or something when you tell an untruth?'

'I think that's in a court of law and it's not an untruth. It's as clear as the nose on your face. You must have been blind all these years not to have noticed,' she said stubbornly. 'He was devastated when you came in flaunting that engagement ring and he had to accept he'd missed his chance. I don't think he ever really knew much about the first brother, because Samantha covered up the fact that you'd run off to be with *him*.'

'*Simon*?' I said again, hearing the amazement in my own voice.

'Yes, *Simon*,' she said back firmly, 'and he's a good man. His one fault would appear to be that he's too willing to let the grass grow under his feet where you're concerned. He should have made his move years ago. You could do far worse, you know.'

I couldn't think of anything to say to that, so we completed the rest of the journey in near silence.

There were just the two of us in the office, because Sam was off on her annual break and Simon wasn't in yet. It was a quiet time of the year because, with Christmas approaching, people had other things on their mind than financial planning — there would be time enough for that in January when the bills came in.

I wandered out into the reception area, which was Valerie's domain. 'I've been thinking, Valerie, that while it's a bit slow I could show you some of the ropes. You know, the basics of my job. You're more than capable; after the years you've spent with the company you probably know more than I do.'

Valerie's face flushed, and I half expected her to bite my head off, but she surprised me by saying, 'Oh, would you do that, Stacey? I'm sure I could cope with some of the simpler tasks, which would leave you, and Sam, too, more time to deal with the rest. You're not doing this because you feel sorry for me, though, are you?'

'Not at all,' I insisted, not altogether truthfully, because a better understanding of what her life was like probably had provoked a more sympathetic attitude on my part. 'I'm not sure why you haven't been given more responsibility over the years and a salary to match, but we'll see how it goes and then perhaps I could have a word with Simon on your behalf.'

It was my turn to flush just from mentioning my employer's name in the light of Valerie's recent revelation, and I hurried on, 'I don't want you to think this has anything to do with your offer of a temporary roof over my head. It actually has more to do with a better understanding between us and a feeling that we could actually work together because of it.'

She smiled. 'Oh, I know I'm my own worst

enemy, but my bark is usually worse than my bite.'

'I'll bear that in mind,' I said, feeling conscious that I might sound stuffy and a bit officious, but also feeling I should point out: 'this is a small company and it's bound to be better for all of us if the atmosphere in the office improves. I will certainly try harder, if you will.'

'When can we start?'

I had never seen Valerie appear so enthusiastic and, eager to capitalize on that, I suggested, 'No time like the present.'

She was a revelation, absolutely came into her own given a bit of responsibility, and was excellent with the clients — despite Simon's comments to the contrary — especially the elderly ones, where obviously she had plenty of experience and had learned endless patience.

Towards the end of a very productive day, heads together, we were poring over a spreadsheet — the one thing Valerie was having a bit of trouble understanding, when we became aware of someone standing in the doorway.

'Sorry to barge in,' Lex said smoothly, 'but there was no one at the front desk.'

'Oh,' Valerie was flustered, 'that's my fault, I'm afraid, but we weren't expecting anyone this late in the day. Can I help at all?'

'I'm here to see Stacey,' he said, and turning his full attention on me, added, 'I was hoping we could talk.'

'I'll leave you to it,' Valerie said, skipping smartly out of the room and closing the door behind her.

'I don't believe we have anything to talk about,' I said coldly, listening to my head and relieved he couldn't see the way my heart was reacting to having him standing so close. In spite of his deceit I knew I still loved him and my treacherous body still wanted him.

'You discovered there was a bit of history between Anthea and me?' he speculated, and I nodded. 'Eleanor said I should have told you right from the beginning and, of course, she was right. She usually is.'

'What a fool you all must have thought me,' I said bitterly, and sliding the ring I hadn't been able to bear to part with from my finger, I placed it firmly on the desk with a sharp and very final sounding tap. 'I've just been a pawn in some kind of tit-for-tat game between you and Nick. He stole Anthea from you and you've used me all this time to get back at him.' A thought suddenly occurred to me and it made me feel sick. 'You probably even used the same bloody ring.'

'No.' Lex's tone was loud, harsh even, then

314

he added emphatically, but more softly, 'No, I did not.'

Ignoring him, I asked, 'How long has it been going on — this competition between you and Nick? How many other women have there been?'

'It wasn't like that,' he insisted, taking a step towards me.

I took a step back and held my hands, palms outwards towards him, as if to fend him off. 'How exactly was it, then?' Even as I said it I was telling myself I didn't want to know, and I hurried on, 'I was always so concerned about your feeling second best because I knew Nick first — and all the time — all the bloody time that's exactly what *I* was to you.'

'You've *never* been second best. I made a mistake with Anthea, just as you did with Nick. We were totally wrong for each other. It might have amused Nick to think he 'stole' her from me, but nothing could have been further from the truth. Our romance, if you can even call it that, was extremely short-lived and was as good as over by the time they got together. Anthea knows that, even if Nick doesn't. It was wrong of me not to tell you, but, in my own defence, you did say you weren't interested in my past.'

I couldn't believe *he* was blaming *me* for

his deceit and now I lost it totally, 'Oh, get out, Lex. Everyone I ever thought was too good to be true always was and, though it pains me to say it, you're no better than all the bloody rest.'

He gave me a long look and then turned to go.

'Oh,' my voice rang out as he reached for the door handle, 'don't forget the ring, you'll need that for the next one.'

I threw the ring, he caught it deftly, pocketed it, and then left without looking back again. The sound of the door closing had a very final ring to it and, though I hadn't done anything wrong, I was still left wondering if I'd just made the biggest mistake of my life.

20

'Are you *sure* you've done the right thing?'

It was a question I'd been asked repeatedly by Valerie over the last week, and now Sam was back from holiday, she'd wasted no time jumping on the bandwagon.

'What do you think *would* be the right thing?' I demanded. 'Should I ignore the fact that Lex lied to me about Anthea?'

'Only by omission,' she excused him, making me furious, 'and are you sure they were actually engaged?'

'I've asked her that, too,' Valerie put in helpfully. 'Perhaps they only saw each other a few times.'

'What difference does it make? They were *involved*, in whatever capacity, and then Anthea dumped him for Nick. If that hadn't happened she might very well still have been with Lex. Something like that shouldn't have been kept a secret from me. It's totally obvious — to me if not to anyone else — that he's been using me to get his own back on Nick. I've been made to look a fool by the whole Cable family and, anyway, Valerie, why are you sticking up for Lex when you've

317

made it perfectly clear you always thought Simon was the one for me?'

'Simon is . . . ' she began, then a voice from the doorway said, 'Do I hear my name being taken in vain?'

Three startled faces twisted round to find Simon standing there wearing a quizzical expression, and I'm quite certain each of ours showed guilt and embarrassment in equal measures. Just how much he had heard was questionable — that we had been talking about him was patently obvious.

'Simon is . . . ' he prompted, and we shared a hefty sigh of relief at what could hopefully be taken as evidence this was all he had heard, and tried to come up with a suitable and completely harmless way to complete the sentence.

'Simon is always ready for a breakfast doughnut,' Sam finished, not very convincingly, I thought, but it seemed to do the trick — in fact he offered to go out and buy them and then left to do just that.

'We'll have to watch that,' I warned, and then smiling to soften the words, I added, 'Now we've all got to eat huge sugary buns very convincingly.'

'He's such a nice man.' Valerie was obviously hedging her bets and wasn't about to give up on Simon as a contender for my affections just in case Lex didn't work out.

'He is,' Sam agreed, and I braced myself for the 'but' that I was sure was coming, 'but I have the advantage of having seen Stacey and Lex together in a social setting and, please believe me, when I say they are absolutely made for each other, you will never hear me speak a truer word.'

'That's what I thought,' I said sadly. 'It just goes to show how wrong you can be.'

'He absolutely adores you, Stacey, I'm certain of it. You could at least give him the benefit of any doubt,' Sam insisted stubbornly, 'and the opportunity to explain.'

Luckily, Simon returned then and, as Valerie hurried off to make coffee he gave us something else to think about, ripping open the bag of cakes and saying, 'These could be by way of a celebration.'

Having captured our attention, he continued, 'I've been thinking for some time about expanding, perhaps going for slightly bigger premises and taking on at least one more member of staff.' He turned as Valerie came back with a loaded tray, and included her by saying, 'You should also hear this, Valerie, because Stacey had a point the other day when she indicated that as an experienced member of staff you're undervalued here and that your undoubted skills are underused, but that's all about to change.

'As a smaller, perhaps more people-friendly and approachable firm we've always done well — often when many bigger firms offering financial services have struggled. Simply by lowering our sights and targeting the family man or woman in the street we had already managed to tap into a whole new market, but things have really picked up lately.

'Joe Public might not bring big money contracts, but a steady flow of smaller customers has been proving extremely lucrative for us. With the credit crunch everyone is feeling the pinch and looking for ways to make their money go further; we're well established now as the ones to approach regarding family finances, and word of mouth is bringing new customers to our doorstep.

'We've done better than I ever expected in the early days to be honest, especially given the competition. I should have been looking to improve some time ago, but I'm not a great one for change — as you probably all know. Over-cautious, actually, and I've always tended to think if it's not broken, why mend it? But I've been turning work away, which is not exactly clever. I think Mannings can do better, a lot better, but I need to know you are all with me, because I can't do it without you, and I wouldn't want to. I'm well aware that a business is only as good as the staff who run it.'

I hoped I was imagining that he'd been looking at me in particular when he said, 'I can't do it without you, and I wouldn't want to', but remembering Valerie's words, I rather thought not. He was very, very nice, but he wasn't Lex. The familiar feeling of devastation swept though me at the thought of him, and I had to force myself back to the here and now, and to concentrate on what Simon was saying.

'What I'm proposing,' he was saying, 'is to move everyone up. Stacey, I would like to offer you a full partnership — you've more than earned it. Through sheer hard work I think you've managed to bring in more new accounts than the rest of us put together.

'Should you accept, which I hope you will, that leaves your position in the firm vacant for Samantha to step into, if she is agreeable, and I'm sure Valerie is perfectly capable of taking over Sam's role with the right training. Of course, your new status within the firm will be upgraded accordingly for each of you and I will be speaking to you all individually about the changes and what they will mean to you personally.'

The three of us were shocked into silence for a moment, then everyone started talking at once and the next minute Valerie horrified us all by bursting into tears, sobbing in a way that bordered on hysteria.

'I'm so happy,' she wept, grasping a handful of tissues from the box on Sam's desk.

I expect I was the only one present who really knew just how much the recognition — and the pay rise — would mean to her. As I reached out instinctively to hug her I reflected it was the very last thing I would have dreamed of doing just a few short days ago, but she hugged me back, quite fiercely.

'Come on through, once you've enjoyed your coffee and doughnut, Stacey,' Simon invited, 'and we'll talk about this further. Meanwhile, I'm happy for you to discuss my proposition between yourselves, make sure you realize the implications that greater responsibility will have on your lives and decide whether you can welcome the changes or not. So far I have only made suggestions, but remember nothing is set in stone, and negotiations can be made. We are a team — a good one — and will continue to work as one, I hope.' With that he left us to it.

'I didn't know you'd been talking to Simon about upgrading my job, Stacey, but I don't deserve this,' Valerie protested, 'not after what I did to you.'

'You had your reasons for disliking me and, probably quite rightly, thought I had got what was coming to me,' I pointed out. 'As a senior colleague I could have been a lot more understanding of your particular circumstances in the past. I never expected Sam to work outside of Poppy's nursery hours, yet I didn't think twice about expecting you to work late or even stop to wonder if it might be inconvenient for you to do so.'

'You couldn't have known,' she pointed out, wiping her eyes and blowing her nose on the wad of crumpled tissue.

'We work together and have done for a very long time, perhaps it's time we learned to trust and respect each other a bit more.'

I did go through my mind that if she was appreciated more at work she might even learn to value herself more in her private life and insist on respect from her family. Whatever her failings, I appreciated greatly the fact that Valerie worked harder than anyone I knew. She deserved to be rewarded for that alone.

'Right.' I chewed the last piece of doughnut and swallowed. 'Into the lion's den.'

To begin with Simon was very professional, outlining his plans for the company and inviting me formally to be part of the expansion as his partner. He said I had more than earned my place in the firm with all my hard work and loyalty in the past, invited me to accompany him to view suitable premises, insisted he was open to any suggestions I might make and that he was always ready to listen to my views.

Then the tone changed somewhat and, with a telling glance at my naked engagement finger, Simon said how much he had always respected me as a person and how much he was hoping a brand new future might mean a closer working and perhaps — there was a hesitant question in his voice — even the chance of a personal relationship for the two of us.

I'll admit I was flattered — and why shouldn't I be? Simon was quite a catch, after all. I can't say I was surprised — given Valerie's very clear indication that he was interested in me — though even quite a short time ago I'd have been completely shocked because there'd never been any indication that he saw me as anything other than a valued employee. I can't say I wasn't tempted either because, quite suddenly and quite definitely, I was — and that surprised me. Until quite recently I wouldn't have considered the notion with a second thought.

Why not? I thought now. Why the hell not? I was a free agent.

Lex and his deception had been the final straw for me. He had hurt me far more than he would ever know and more than I was prepared to admit. At times I was aware that it was only my pride that kept me upright and functioning and giving the appearance of a normal human being. Despite everything — the questionable way we had got together, the short time we had known each other — I had loved him, really loved him, trusted him implicitly, and look where it had got me.

Well, I had been made a complete fool of for the very last time. I'd had enough and was ready to accept that fairy-tale endings just weren't for the likes of me. I didn't want to spend what was left of my thirties and then my forties going from one unreliable, two-timing man to the next or, almost worse in a way, give up on the idea of a relationship completely, and look forward to living the rest of my life alone.

Accepting what Simon was offering would be the answer to everything for me — there was no doubt about that. He was a good friend and respected colleague, and a life with him would undoubtedly give me the stability I had always craved. Together we could raise the family I had always dreamed of having. I already liked him, respected him and was very fond of him — it was quite possible that, given time, I might even come to love him.

My immediate instinct was to give him every indication that there was very definitely a chance for us on a personal level, but something held me back and I couldn't have said what exactly.

'You've given me a lot to think about,' I said carefully, 'but as you know I'm not normally one to act on impulse,' I didn't add that acting on impulse had recently proved to be disastrous for me, particularly because Simon clearly didn't know the half of it, but I continued, 'so I think we'll both just see how it goes, shall we? There's no rush, after all, but, Simon, I have to ask — does the offer of a partnership come with strings attached?'

'Absolutely not,' he insisted, seeming happy to accept my answer and probably respecting my caution; being a cautious man himself he would understand it. Had he tried to rush me into something I wasn't sure I was ready for at that point, I might have had second thoughts about the wisdom of offering him any encouragement but, as it was, I began to feel more and more that his tentative offer was the answer to everything for me.

'I hope I haven't offended you by speaking out,' he said.

'You haven't offended me at all,' I assured him, and smiled. 'Whatever happens between us in the future, I'm sure that we'll never be less than professional in our working relationship.'

★ ★ ★

'But I thought you, of all people, would be happy for me.' I almost felt like telling Valerie to get out of the car and walk home. Only the realization that I was still living in her home kept me silent. I couldn't understand Valerie's attitude to my decision to consider seriously a future with Simon and I didn't hesitate to say so.

'I am,' she said, though happy was the last thing she sounded, '*if* you're completely sure this is really what you want and you're not just settling for second best by choosing Simon.'

'That's what I would have been settling for if I'd stayed with Lex — *his* second best.'

'Are you sure? Or are you just guessing? If he'd really wanted Anthea, wouldn't he be with her right now and not still trying every which way to get you to talk to him? He's phoned three times again today.'

'She might not want him,' I pointed out, quite reasonably, I thought, and was so shocked when Valerie raised her voice, almost shouting in her exasperation, 'For God's *sake*, Stacey,' that I pulled over without indicating and bumped to a stop half on and half off the kerb. The irate driver behind sounded his horn furiously — as well he might — and I felt only relief that the horn, accompanied by a rude one-fingered gesture, was all he did.

'For God's sake what?'

'For God's sake, stop bloody well second-guessing what the man might or might not want. You can't possibly know what's inside his head, but you're doing exactly what I did with John and making his decisions for him. Please try and learn from my mistake.'

I stared at Valerie, who had begun to cry silently. 'What on earth do you mean?'

'I told my John that, as Joan's only daughter, I had to take responsibility for my mother's care after her stroke, but that he didn't have to and must feel free to go and get on with his life. He insisted he was quite happy to share the load, that we were a team and would manage together, but I was adamant that he'd be better off without us and we without him.'

'I can see now that I pushed him away and left him with no choice but to leave. He probably thought I didn't want him, but I only really wanted what I thought was best for him. That shouldn't have been my decision. I know it's not exactly the same scenario, but the principle is the same. Hear Lex out, let him have his say before you do anything rash — *please*.'

We were still arguing, if only mildly, when we arrived home and it didn't take long for Valerie's mother to get the gist of what it was about. Frail she might have been, but feeble-minded she certainly was not.

'Are you saying it's my fault your marriage broke up?' Joan demanded, obviously incensed by the very idea.

'No, I'm saying it's mine. John didn't just up and leave — as you've always claimed — he was pushed and it was me doing the pushing. Don't look so shocked, Mother. You must know it's not every man who would want to share a home with his partner's ageing parent — but then John wasn't every man, was he? But there, I made my decision long ago and now I have to live with it.'

Her mother harrumphed a bit, but I noticed she didn't try to argue, which was unusual for her. While Valerie was taking a shower I took the opportunity to say, 'She gave up a lot for you, you know,' and waited for the bad-tempered fall-out and the direct advice that I should mind my own business.

For a moment Joan was silent and I carried on peeling potatoes, then I almost cut my finger off as she said, quite humbly and in a very different tone, 'I do know that.'

I stared at the old woman, willing her to continue, and eventually she did.

'How do you think it makes me feel knowing I have no choice but to take advantage of her generosity?' she asked and then added thoughtfully, 'But I could show my gratitude more. I can also make sure I'm the *only* one who takes advantage of her, by making it clear to her brother — when he shows his face again — that from now on he stands on his own two feet. I should have done it long ago.'

I was surprised, but very pleased, and we sat in companionable silence for a moment or two. Then I stood up to put the potatoes on to boil.

'Oh, dear, I'm sorry, Stacey, I almost forgot — some agency phoned and left a message for you, they said something about your flat being vacant by the end of the month.'

I wrapped my arms around her in a big hug and kissed the wrinkled cheek. Then we pulled apart quickly and stared at each other. I wasn't sure who was more shocked, then I surprised myself even more when I said with total honesty, 'Family life isn't always plain sailing, I know, but I do envy you and Valerie. I know I will never have the relationship with my mother that Valerie has with you. I'm well aware that, whatever your differences, you do love each other very much.'

'You've been a breath of fresh air,' the old lady said smiling and nodding. 'Probably just what we needed and we're going to miss you.'

I laughed. 'I'm only going back to my life, not to Timbuktu, so I'm sure you haven't seen the last of me.'

'You sound happy.' Valerie came into the kitchen with her hair wrapped in a towel, and pushed past me to turn the boiling potatoes down.

I looked up from arranging sausages in rows on the grill pan, aware that I was positively beaming. 'I can have my flat back at the end of the month and then it will be just as if the past weeks had never happened.'

'Really?' she said, clear doubt in her tone.

'Really,' I insisted firmly, and I meant it.

'Please don't do this, Stacey. Please.' She sounded so desperate that I looked at her — really looked at her. I could see how upset she was as she continued. 'Don't make a decision you will come to regret bitterly, as I have and still do years later.'

I could feel myself relenting even before I asked the question, though I already knew the answer. 'What do you want me to do?'

'Speak to Lex. Just speak to him.'

I stared at her thoughtfully and then said, very quietly, 'I will speak to Lex, but only if you will speak to John.'

21

I don't know what made me say it — desperation maybe. I had no intention of speaking to Lex ever again, but Valerie obviously thought it a good idea. Consequently she was becoming like a dog with a bone, coming back to the same subject again and again. It had become clear she wasn't going to give up easily, but I believed I had come up with a way that would give her little choice but to let the matter drop. There was no way in the world she would be speaking to her estranged husband — not after all this time.

Satisfied that I had got the better of her, I gave my attention to turning the sausages now sizzling on the grill pan, saying over my shoulder, 'Did you say you liked these well done?'

'I do,' said Joan, and I noticed she was careful to keep any comment confined to the food, so she was learning.

'I wouldn't even know where to start looking for John,' Valerie said suddenly, and I don't mind admitting I was shocked to the core that she was apparently giving doing so some serious thought. So shocked that I allowed a sausage to roll out of the pan and on to the floor, though no one apart from me and the cat who quickly pounced and made off with it appeared to notice.

'You could start with Friends Reunited or Facebook,' I pointed out helpfully, beginning to wonder what I had started and where, exactly, this was all going to end up. 'We'll go in early to work tomorrow and take a look.'

Nobody ate very much, though Joan tried her best. I think we were all too churned up at the thought of what lay ahead to have any appetite left for food.

★ ★ ★

That John Winstanley had the look of a really nice guy, was my first thought when his face popped up on the computer screen. From the head-and-shoulders snapshot of his profile he appeared quite ordinary, with his greying hair and clean-shaven face, but he had a pleasant smile and warm brown eyes. I had a feeling I would like him.

'Is that your John?' I asked just to be certain.

Valerie leaned over my shoulder and stared at the screen. She stared some for quite a long time before she nodded slowly. 'He's not 'my' John, but yes,' she said, 'that's him.'

'He looks nice.'

'He is — was,' she agreed without hesitation. 'Very nice.'

'It doesn't say he's married again or even in a relationship, though it looks as if he's done a fair bit of travelling.' I went through his profile carefully and read out some of the relevant facts.

'He always wanted to see the world — for us to see it together actually — but by the time we could afford to think about making a start, my mother had had the stroke and everything changed,' Valerie sounded sad for a moment, but then she said, 'I'm glad he realized at least part of his dream.'

'Well, here's your chance to tell him so.' I turned the screen towards her.

She hesitated, 'And if I do this you promise you will speak to Lex?'

I knew if I backed out now, so would Valerie and, having gone this far down a road I hadn't even imagined we'd be travelling, I had no choice but to say a firm 'Yes'. If there was the slimmest chance of reconciliation for Valerie and John, talking to Lex was surely a small price to pay I reasoned.

I would do it. I would talk to Lex, but that was all. I could manage that, hear what he had to say, meet my obligation to Valerie and clear the way for a future with Simon with a clear conscience. I carefully didn't examine my feelings too closely but turned my attention quickly back to Valerie.

Having gained the required promise from me, without further hesitation she sat down, her fingers flew over the keys, clicked the mouse to send the message and then she sat back in the chair.

'What on earth did you say after all this time?' I asked curiously, and then said immediately, 'No, forget I said that, it's none of my business.'

'I just said I hoped he was well and happy and wondered if he thought there was any point to us having a chat. He'll probably think I want a divorce,' she added ruefully.

'You mean you're still *married*?'

'Mmm.' Valerie turned the screen back towards me and, refusing to be drawn further, declared in a firm tone, 'Your turn now.'

I tried not to deliberate, just took a deep breath and a leaf out of Valerie's book, Googled the Cable Construction website for contact details, typed quickly and sent the message on its way. I knew Lex would pick it up via his Blackberry — one of the things I learned about him during our time together was that he was meticulous about keeping on top of emails. What his response would be, I had no idea.

'What did *you* say?' Valerie asked curiously.

'Pretty much the same as you, though I've suggested a time and place to meet.'

'Because you didn't need to ask if he wanted to talk, since he's made it abundantly clear that he does.' Valerie nodded, then she stood up. 'Well, I've got a pile of filing waiting with my name on it. I can't hang around waiting to see if I get a reply. I'm well aware a lot of water has gone under the bridge since we separated and John may well decide to ignore me — I wouldn't blame him at all. I may check before I go home tonight or if not it can wait until Monday. I certainly don't intend to put my life on hold or build up any expectations either.'

Something told me we weren't being entirely truthful with one another but I supposed there was no real reason we should be. I guessed, having been forced into making these contacts against our better judgements, neither of us was expecting a happy outcome, so we saw no point in discussing things further. When I went out later that evening I didn't even tell Valerie what my plans were, and she didn't ask.

★ ★ ★

The house looked large and imposing — and totally deserted, which I hadn't been expecting for some reason. Even though my message had been abrupt I had been so sure that Lex wouldn't hesitate since he had seemed so keen to be given the chance to explain, but perhaps telling him just to be there or forget it hadn't been such a good idea after all.

I'd known he wouldn't take kindly to what amounted to being given an order, could only guess he'd reached the point of being sick to the back teeth of me and had finally made up his mind he didn't want to see or speak to me ever again. So be it. I'd already decided my future didn't lie with Lex anyway.

Even so, standing there in the black darkness, surrounded by the tall trees I knew to be so beautiful by day, I felt very close to tears as I faced the fact that history really was going to repeat itself. I had been stood up.

It took a moment or two of reflection before common sense prevailed, and I reminded myself that Lex was *not* his brother. If Lex had insisted he was prepared to meet me any time any place, then he would, and he would simply have been held up. All I had to do was go inside and wait. Perhaps there was even a message on the answer phone.

I eyed the porch and the open window above that had allowed me access to the house that very first time. I can't say I wasn't a little tempted to make the climb all over again, just for old times' sake, but since I still had a key I knew common sense really should prevail and it did.

Once inside I checked the phone, but the line was inexplicably dead so I settled myself to wait — and wait I did. I waited and waited and waited. Evening gave way to night, but I never once gave up on the idea that Lex would eventually come because he had said he would and, unlike his brother, he was a man of his word.

I could have left, just jumped in the car and driven away. It would have been an end to the matter. After all, I had met my obligation just by turning up it was hardly my fault he hadn't. I owed nothing to Lex and leaving while I had the chance would surely be the sensible thing to do. Something kept me there though and I wasn't quite sure what.

The long wait gave me time to do the thinking I had so carefully been avoiding, particularly about the future and about Simon — it also gave me the time to be scrupulously honest with myself for the first time and to examine my real feelings for him in minute detail.

After endless soul-searching I began to question the fact that I'd seriously contemplated the possibility of the two of us making a lifelong commitment. I *was* very fond of Simon but in all honesty fond was all I ever would be, and what about his feelings for me? I suddenly wondered why I hadn't thought to question why he had taken years — yes, *years* — to make his move. Hardly the actions of a man who couldn't live without me, I could only guess he'd been weighing up the pros and cons for all that time before eventually making his decision.

Once upon a time Simon's natural caution might have appealed to me. I was honest enough to admit that, had I never met Lex and experienced the roller-coaster that life with him could be, I might have been more than happy to settle for life with someone like Simon, and would probably have been content, but I had met Lex, everything had changed and it was far too late to change it back. I was only surprised I hadn't recognized that simple truth before.

The thought of Lex was my undoing and I realized in that moment that if I didn't give our relationship the chance it deserved I was going to spend the rest of my life trying — and probably failing abysmally — to recapture what I had so unexpectedly found with him. I had imagined myself in love before — and perhaps would even do so again — but the elusive spark that had been there between us from the time we met, whether we were fighting or loving, was always going to be missing.

With Lex, and only with him, I had known a desire so strong it made me forget everything but the way he made me feel — after that I couldn't even begin to imagine settling for lukewarm affection. Simon was a good man and he deserved more than to be always a poor second best in my life — because I knew without a doubt that that was all he would ever be. I recalled Valerie's words, 'You're a long time married to the wrong person,' and Simon was definitely the wrong person for me. I would have to be totally honest with him — he deserved that much at least. Whether we could still work together remained to be seen, and it was a decision best left to him.

* * *

There was no warning, none at all. One minute the room and, as far as I was aware the house also, was dark and completely silent, the next the door flew open and a broad beam of light spilled across the bed where I had been — until that very minute — sound asleep.

'*There* you are,' a deep voice exploded and I shot up in the wide bed, heart hammering and adrenalin coursing through my veins.

I'd eventually taken myself off to bed, certain there would be a sensible explanation and that Lex would turn up in the morning. I'd steadfastly refused to contemplate any other scenario than that of him turning up but I still couldn't believe it wasn't Lex but *Nick*, of all people, standing here in the room with me in the middle of the night.

Belatedly grabbing at the duvet, I clasped it tightly to my breast, and glared at him, demanding furiously, 'How dare you creep around like that? What the hell do you think you're playing at, Nick? And where is Lex?'

'How should I know?' He shrugged nonchalantly. 'And why should we care? Isn't this what we both wanted right from the start?'

I stared at him speechlessly, and feeling like a complete fool could only mutter, 'What? What do you mean?'

'Us. You and me together, my love. My marriage is over and we can be together at last, just as we were meant to be. You don't have to settle for Lex now, Annie, when we both know it was always me you wanted.'

His sheer arrogance, together with the unshakable belief that he could turn the clock back, just like that, took my breath away.

I rose to my feet with all the dignity I could muster, dragging the duvet with me, and said, 'Go back to your wife, Nick, while you still can. She still loves you, though God knows why; my feelings for you are nothing but contempt. There is no 'you and me'; there never really was. I accepted that long ago and suggest you do the same. I despise you. In fact, had I met Lex first, I wouldn't even have noticed you. It's as simple as that.'

'You're just saying that because you're angry with me,' he said with the supreme confidence of a man who was far too used to getting his own way to let a small thing like someone else's wishes obstruct his desires, 'and I don't blame you. I treated you badly, and I admit it, but I'm here to make it up to you. With my share of the business and vision of the future we can make a fresh start, miles away from here. Let Lex keep the family firm and the old folks happy. I have plans, big plans — '

I'd had enough. 'You,' I said, jabbing a finger in his direction, 'can take your bloody plans and share them with somebody who gives a toss about them — because that certainly isn't me.'

He moved with a speed that was frightening, wrenching the duvet from me. 'You've always wanted me. Don't even try to deny it. You want marriage, it's yours. Anything you want is yours, but first I want what's due to me.'

'No!'

'I think you've kept me waiting long enough, don't you?'

'No!'

I pushed against his chest, but he was too strong and his mouth came down hard on mine, crushing my lips until I could taste blood. One minute he was forcing me relentlessly towards the bed and the next he gave a harsh shout and suddenly I was free.

We stood practically chin to chin, panting, both furiously angry. Slowly, Nick put a hand to his face, felt the scratches, deep and bleeding profusely, and said savagely, 'You vicious little bitch you.'

'So,' a deep voice drawled from the doorway, 'you finally met your match, eh, Nick?'

Nick's recovery was immediate. 'It's not the way it looks, Lex. She's just making me pay a little, but you know as well as I do that I'm the one she really wants. You've always known it.'

My first instinct was to rush to defend

myself as I had in the past. My second was to trust that Lex, after everything that had happened between us, would know better than to believe every damning word Nick said. If he did believe Nick, then so be it and I would know it was all over between us.

'You know what, Nick,' Lex said with a nod, 'I have everything to thank you for.'

He sounded so calm and yet there was barely suppressed anger in his tone — an anger that was obviously directed at me, and what he would see as my duplicity. I really had believed he knew me better. My heart gave a painful lurch and in that moment I accepted it had been the biggest mistake of my life to come back to the house in the forest. But at least now I had all the answers and wouldn't spend the future — as Valerie had done — wondering whether things might have been different.

'I knew you'd see sense, Lex.' Nick's good-looking face took on a smug expression.

I watched Lex turn, reach out and place his hand on the door handle and it was all I could do not to run after him. I could scarcely believe that he thought so little of me that he would actually go and leave me to Nick's far from tender mercies. With all the dignity I could muster, I reached for the duvet and wrapped it tightly around myself.

And then Lex turned again and I braced myself for some sarcastic comment about false modesty. Instead he spoke directly to his brother and without raising his voice once he said, 'Yes, I have you to thank for bringing Stacey into my life but,' he put up his hand when it seemed Nick would have spoken, 'that's all I have to thank you for, and by trying to destroy what we found together you've just proved, beyond the shadow of a doubt, that you are not the brother I hoped you were and that you never will be.'

'This is my house, Nick, and you are no longer welcome in it. Now get out and don't ever come back. I'm a fair man — which is more than can be said of you — and you will get your share of the business. Do with it what you will. Go back to that wife of yours, because you surely deserve each other. If you and Anthea couldn't be happy together, the least you could have done was to wish us well, but you couldn't even manage that, could you? But you know what, Nick,' Lex came to stand beside me and, smiling into my eyes, he said, 'we don't need your permission to be happy.'

Nick seemed to accept defeat, at last. He walked towards the door, but he wasn't quite finished. He turned with a sneer to say to me, 'You'll be sorry. You could have had the best but chose to settle for less — and you,' he stabbed a finger in Lex's direction to remind him, 'you will never be more than the consolation prize — the second-best brother.'

I was so proud of Lex when he said with a shrug, 'You can believe that if you choose, but I happen to know better.'

'You know what, Nick.' I lifted my chin and looked him right in the eye. 'Because of you and others like you, it's taken me a while to learn to put my trust in a good man like Lex, but that's my only regret. From the moment we met it took no time at all to learn to love him — and I do with all my heart. It's you I feel very sorry for, because a love like that is something you will never know.'

I knew he wouldn't be able to help himself, and I was right; Nick had to stop on his way out of the door and ask, 'Oh, and why is that?'

'The love of *your* life is standing right here in this room, Nick, because for you Nicholas Cable comes first and last and in the middle. There's not a woman in the world who could love you more than you love yourself — and no one likes to be second best, do they?'

We do hope that you have enjoyed reading this large print book.

Did you know that all of our titles are available for purchase?

We publish a wide range of high quality large print books including:
**Romances, Mysteries, Classics
General Fiction
Non Fiction and Westerns**

Special interest titles available in large print are:
**The Little Oxford Dictionary
Music Book
Song Book
Hymn Book
Service Book**

Also available from us courtesy of Oxford University Press:
**Young Readers' Dictionary
(large print edition)
Young Readers' Thesaurus
(large print edition)**

For further information or a free brochure, please contact us at:
**Ulverscroft Large Print Books Ltd.,
The Green, Bradgate Road, Anstey,
Leicester, LE7 7FU, England.
Tel:** (00 44) 0116 236 4325
Fax: (00 44) 0116 234 0205

Other titles published by
The House of Ulverscroft:

A BLESSING IN DISGUISE

Pamela Fudge

When Alex Siddons becomes pregnant after twenty-five years of childless marriage, her life is turned upside down and her relationship with her husband, Phil, hangs in the balance. A child at their time of life is the last thing either of them wants or needs and yet, despite pressure from Phil, Alex cannot bring herself to terminate the pregnancy, even if it is the only thing that will save her marriage. Facing the prospect of life as a single mother, Alex finds unexpected support from within the Siddons family. Now she finally learns the true meaning of family and love.

HIGH INFIDELITY

Pamela Fudge

When a brief affair in Tina Brown's past resulted in an unplanned pregnancy, the decision was made not to share the news with the father, Calum Stacey. Tina raised the child alone, having decided to provide her with the full facts when she is eighteen years old. With her birthday just months away, Leanne is rushed into hospital with suspected meningitis and Tina feels she has no choice but to contact Calum without delay. Calum's engagement to a famous celebrity makes him newsworthy and there is mounting speculation surrounding his past. Can Tina and Calum protect their daughter from sudden media intrusion?